ARIFURETA: FROM COMMONPLACE TO WORLD'S STRONGEST

ryo shirakome   takayaki

KAORI
SHIRASAKI

SHEA

HAJIME NAGUMO
"I'D LIKE TO SEE YOU TRY, GOD'S PUPPET!"
AIKO HATAYAMA

"I AM NOINT. AN APOSTLE OF GOD. MY DUTY IS TO REMOVE UNWANTED GAME PIECES FROM MY LORD'S GAMEBOARD."

ERI NAKAMURA

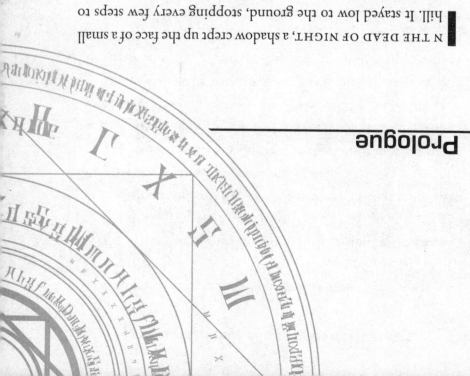

Prologue

IN THE DEAD OF NIGHT, a shadow crept up the face of a small hill. It stayed low to the ground, stopping every few steps to examine its surroundings. The monster looked vaguely like a dog, and a chill wind ruffled its black fur.

After some time, it crested the hill and stared at the sea of lights in the distance. They were manmade. The glimmering flower of the night was the capital of the kingdom of Heiligh.

Most of the capital's citizens were fast asleep. But for the city's thieves, black market merchants, and other unsavory types, the night was just beginning.

The city's watchmen and throngs of adventurers also walked the streets, and some enterprising merchants kept their stores open late. However, it was a far cry from Fuhren. That city never slept.

Every few minutes, another light winked out of existence, until finally the capital was shrouded in darkness. Only the distant twinkling of the stars and the moon's cruel light could be seen.

It whipped around and looked warily at the newcomer.

"Grr...!"

The newcomer didn't respond to the growled challenge.

But then, it was no living creature.

The ground in front of the monster glimmered with light.

The presence it had sensed consisted of mana.

The monster stared warily at the light, unsure what to do, then cautiously approached. It seemed as though the mana was stored underground, and only some was leaking to the surface.

The monster dug with its front paws, and its claws eventually struck something hard: a stone slab engraved with unnatural geometric patterns.

Curious, the monster started digging it out. A second later, it leaped back in surprise. Another section of ground was glowing. Yet another glowing circle appeared after that, and then a fourth. The monster's instincts screamed at it to flee. It dashed off, running as fast as its legs would carry it.

It made the correct choice. Once it had put some distance between the anomaly and itself, it turned around to see more than a hundred lights dotting the hilltop. The lights joined together, creating a massive magic circle.

The strange carvings on the slab were a miniature version of the pattern on the circle. Had a certain vampire princess been present, she would have recognized the design.

It was the magic circle for teleportation.

And, unfortunately for the capital's citizens, it was big enough to transport an entire army.

"Hajime-kun, please! We have to save them! What if..."

Hajime didn't wait for her to finish. He poured more mana into Brise and sped up. The merchants would be doomed if he wasted time debating whether to help. He'd hear Kaori's explanation later. First, he needed to act. If there was one thing Hajime prided himself on, it was decisiveness. Especially when it came to his comrades.

Brise roared down the plain, a trail of smoke rising in its wake.

"Hajime-kun... Thank you."

Kaori smiled, glad that Hajime was willing to listen. Hajime just shrugged.

Yue and the others hurriedly strapped on their seatbelts. They knew what Hajime was about to do.

"U-umm, Hajime-kun? You aren't planning on..."

Kaori's face froze as Brise hurtled toward the bandits. She had asked Hajime for help, but as someone who had lived in a world with cars, she assumed he would hesitate before doing something so unethical.

"When you see criminals, you run them over," he replied with a straight face. "Isn't that what they teach in driving school?"

"No! Stop making up your own traffic laws! Look, even the others agree with me!"

Hajime ignored Kaori and drove Brise straight toward the bandits, aiming for the one that appeared to be their leader. He clearly thought vehicles existed to run bad guys over.

The bandit leader noticed Brise too late. He shouted pan-icked orders to his men and began casting a spell. He was sure this strange black box was some kind of new monster, and would never have guessed that it was actually a metal vehicle made for transporting people.

Hajime poured more mana into Brise and activated one of its gadgets. Meter-long blades popped out of Brise's sides and hood.

The bandits hurled fireballs at the monstrosity bearing down on them, with no noticeable effect. Hajime powered forward, and ignored their pathetic attempts at resistance.

The bandits trembled as they watched the black box shrug off their best attacks. There was a sickening crunch as Hajime drove into the mass of unarmored bandits. Despair and confusion appeared on the men's faces as Brise struck them.

A few were pushed onto the hood and sliced apart by blades. Others tried to dodge out of the way and were sliced apart on either side of Brise. Those fortunate enough to avoid that death were crushed by the force of a giant truck slamming into them at eighty kilometers per hour, their bodies utterly pulverized. In the span of a single second, seven bandits were killed. After destroying their backline, Hajime drifted Brise to a halt.

Both the bandits and the merchants stared blankly. The sudden carnage left them speechless. Some guards and bandits even stopped fighting mid-swing.

Hajime ignored them and turned to Kaori.

"If we're doing this, I'm not going to show mercy. I'll kill them all. No healing any of them. You get that, right?"

Kaori took a deep breath and nodded. "Yeah, I understand."

Hajime knew how kind Kaori was, but he had no intention of letting her heal his enemies. If she did, she'd no longer be his comrade.

"All right, then go. I won't get in your way."

"Okay!"

Kaori leaped out of Brise and ran to the injured merchants. The bandits were shocked senseless when Brise showed up. However, Kaori just looked like an ordinary girl. That was something they could handle. They let their anger fuel them and attacked.

"Die, you bitch!" One bandit brandished his sword.

Kaori only spared the man a glance before turning her attention back to the injured. She reached the merchants, chanting a healing spell.

That only made the bandit angrier, but before he could vent his frustrations, he was slaughtered. Hajime blew his head clean off.

Bang! Bang! Bang! Bang! With each gunshot, another bandit lost their life. Even the rescued guards shivered in fear as they watched Hajime slaughter the bandits.

It was just so merciless. In the span of a few seconds, Hajime executed over half of the forty-odd men.

Some of the bandits panicked and tried to take the merchants hostage, but Shea leaped in front of them.

A guard shouted a warning to her, but it was unnecessary. Shea was so overpowered now that she could even give Hajime a run for his money. This fighting rabbit had no blind spots. She summoned Drucken from her Treasure Trove and held it aloft.

Then, she swung it with such force that a wall of air shot forward. The three bandits charging the merchants crumpled to the ground, the upper halves of their bodies missing.

"Huh? Wah! Look at all that blood!"

It was so long since Hajime's party had fought a weak enemy, none of them were able to hold back. Shea only planned to send the bandits flying, but she accidentally cut them in half. It was quite a gruesome sight. She jumped away from the sudden fountain of blood.

Yue and Tio spared Shea a single glance before obliterating the remaining bandits in a storm of magic.

Hajime blew the heads off the few who tried to escape. They didn't even have time to beg for their lives. Their punishment was swift and thorough.

Kaori used Holy Blessing, an AoE healing skill, to heal the injured merchants and adventurers simultaneously. Unfortunately, a number had already died. Not even restoration magic could bring back the dead.

She ground her teeth, frustrated that she hadn't been able to save everyone. As she lamented their deaths, someone came running. They wore a cowl over their face, their features unrecognizable. However, Hajime could tell by the color of the mana surrounding this figure that they had cast that barrier. He saw no reason to stop them.

"Kaori!"

The girl threw herself into Kaori's arms. Kaori was surprised. Her guess had been correct.

"Lily! Did you really have to bring that up?!"

to see Kaori's state when she thought you were dead."

strong will to escape the labyrinth. I'm glad you survived. It hurt told me you were still alive. It must have taken an unbelievably

"You must be Nagumo-san, correct? It's been a while. Shizuku dawned on her.

to her. She stared at Hajime for a few seconds before recognition

Liliana squealed in surprise upon hearing a voice right next

walking over.

"Kaori, have you finished healing everyone?" Hajime asked,

ney. The two looked at each other for a few seconds.

have happened for Liliana to embark on such a dangerous jour-

attendants. Kaori's expression grew grim. Something serious must

It appeared that Liliana was traveling incognito, without any

finger to Kaori's lips and implored her not to use her real name.

thing, Liliana covered her face with the cowl again. She put a

Kaori looked worriedly at her friend. As if just noticing some-

"Lily? What's happened...?"

you were passing by. It seems my luck hasn't run out just yet."

"I didn't expect to see you here either, Kaori. Thank goodness

Kaori in admiration and whispered something to her.

reveal dazzling blond hair and sparkling blue eyes. She looked at

Liliana breathed a sigh of relief and pushed back her hood to

Heiligh.

It was the princess of the Heiligh Kingdom, Liliana S. B.

I wasn't sure. I can't believe you're out here!"

"Lily, is it really you?! I thought I recognized that barrier, but

CHAPTER 1: A DISTURBING DARKNESS

"Hee hee...! I heard about your confession from Shizuku, too. Later, you should tell me all about the *adventures* you've had."

Kaori blushed, and Liliana smiled at Hajime from beneath her hood.

Most people couldn't resist her smile. It had grown famous throughout the kingdom. It captivated men and women, old and young.

However, Hajime didn't seem affected. He gazed suspiciously at Liliana.

"Wait, who are you?" he asked, his words echoing his confusion.

"Huh?"

Kaori and Liliana had been friends even while Hajime was still in the capital. In fact, Liliana made an effort to talk to every member of the hero party at least once. Since the others hadn't looked favorably on Hajime, she didn't have as many chances to speak to him. Still, they conversed a few times when he was with Kaori.

Liliana wasn't used to being forgotten. Not only was she royalty, her affable personality made her memorable. She was honestly stunned when Hajime didn't recognize her. She stared at him, dumbfounded.

Kaori stepped in, whispering the explanation in Hajime's ear, since Liliana had told her she didn't want her identity revealed.

"H-Hajime-kun! She's the princess! The princess of Heiligh! Liliana! You've talked to her before, remember?!"

"Oh."

"*Hic...!* I never knew being forgotten could hurt so much... *hic...*"

"Lily, don't cry! Hajime-kun's just a bit, you know, dense. No normal person would ever forget you! Please don't cry!"

"Hey, did you just insult me?"

Hajime hadn't expected Kaori, of all people, to casually disparage him like that.

Even more surprising, Kaori snapped back, "Shut up for a bit, Hajime-kun!"

"No, no, it's fine, Kaori. I shouldn't think so highly of myself."

Liliana smiled bravely, and Hajime found he couldn't really say anything back. Besides, it was his fault he'd forgotten about her.

Yue and the others walked up, bringing along the merchants' leader. "It's been some time, hasn't it...?" the man greeted Hajime.

"You seem to be in good health."

To Hajime's surprise, he recognized the man. "You're the energy drink guy!"

"Energy drink? I do sell those, among other things, but... I don't think my energy drinks are particularly famous."

"Ah... Sorry, just talking to myself. Your name was More, right?"

"Indeed. I'm honored you remember me. More Nos, of the Nos Trading Company, at your service. This is the second time you've saved me from certain death. I'm beginning to think we're connected by fate."

This merchant caravan's leader was the same man Hajime escorted from Brooke to Fuhren.

Hajime still remembered that trip, during which he learned just how far this world's merchants were willing to go to make a sale. More's mercantile spirit hadn't waned one bit, and he thumbed the ring on Hajime's finger as they shook hands. It looked as though he still hadn't given up on buying Hajime's Treasure Trove.

Shea explained More's identity to Kaori and Liliana. The princess sank further into depression.

"He remembers someone he met just once, but not me...the princess..." she mumbled.

Kaori tried everything she could to cheer Liliana up, while Hajime continued his discussion with More.

It turned out that More was en route to Ankaji via Horaud. Everyone had heard of Ankaji's plight, and More hoped to make a huge profit selling food to the starving city. He'd already finished one trip, gone back to acquire more food from the capital, and was on his way to Ankaji again. Judging from More's smug expression, Hajime guessed that he had already made quite a profit.

On the other hand, Hajime and his comrades were traveling to the Haltina woods. However, they planned on passing through Horaud and Fuhren first. Horaud was on the way, and they needed to tell Ilwa that they'd successfully reunited Myu with her mother.

Since they both needed to pass through Horaud, More asked Hajime if he'd be willing to guard them until then.

However, Liliana interrupted. "My apologies, good merchant, but I would like to hire their services myself. I understand I'm being presumptuous, especially as you were so kind as to let me join your convoy, but..."

"Oh, you no longer need to go to Horaud?"

"Yes, this is far enough. Of course, I will still pay you the full fee."

Liliana had originally planned on going to Horaud. However, now that she'd found Hajime and his friends, there was no need. Hajime wasn't sure that he felt good about Liliana's plan, but he knew if he said anything now, Kaori would just yell at him for being mean. He held his tongue.

"I see. I'm happy to know I was of assistance. You don't have to worry about paying me."

"Huh? But I can't just not pay you."

Liliana seemed at a loss. The caravan had provided her with food and lodging, and she couldn't imagine not repaying their hospitality. In fact, she'd expected him to ask for more than usual. After all, she'd promised to pay upon reaching Horaud, rather than upfront.

However, More simply smiled.

"I doubt I'll ever say those words again. Let me give you one piece of advice before you go. Normally, you pay up front when asking to join a caravan. If someone doesn't ask to see your money right away, then they're either up to no good, or they have their own reasons for not wanting to take your cash. Fortunately for you, this time it was the latter."

"Wait, does that mean...?"

"I have no idea why someone of your standing needed to sneak out of the capital, but I have no doubt it is a matter of utmost importance. If I didn't assist you in your time of need, then I could hardly call myself a proud citizen of Heiligh. I may be a merchant, but I'm a patriot too."

So, he knew from the start...

Despite that, More hadn't revealed Liliana's identity, and had tried his best to help her.

"In that case, I owe you my gratitude. It was only thanks to you that I was able to leave the capital."

"I see. I'm sorry to change the topic so suddenly, but do you know what a merchant wants most, but finds hardest to obtain?"

"Huh? No, I don't."

"It's trust."

"Trust?"

"Yes, trust. Without it, we would be unable to conduct any business. At the root of every merchant's profits lies a relationship built on trust. Furthermore, even if a merchant finds themselves penniless, as long as they have the trust of others, they aren't ruined. After our little trip, wouldn't you say that the Nos Trading Company is trustworthy? If so, I've already made a far greater profit than any amount of money you could provide."

Liliana smiled to herself. More certainly knew how to give a speech. If she paid him now, it would be the same as saying she didn't trust him. Her thanks would backfire.

Liliana pulled back her cowl and looked More in the eyes.

"I would trust your company with my life. I swear that I, Liliana S. B. Hellish, will never forget the kindness you showed me. I thank you from the bottom of my heart."

"You are far too kind."

More, along with the rest of his merchants, bowed deeply to her.

After that, the merchants left Liliana in Hajime's care and continued down the road to Horaud. Just before they were out of sight, More turned around and yelled one final warning. He'd heard that Hajime was a heretic, but chose to believe in the man who saved his life twice. He informed Hajime that something sinister was happening in the capital, and that he should be careful. In return, Hajime told More that his party had purified Ankaji's oasis, and that the city was no longer in dire need of food. That was all the information More needed to guess why the Holy Church had turned against Hajime.

He left with a final, "If you ever find yourself in need of supplies for your journey, please come to the Nos Trading Company first."

He really is a merchant through and through, Hajime thought.

Once More was gone, Hajime and the others took Liliana back to Brise and asked what she'd come for. The tension in her voice did not bode well, and Hajime was worried he'd get dragged into something he didn't want. However, the first thing she said took him completely by surprise.

"...ko-san...has been kidnapped..."

Worse than anything Hajime could have imagined.

Liliana explained her story.

For a while, she'd been worried about the strained atmosphere the palace. Her father, the king, was spending more and more th with the pope, and had grown far more religious. He often praised Ehit during meals or conversations, and his piety influ- the ministers and nobles to become more religious as well.

Liliana kept trying to tell herself that it was just a side effect of all the time her father was spending with the Holy Church. Humans needed to unite in this time of crisis, or the demons would overrun them. However, things steadily got worse. Many soldiers started looking listless, as if someone had sucked out their souls. Whenever she asked the knights how they were doing, they always replied that they were fine, but they all looked seriously ill.

She tried to consult Meld, the knight she trusted most in the palace, but he had vanished. He still showed up from time to time, when the others trained. Whenever she managed to catch a glimpse of him, though, he disappeared before they could talk. In the end, she never got a chance.

Then, Aiko returned to the capital. She gave the king a report on what happened at Ur.

Liliana was in the audience chamber and heard the whole story. An emergency vote was held.

That was when they decided to declare Hajime a heretic. They ignored Aiko's protests and the fact that Hajime saved both an entire city and the hero party, declaring him an enemy of mankind. Liliana found the vote absurd, and said as much to her father. However, the king seemed convinced that Hajime was Ehit's enemy. His hate was so vehement that Liliana feared her father was possessed. As a matter of fact, he claimed Liliana herself lacked faith when she even suggested that Hajime was innocent, as if meeting progressed, he began looking at his own daughter as if she were the enemy.

Terrified, Liliana pretended to agree and fled his chambers. She ran to Aiko, hoping to share her worries.

During dinner, Aiko planned on telling her students what Hajime confided to her about the gods, and the true goal of his journey. She expressed her hopes that Liliana would join them.

So, that evening, Liliana headed for the dining hall where the students took their meals. On the way there, she heard Aiko arguing with someone. She peeked out from the hallway to see what was going on, and watched as a silver-haired nun incapacitated Aiko and took her away.

Liliana was terrified of that nun, and hid herself in a nearby guest room. Inside, she entered a secret passage that only royalty knew about. The nun came looking for her, but couldn't find her. Fortunately, the passage was an artifact that hid the presence of its occupant.

Liliana knew she had to tell someone. The nun was clearly behind the castle's strange atmosphere. Or, if not behind it, working for whoever was.

However, if Aiko had been taken, then it was likely that the students were under surveillance. Furthermore, Captain Meld was still nowhere to be found.

After a lot of worrying, Liliana decided to turn to the one friend she knew outside the palace.

Kaori. Liliana knew that Kaori would be traveling with reng. These two were the only people left that Liliana could rely so she followed the secret passage out of the castle and tried find someone willing to take her to Ankaji.

Liliana knew the Zengen family would be willing to help her, and they were far enough away that they were likely still unaffected by the darkness hanging over the capital. Most importantly, Liliana guessed that she'd run into Kaori there.

"After that, I joined More Nos' caravan and traveled with him out of the capital. I didn't think he'd recognize me straight away, or that we'd be attacked by bandits, or that the people I set out to meet would be the ones to save me. A few weeks ago, I would have said that this was all because Ehit was watching over me. But now...I'm...afraid of the Holy Church. I don't know what's happening anymore. I have no idea who that silver-haired nun is... or what's wrong with my father..."

Liliana hugged her knees and trembled. She looked less like a wise and confident princess, and more like an ordinary, frightened girl. Hajime couldn't blame her. Everyone she knew and loved had either gone insane or disappeared.

Kaori hugged Liliana tight. That was all she could do to ease her friend's worries.

Hajime shook his head. Liliana's story bore a surprising resemblance to the visions they'd seen in the Sunken Ruins of Melusine. Ehit was starting to possess people, one by one. Things didn't look good.

Under most circumstances, Hajime would just wash his hands of this and say it had nothing to do with him. He would have sped up his schedule, conquered the labyrinths as quickly as possible, and left this world without a second thought.

However, he could guess why Aiko had been kidnapped, and

couldn't say her capture had nothing to do with him. Someone affiliated with the Holy Church took her because she tried to tell the others what Hajime told her. Ehit likely didn't want his own pawns, Kouki and the others, to stop following his script.

Aiko had been kidnapped because Hajime tried to use her for his own gain.

Hajime doubted they intended to kill her, or they would have done so already. Still, he didn't want to imagine what kinds of things they might do. After all, the so-called gods had no qualms about manipulating people like pawns. He doubted they'd shy away from torture.

Most importantly, he owed his happiness to Aiko. She was the one who advised him to change. Even if her kidnapping wasn't his fault, he wouldn't abandon her.

There was only one option. I won't abandon her. This isn't someone else's problem, it's mine. Hajime made his decision. "Guess we've gotta save Sensei."

Liliana looked up at him, relief flooding her face. She'd expected him to refuse. Shizuku told her how Hajime said that this world's people, and even his own classmates, meant nothing to him anymore. The princess was prepared for a long debate.

"You'll come back to help?" Liliana asked, just to be sure.

Hajime shrugged. "Don't misunderstand. I don't give a damn about the kingdom. I'm only going back to save Sensei. It's my fault she got kidnapped, and even if it wasn't, I owe her."

"Aiko-san's..."

While it was unfortunate that Hajime cared nothing for

Liliana's kingdom, it didn't change the fact that he would return. She settled for that.

Hajime's next words brought a smile to her face.

"And, well, if whatever's messing up the palace tries to get in the way of saving Sensei, I'll beat the shit out of it for you."

"You'll... Hee hee! In that case, I pray it *does* try to get in your way. Thank you for agreeing to help, Nagumo-san."

Aiko was being held captive by a nun. That, plus the king's strange fanaticism, likely meant that the Holy Church was behind this.

Saving Aiko would almost inevitably entail fighting the Church. Hajime knew that. He understood that accompanying Liliana back to the capital would mean he'd end up having to save her kingdom.

The corners of Hajime's mouth inched upward as he watched Liliana and Kaori smile at each other.

He had a second reason for going back. After all, the Divine Mountain housed its very own labyrinth. He needed the ancient magic it contained. However, he had absolutely no idea where its entrance was. Searching the area would be difficult with all the priests and clergy running around.

He'd already decided to ignore the mountain and head for Haltina first to avoid starting a fight with the Holy Church. But, with the situation being what it was, he had ample reason to conquer the mountain immediately.

Rescuing Aiko would put Hajime in direct opposition with the Holy Church. In that case, it made sense to launch a preemptive strike. Plus, he'd be able to get his hands on ancient magic. This approach killed two birds with one stone.

Liliana's silver-haired nun reminded Hajime of the hooded figure at King Aleister's side in Melusine's visions. When the figure and Aleister disappeared below deck, Hajime remembered seeing a flash of silver hair. He wasn't sure if that could be the same person. Centuries had passed since then. But, for some reason, Hajime had a feeling it was... And he was sure they'd soon find themselves at odds.

He was raring for this fight. The monster incubated in the abyss thirsted for blood. Anything that stood in his way would die, no exceptions.

He cracked the same fearless grin he usually showed when he was up against grim odds.

"Hajime, you're amazing."

"Whoa, Hajime-san's making that face. I'm falling for him all over again!"

"Hm...Master? If you keep grinning at me like that...my panties are going to get soaked."

The trio of girls drooled over Hajime and ruined the tense atmosphere he was building.

❖ ❖ ❖ ❖ ❖ ❖ ❖ ❖ ❖ ❖ ❖ ❖ ❖

Let's turn back the clock, to a few days before Liliana met up with Hajime and the others.

A lone figure stood near the outskirts of the royal palace, in an empty, quiet clearing. It was a solemn place, the silence punctured only by the night breeze. Crisp moonlight illuminated the area.

In fact, the figure was standing in a cemetery. However, since the cemetery was near the palace, it was no mere graveyard for the masses, just a single stone monument carved directly from the mountainside. The towering edifice immortalized the sacrifices of the brave souls who gave their lives for the kingdom. The names of those who died fighting for the kingdom were engraved there.

The figure standing in the cemetery was Heiligh's knight captain, Meld Loggins. Although his expression was neutral, there was a deep sadness in his eyes.

This late at night, the only people wandering the palace grounds were soldiers on patrol, but none passed through the graveyard.

That made it the perfect place for clandestine meetings.

"Captain."

The whisper was so quiet that the wind nearly snatched it away. Meld turned around and saw the man he was waiting for. The newcomer walked up without making a sound. His name was Jose Rancaid. He was the vice-commander of the knights, and Meld's right-hand man.

"Were you followed?"

"No, I didn't meet a soul. Still, it would be unwise to linger too long."

"We wouldn't want people starting rumors that the two most important knights in the kingdom are plotting something, especially considering the current state of the court. The ministers all suspect their own shadows."

Meld smiled bitterly, and Jose smiled back.

"How are the soldiers?" Meld asked, his expression serious once more.

Jose was pale. "Including the captains, over sixty percent of the soldiers are showing signs of 'Hollowness.'"

The Hollowness was a strange phenomenon that had appeared over the past few days. It spread quickly through the ranks of common foot soldiers and knights. Put simply, the odd affliction made the soldiers and knights lethargic.

They continued doing their jobs, and responded to direct questions. However, they were clearly more listless than usual, and none smiled. They became social recluses, leaving their rooms only to work.

The epidemic spread fast, and now it was affecting even nobles and commanders.

Naturally, Meld had launched an investigation. He was worried about his men, and feared that the Hollowness was worse than simple lethargy.

"Already? I should be thankful that only ten percent of my knights are affected. And none of my captains seem to be ill yet."

"Captain, I'm not quite sure how to put this, but...should we really assume this is an enemy attack? Couldn't it simply be that the men are burnt out?" Jose's tone was hesitant.

"Kouki's been beaten, we've lost many of our best knights, and the demons overturned our advantage in numbers. Do you really think this is a coincidence? I understand how you feel, Jose, but blind optimism will get you killed."

"My apologies."

Jose was by no means being optimistic. It was his job as Meld's confidante to offer alternate viewpoints and contradict any potential flaws in Meld's ideas. Jose cleared his throat and continued.

"How are things on your end, Captain? Has the king been affected as well?"

"His Highness is safe for now. He shows no symptoms of Hollowness. If anything, he seems livelier than ever. He swears by Ehit that he won't let the demons' atrocities continue. However..."

"What is it?" Jose wasn't used to seeing his commander hesitate.

Meld searched for the right words. In the end, he couldn't find them. He shook his head.

"It's nothing." He could hardly tell his vice-captain that the king was *too* religious. That would be blasphemy, both to Jose, and to his own faith. "The prime minister seems unaffected as well. However, some influential nobles haven't been so lucky."

Jose staggered as Meld rattled off a list of people who'd become Hollow. The government's integral nobles were fortunately still safe, but many other highly powerful people had been laid low.

"I've given His Highness a full report, and he's guarded by a contingent of knights day and night. I don't trust the templar knights or the royal guard. My men have orders to come see me the moment they sense anything even slightly out of the ordinary."

"What does His Highness say about the Hollowness?"

Meld had informed King Eliheid of the possibility of a mental attack, orchestrated by some unknown enemy.

Even if the Hollowness was just apathy, the number of sufferers spoke for itself. Meld was certain this outbreak required a swift response. However, the king had disappointed him.

"The fact that the two of us are speaking in secret here is answer enough, isn't it?"

"He rejected your request to start an investigation, didn't he?"

The king had ordered Meld to stop worrying about foolish things like apathetic soldiers, and start building up the country's army.

Although forbidden to conduct an investigation, Meld couldn't let his worries go. His instincts told him that this Hollowness was dangerous.

"The demons have grown more powerful than ever. His Highness has more important concerns than unmotivated soldiers and some vague hints that this might be an epidemic."

"Still, the king heeds your words, Captain. Normally, he'd never dismiss your concerns out of hand..."

Meld cut Jose off with a look. Although Eliheid may have been acting strange recently, Meld didn't want to hear any insults to the king. He was, at heart, a loyal man.

"That's why we need to gather proof. Jose, talk to all the dark magic experts you know. Figure out what this Hollowness really is, and devise countermeasures. Also, try and convince the guards to open the royal vault. Surely it contains an artifact that can deal with mental attacks like this. At the very least, get a catalog of items from the vault manager."

"Yes, sir. What about Kouki-kun and his friends?"

"Let me worry about them. They're in a delicate state right now. I didn't want to burden them with more worries than I had to, but... I suppose I have no choice. I'm really not cut out to be a teacher."

Meld sighed, and Jose smiled at him.

"I'm sure those kids understand how hard you're trying."

"Who cares if they understand me? The problem is that I don't understand them. It's honestly my biggest worry. Fighting is so much easier than this."

"Still, I think it would ease some of their concerns if you talked to them."

Prospective knights knew what they were getting into, so Meld's way of cheering them up usually consisted of training them until they collapsed, then sharing a few drinks. It generally worked. However, applying that approach to Kouki and the others wouldn't be a good idea. They were students who'd been dragged against their will into the war in Meld's world, and they were only fighting to go back home.

Meld didn't know how to help the students come to terms with the fact that they'd have to kill. Jose snickered. Meld was acting like a father who wasn't sure how to teach his kids.

The two of them talked a bit longer about less pressing matters. Once they gave their respective reports, they melted away into the darkness.

Meld snuck back to his room, keeping an eye out for patrols. As knight commander, no one would challenge him, even if they did spot him. However, he didn't want anyone wondering what he was doing so late at night.

I can't believe I'm acting like an intruder in the palace I'm supposed to protect. Meld smiled to himself. A second later, his heart leaped into his throat as someone called out to him.

"Captain Meld—!"

Meld looked around, but saw no one. Although he was on high alert, someone had snuck up on him. In fact, they got so close that they managed to tap his shoulder. They could have killed him if they chose to.

"Zaaah!" Meld's overblown reaction was a symptom of his nervousness. The moment he felt a hand on his shoulder, he pulled out his sword. It drew a silver arc through the air as he turned it on his assailant.

"Hiii...?!" Meld's sword met only empty air. Whoever snuck up on him had good enough reflexes to dodge. Or, at least, trip over himself. Meld looked down to find his attacker in tears. "K-Kousuke?!"

The boy Meld had mistaken for an attacker was Kousuke Endou, the hero party's scout.

He nodded, terrified. "C-Captain. D-did I do something to make you mad?"

Realizing his mistake, Meld sheathed his sword and helped Kousuke up.

Everyone knew how difficult it was to notice Kousuke. Even when he talked with his friends, they sometimes forgot he was there. Back in Japan, automatic doors often wouldn't even open for him. He was almost always omitted during roll call in class. He was a natural master of stealth.

Meld understood why he hadn't sensed anyone. "N-no, sorry. I was just surprised to find someone behind me, and kind of…"

"You sound like Golgo, Captain."

You "kind of" almost chopped my head off!

Meld cleared his throat and changed the subject.

"Anyway, what are you doing out so late, Kousuke?"

"After practice today, I fell asleep in my room. We went pretty hard, and I was exhausted. But it was still early, and…"

Meld looked pityingly down at his pupil. He could tell where this was going.

"And no one thought to wake me up for dinner or anything, so I slept until now."

"I-I see."

"When I finally woke up, I hurried over to the dining hall, but everyone had already finished. They noticed another meal laid out, but they thought the chefs made extra by mistake, and they ate it. No one even realized I didn't come to dinner."

"I-I see."

"Well, I guess it was partly my fault for not arriving on time. I felt guilty about asking the servants to make food just for me, and I figured skipping one meal wouldn't be a big deal. But then, I got so hungry I couldn't sleep… Which is why I figured I'd go to the kitchens to see if they had anything. I found some leftover vegetable scraps and ate those, but…"

"But?"

"Whatever they were, they didn't sit well in my stomach…

I spent two hours in the bathroom. You really don't want to go in there right now."

"What a night."

"Anyway, once I finished, I realized there was another problem."

"Your story's not over yet?! And what on earth is in that bathroom?!"

"It's not what's in there, but what isn't. There wasn't any toilet paper."

"......"

Kousuke didn't explain how he eventually managed to find some toilet paper, but considering how far from the kitchens he was now, Meld guessed he must have spent a long time searching.

"Kousuke... Go rest."

"Will do. Good night, Captain."

Kousuke had been forgotten, had his dinner eaten by someone else, gotten sick from the leftovers he found, and then spent the night wandering the halls looking for toilet paper, only to nearly be killed by his teacher. Meld felt for the poor boy.

As he watched Kousuke totter off to his room, Meld gave him a crisp salute.

Meld made it the rest of the way back to his room without incident. He heaved a heavy sigh and put his sword on the stand on the wall. After disarming, he flopped onto his sofa and massaged his temples.

Once he'd rested, he started planning.

"Magic that only affects troops' morale... It would make sense if demons are behind it, but I can't believe they've infiltrated the

capital. If they have, why not try something bolder than just hitting our morale? And why only target our rank and file? If they can cast spells undetected, why not come for me? Killing me would remove a powerful enemy *and* lower our army's morale. So, why? What on earth is going on?"

Meld spoke his thoughts aloud. He was extremely worried about the unknown threat that had wormed its way into the palace. He wasn't exactly at his limit, but the constant planning and worrying took its toll. Doubly so, since his fellow palace officials didn't seem to share his concerns.

Worse, the problems kept piling up. Meld could feel his impatience permeating his thoughts, like an ink stain spreading through paper.

Meld thought of the boy he'd reunited with in the Orcus Labyrinth. The boy he'd believed he failed to protect. The boy who used legendary medicine to save his life. "I wonder what he's up to right now?"

After reminiscing for a few minutes, Meld stood up and walked to his desk. He pulled out two pieces of paper and as many envelopes. With a conflicted expression, he began to write.

He needed to be ready for the worst. The first letter was addressed to the duke of Ankaji. The second, to Hajime. Meld hoped Duke Zengen would know how to get in touch with Hajime, and pass the letter on. That way, even if something happened, the kingdom would stand a fighting chance.

Glimmering moonlight illuminated Meld's room as he wrote.

He'd just finished, and was going over the letters again, when there was a knock on the door.

Meld warily grabbed his sword off the wall.

"Who is it?"

"Umm... It's me, Captain Meld. Hiyama."

"Daisuke? What are you doing up at this hour?"

"Well... There's something I really need your advice on."

Wondering what could make the boy sound so desperate, Meld slowly opened the door. Hiyama stood in the hallway, his head bowed low.

"You said you needed my advice, but...why this late at night?"

"I'm sorry. I know I'm being a bother... But I don't want any of my classmates to overhear."

"I see... Well, it's no trouble for me. Come in."

Meld thought he had a good idea of what Hiyama needed advice about.

Hiyama's social standing among his classmates was tenuous. His carelessness nearly got Hajime killed. Hiyama had apologized profusely, and the other students all agreed not to bring it up again. No one blamed him for anything. Still, that was only on the surface. Most of the class generally kept their distance from him.

Especially now that they'd learned Hajime was alive.

Meld was a little worried about him, so he was glad Hiyama came to him for advice. At least, that was what Meld assumed Hiyama had come for.

Hiyama kept his head bowed low, so Meld couldn't make out his expression, but Meld didn't like what he saw. Hiyama seemed to be on the verge of doing something drastic.

Meld ushered the boy over to his sofa. He waited patiently, but Hiyama didn't say anything. He simply sat there, wringing his hands and tapping his foot.

"Daisuke, I think I know what you wanted to talk about. You don't have to sugarcoat anything. Give it to me straight. Tell me what's troubling you, and we can come up with a solution together."

Meld's reassuring words did nothing to ease Hiyama's apparent nerves. He kept his head bowed, unwilling to meet Meld's eyes.

This must have been eating away at him more than I thought.

Meld tried to reassure Hiyama again. Before he could get more than a few words out, there was another knock at his door. *I sure am getting a lot of visitors today.*

Meld called out to ask who had knocked. Surprisingly, Jose's voice answered. He apparently had an emergency report.

Jose's timing couldn't have been any worse. Hiyama was still in Meld's room, and it was entirely possible that Meld wouldn't want the student to hear what Jose had to report.

Hiyama noticed Meld's hesitation.

"It's fine, Captain Meld. I'll just wait in the hallway until you're done."

"If you're sure... Sorry, Daisuke."

"It's fine," Hiyama replied curtly, and stood up.

Meld walked to the door and turned the knob. The door opened with a soft click. Jose stood in the hallway, but he'd gone Hollow.

Meld felt goosebumps along his back. His instincts screamed at him to run.

"Wha...?!" he gasped, and leaped backward.

A second later, a knight's sword whistled through the air where he'd stood.

"Jose, what's gotten into you?!" Meld yelled to his vice-captain.

The only response Meld got was a diagonal slash aimed at him. He rolled out of the way, pulled his sword free, and blocked Jose's follow-up attack. The two swords met with a resounding clang.

"Crap... So it was a form of brainwashing after all?!"

Up close, Meld could tell Jose's eyes were blank. That was one of the symptoms of Hollowness. However, the other Hollow soldiers hadn't tried to attack him. That meant that Jose was following someone's orders, and other Hollow soldiers could be made to do the same.

Meld shivered. *I knew it wasn't something as innocent as apathy!* To cure Jose of his brainwashing, Meld needed to immobilize him. He yelled and shoved Jose's sword back.

"This might hurt a little, old friend!"

Meld rushed at Jose while the vice-captain was off-balance, and hoped he could pin his opponent in place with a tackle.

Jose didn't move according to plan, though. Meld had been assuming that he himself was the target. However, Jose ignored him and turned his gaze to Hiyama, who stared at the two of them, dumbfounded.

Jose's sudden change of target made Meld hesitate. He turned to see Hiyama take a few steps backwards and trip over himself. Meld couldn't believe it.

Hiyama was one of the hero party's frontliners. Moreover, he had an extremely powerful job. He shouldn't have lost his courage when faced with a single measly knight. *No, wait… Maybe this was what he wanted to talk to me about!*

Meld clicked his tongue and changed directions. His legs screamed in pain as he pivoted without losing momentum. The sudden movement required him to step with such force that his floorboards snapped, but he got between Jose and Hiyama.

"Ngh… Such power."

Meld and Jose's swords met in a flash of sparks. Meld's stance was in shambles from the sudden change of direction. Still, Jose's blows were more powerful than they had any right to be. Meld's arms numbed with the impact.

Jose was a master of the sword. However, his style favored speed over strength. Technique and agility were his weapons, not raw power. Yet, somehow, he rained down blows that matched Meld's.

Meld couldn't dodge, since he was covering Hiyama. He couldn't push Jose back, either, since his stance was wrong. His full strength was utterly beyond reach. *I've got no other choice. I'll have to use magic.*

"Sorry about this, vice-captain!"

Meld might severely injure his right-hand man. He put his faith in Jose's resilience as he held out his free hand and prepared a blast of wind.

"Heed my call, O wind—Blitz—?!"

However, Meld never got a chance to finish speaking. He stopped chanting midway through...when a sword stabbed into his side.

"Daisuke?"

"Tch... I can't believe you managed to dodge that."

Meld turned around in disbelief. Just as he'd thought, none other than Hiyama had thrust the sword into his side. And Hiyama's eyes weren't blank. They were bloodshot.

"Daisuke, you..."

Meld didn't know the details, but he was certain that Hiyama had something to do with the Hollowness. If Meld hadn't dodged sideways, Hiyama's sword would have pierced his heart. He could thank his uncanny instincts for his survival. Hiyama had aimed to kill.

Hiyama ignored Meld's words, yanked his sword out, and tried again to drive it through the captain's heart.

The mana from Meld's unfinished spell was still primed, and Meld called out the trigger to cast it. "Blitz Hammer!"

He aimed, not at Hiyama, but at the floor below. A ball of compressed wind slammed into the boards with tremendous force. Wood fragments struck all three of them, and the gust blew them in different directions.

Meld rolled across the floor, a trail of blood behind him. The pain was so intense that he should have fainted, but the captain stood up as if his wound didn't even hurt, then charged at Hiyama.

Jose was just a knight, but Hiyama was a frontliner who'd

delved deeper into the Great Orcus Labyrinth than Meld ever had. He was definitely more dangerous.

Unfortunately for Meld, even more enemies joined the fray. A horde of Hollow soldiers poured into his room.

"Tch," he muttered. "Looks like they planned this well."

Meld swept aside three soldiers' blades with one stroke of his sword. He stepped to the side, avoiding Jose's overhand slice. Hiyama rushed forward and launched a furious assault, which Meld parried with the flat of his blade.

Following that attack, Meld used another blast of wind to blow away the soldiers who had circled to his rear. He'd shortened the incantation so much that he only had to say the spell's name.

Taking advantage of the opening, Jose swung his sword, but Meld kicked a chair, tripping him. Irritated, Hiyama tried to chant a spell, which distracted his attention for a moment.

Meld was waiting for that. His blade danced through the air, circling Hiyama's shortsword. He slapped the weapon out of Hiyama's hand and rushed forward.

Meld ducked under Jose and tackled Hiyama. "Haaah!"

Meld's shoulder connected squarely with Hiyama's stomach, knocking the air out of Hiyama's lungs as the student slammed into the sofa, then tumbled over it. "Wha...?!"

Two soldiers tried to pincer Meld, but he rolled underneath them and blocked Jose's next attack with his sword. The blow sent Meld flying backward, but he used the distance to straighten his stance.

"Scatter—Wind Wall!"

With the precious seconds he'd gained, he summoned a barrier of wind.

Jose, who'd been in the middle of launching another attack, was knocked off-balance.

Meld blocked one soldier's swing and threw an uppercut at another. Although the soldiers' blows were powerful, their movements were clumsy. Meld knew he could handle them. The uppercut connected squarely with a soldier's jaw and knocked him clean off his feet.

The captain swept his leg out, tripping Jose. While the soldier was still off-kilter, Meld slammed the flat of his sword into his head. There was a sickening crunch, and the man fell to the ground.

"Come on, Jose, I know you can do better than that."

Normally, Jose fought with more finesse. Now, he let his weapon swing him around. Meld parried another of his blows and threw Jose over his shoulder.

Jose gasped as the air was forced from his lungs.

"You stay quiet for a bit."

Meld slammed his fist into Jose's stomach. The man spasmed, then went limp. Meld spared him one last glance before standing and punching behind him, vanquishing the last remaining soldier.

"Goddammit. I even brought the vice-captain to deal with you." Hiyama coughed and stumbled to his feet. "How can someone from this world be so strong? Are you some kinda monster?"

Meld looked sadly at his former pupil. "You overestimate

me. I just have a lot more experience fighting people. I *am* still the kingdom's greatest knight, you know. You may have me beat when it comes to fighting monsters, but I've had years of experience fighting people."

So, please, just surrender. Sadly, Meld's unspoken plea didn't reach Hiyama. The young boy tore at his hair and glanced at the unconscious soldiers.

"What, you think you've won?"

Hiyama sounded insane. Meld gasped as he saw the boy's eyes. They held the broken look of a man who'd fallen too far to have any hope of salvation.

"Daisuke, what did—"

Meld saw movement out of the corner of his eye. He couldn't believe it.

They were standing back up. Both the soldiers, and Jose. It was as if they didn't feel any pain. They simply rose with the same blank expressions.

"Give it up. Heh heh heh... Those guys won't stop, even if you kill them!"

"What? What have you done to—"

Before Meld could finish, two more knights walked into his room. At least half a dozen more stood outside, all Hollow.

Whatever this brainwashing magic was, it was extremely high-level. Although their movements were a little sluggish, the soldiers never tired, and their attacks were abnormally powerful.

Suddenly, it hit Meld. Despite the fight's volume, no one had come to see what was going on. His situation was dire. He'd fallen totally into his enemy's trap. There was likely some barrier around his room that kept sound and vibrations from escaping. Chances were, no one even knew he was under attack.

They completely got me. This is what comes of me putting too much faith in the castle's defenses. Meld hadn't expected enemies capable of setting up such an elaborate trap. For the past few hundred years, humans and demons had been relatively equal, and the castle's multilayered defenses had never been breached.

That left only one possibility. Meld looked at Hiyama. Considering the boy's skills, Meld knew he couldn't have been working alone. He was almost certain that Hiyama had an accomplice. Said accomplice was probably the real brains behind this operation.

In that case, this is no time to think of making a valiant last stand. I need to escape alive, and inform someone of this betrayal. Unfortunately, the doorway was filled with knights. Meld backed up. Jose and the others surrounded him.

"Just give up and die already, Captain Meld!" Hiyama's mouth twisted into a sneer.

"I refuse. As shameful as it is, I'm afraid I'll be escaping with my life."

"Wha...? You little—"

Meld turned on his heel and dashed for the window. He slammed through it, shattering the glass with ease. For a moment, he hung suspended in the air. The room was on the fourth floor. A fall from that height would leave him crippled at the very least.

"Wind Wall!"

Meld slowed his descent with magic and landed softly. He knew Hiyama and the others would soon chase after him, so he hadn't truly escaped yet. Not by a long shot.

However, he'd at least bought as much time as it would take to chant a high-level spell. Specifically, a powerful fire spell. With that magic, he'd have a head start on finding someone who wasn't brainwashed, and telling them everything he knew. *I can do this!*

"O crimson—"

He stopped chanting almost as soon as he started. Or rather, something stopped him. He wasn't sure what. Hiyama and the others still hadn't made it to ground level, and there was no one else in the courtyard.

No magic was stopping him from continuing, and no one had fired an attack.

However, Meld's instincts screamed at him to be silent. He *knew* not to make a sound or move a muscle. "..."

It felt as though his heart was caught in a vice. Cold sweat dripped from his chin. He stood stock still, wishing his breathing and heartbeat weren't so loud.

Like an animal sensing a predator nearby, Meld knew his only hope for survival was if this thing passed on.

"First, I had to step in to take care of the king; now, the knight commander. I must say, your performance is quite disappointing. I suppose this is all I can expect from a human. Very well. It seems I must lend you a hand..."

The voice was so melodious that it sent chills down Meld's spine. It was also utterly devoid of emotion.

Meld didn't budge until after hearing the voice. He looked up slowly, his head moving like a badly-oiled machine.

A girl floated in the air, silhouetted by the moon. Wings sprouted from her back. A glowing silver sphere hung in front of her. The sight looked so fantastical that, for a moment, Meld couldn't believe it was real.

However, there was no time to be impressed. His body, his mind, his very soul despaired.

There was an overwhelming difference in strength between him and this creature.

The sphere's silver light intensified. It looked beautiful, like a miniature moon. But the power stored in that light was anything but beautiful. It was cold and merciless.

Meld knew full well what was about to happen. There was no escape.

"Ehit..." Meld, the strongest knight in the kingdom, prayed to the god he'd believed in since childhood.

"Correct. This is what your lord desires."

Ehit didn't stop the girl from bringing the silver sphere down on him. It was no larger than a child's ball, but its glow eradicated all life.

Death's silver light filled Meld's vision.

This is what Ehit wanted? He wanted *me to die?!* Meld recalled what had happened to his subordinates. He was sure that even worse things awaited them.

In his final moment, Meld's thoughts turned not to Ehit, but to someone else. *Please take care of the rest for me... Well, even if I don't ask, I know you'll do that anyway. She's your enemy, after all, so...beat the shit out of her for me.*

The kingdom's strongest knight put his faith, not in god, but in the monster who crawled out of the abyss.

❖ ❖ ❖ ❖ ❖ ❖ ❖ ❖ ❖ ❖ ❖ ❖ ❖ ❖

Soldiers with Hollow eyes silently repaired the window and floorboards of Meld's room. Another figure looked down at the letters still on his desk.

"Oh, my, I guess I should have expected as much from the captain. He didn't miss a thing. That was close."

"Huh? What are you talking about?" Hiyama walked towards the figure, not even attempting to hide his displeasure.

"It's nothing. At any rate, how does your stomach feel? From the looks of it, he hit you pretty hard," the figure said with a sneer.

"This is nothing," Hiyama spat back, grimacing.

The figure's sneer grew. Hiyama turned to watch a soldier fit a new window frame, and something occurred to him.

"What about her?"

"She already left. She said our performance was disappointing."

"I see. Well, I expected her to intervene. I've gotta say, it really feels like we're blessed by god. Hee hee... Never expected her to be such a cruel bitch, though."

Hiyama shuddered as he thought about the girl. Originally, the plan would have taken much longer. Her help, however, had removed the obstacles standing in their way.

Hiyama still didn't know why she chose to cooperate with

them. She claimed her god told her to, but Hiyama had no way of knowing for sure. He didn't even know what she really was, just that she was far stronger than him.

Hiyama shook his head, casting off the fear. He changed the subject. "Well, the biggest problems are solved now. At this point, we'll be fine, as long as Yaegashi doesn't catch on."

"Indeed. Thanks to our little accomplice, both the king and prime minister are effectively our puppets. And the Holy Church was never our enemy to begin with. With the captain gone, there's no one left who can stop me."

A hint of madness tinged the figure's voice. Even Hiyama, who'd already killed someone, took an involuntary step back.

The figure crushed something in their hand. Upon closer inspection, Hiyama realized it was the letter Meld had written to Hajime.

"At this point, things will progress very quickly indeed. The ball's rolling, and it's only going to speed up. There's no stopping now, not until we achieve the future I desire."

The figure grinned, and their pupils shrunk to tiny dots.

Maniacal laughter filled the late Captain Meld's room.

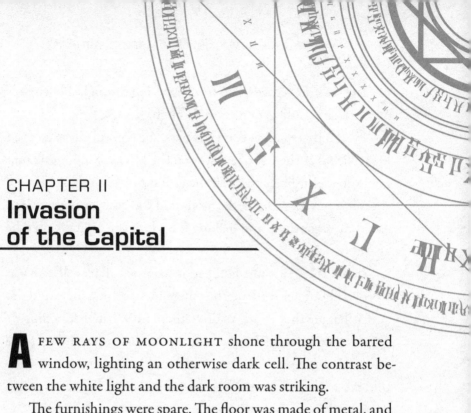

CHAPTER II
Invasion
of the Capital

A FEW RAYS OF MOONLIGHT shone through the barred window, lighting an otherwise dark cell. The contrast between the white light and the dark room was striking.

The furnishings were spare. The floor was made of metal, and the room held only a single wooden pallet, a tiny desk, and a squat toilet. In truth, prisons back on Earth were more comfortable.

Huddled in a corner of the bed, Aiko leaned against the wall, head resting on her knees.

Three days had passed here. Thanks to the bracelet strapped to her wrist, she couldn't use magic.

At first, she tried everything to escape. Even cutting herself and drawing a magic circle with her blood, however, hadn't enabled her to cast magic. She wasn't physically strong enough to break the bars of her cell. Nor was she able to slip past the silver-haired nun who brought her food. The nun was far stronger, and could easily overpower Aiko.

The bars prevented Aiko from escaping through the window. At most, she could get one arm through.

Even if there hadn't been any bars, she couldn't have escaped. Her cell was at the top of a tower on the Divine Mountain's summit. She was unlikely to reach the ground without dying. Even if she did reach the ground, the mountain was crawling with priests. Avoiding all of them and making it back to the capital would be an impossible task.

In the end, Aiko just huddled in a corner of her cell. She was worried about her students, but there was nothing she could do.

"What are they trying to do to them...? What's happening...?"

As Aiko mumbled to herself, she recalled what the nun had said... That the nun's master would find it inconvenient if Aiko told the students what she learned from Hajime. The nun wanted one student's plans to continue unhindered.

Worry and despair swirled inside Aiko's mind. She thought back to the boy who'd died in Ur, Yukitoshi Shimizu. She worried that another of her students might do something they could never take back. She couldn't help but agonize about it.

Stuck alone in the prison, Aiko had plenty of time to think. The more she pondered recent events, the more clearly she realized there had been something wrong inside the palace when she returned. Eliheid and the other leaders acted strangely fanatical.

That silver-haired nun must have done something to them. If the strange spell she'd cast on Aiko was really some kind of mind control, then it stood to reason that the king and his retainers were brainwashed.

However, neither Shizuku nor Liliana had acted unusual. Still, there was no telling what might have happened to them since Aiko's capture.

As she prayed for their safety, Aiko remembered one other thing the nun said. *She needed to eliminate the "irregular."*

That word brought to mind a specific student. The boy who'd saved her life, and killed Shimizu. Despite being strong-willed, the boy had still seriously considered the advice Aiko gave him.

Then...they'd...maybe-kind-of-not-really-sort-of-possibly-almost-kissed.

As much as Aiko had tried to bury that memory, it kept surfacing. She blushed despite her desperate situation.

Aiko shook her head, trying to banish the thought. She was worried for his safety, but she also really wanted to see him again. "Nagumo-kun..."

"Yeah? What's up, Sensei?"

"Wha...?!" Aiko couldn't believe her ears. There was no way Hajime was in the cell right then.

She glanced around the room, saw no one, and tilted her head. *Am I hearing things?*

But it wasn't just her imagination. Hajime called out again. "Up here, Sensei."

"Huh?" Aiko looked up at the window. Hajime's face poked between the bars. *I'm not just hearing things!*

"Huh? What? Nagumo-kun?" she gasped. "How? This is the top floor...on the summit... huh?"

"Yeah, I know. Just calm down, Sensei. I need to make sure there aren't any traps."

Hajime swept his gaze around the room, confirming that everything was clear with his demon eye. There was a flurry of red sparks, and a hole appeared in Aiko's wall, wide enough to let a person through.

Aiko's cell was at least a hundred meters in the air. And yet, Hajime just waltzed in as if the ground rose past Aiko's walls.

Hajime smiled as he saw the shock on Aiko's face.

"Why do you look so surprised? I thought I was doing a pretty good job of hiding my presence, but it sounded like you knew I was already here... You made me lose self-confidence, honestly."

"Huh? I did? How?"

"I mean, you called my name, didn't you? Wasn't that because you knew I was here?"

Aiko had known no such thing. She'd only been thinking of him. Not that she could tell Hajime that. She hurriedly changed the topic. "A-anyway, why are you here...?"

"To save you, of course."

"You came all the way here just to save me? Really?"

Hajime raised an eyebrow. Aiko's odd actions made him wonder if she was already brainwashed. He turned his demon eye on her, just to make sure.

Aiko blushed, and her heart beat faster. The boy she'd been thinking about came to save her just when she needed him, and now he stood next to her bed, staring intently at her.

If they'd had a simple teacher-student relationship, Aiko would simply have asked what was wrong. But they didn't, so she could do nothing more than stare back.

Hajime found no traces of mana and decided that Aiko was likely still herself. He took her by the hand and examined her bracelet. He wanted to remove the artifact that sealed her mana, but that wasn't how Aiko interpreted it.

"We can't, Nagumo-kun! This is too sudden! And I'm your teacher!" Aiko squealed, saying some rather scandalous words.

"Don't you want to be able to use magic again? Or will some kind of trap activate if I break this? It doesn't look like that, but..."

"Huh? Oh, that's what you were doing..."

"What did you think I was doing?"

"Aha ha ha ha...! I'm sorry. It's nothing."

Hajime stared quizzically at Aiko, who tried to play her behavior off with a laugh. She changed the subject again, asking how Hajime knew she'd been captured.

"The princess told me."

"By 'the princess,' do you mean Liliana?"

"Yeah. Apparently, she saw you get taken. She couldn't tell Amanogawa or the others, because she was worried they were under surveillance, so she slipped out of the castle to find us."

"So, it was Liliana-san... You agreed to help her?"

"I guess. This is partly my fault, after all. I know you probably didn't want to see my face again, but...you'll just have to deal with it until we meet up with the others."

Hajime smiled awkwardly, then shattered the bracelet sealing Aiko's mana and stood up.

He probably thinks that because of what happened with Shimizu-kun. Aiko grabbed Hajime's arm. She looked directly into his eyes and told him her true feelings.

"I would never wish not to see your face again. I'm truly happy you came here to save me. It's true that I still haven't come to terms with what happened to Shimizu-kun... Honestly, I doubt I ever really will. Still, I'd like to think...that I at least understand why you pulled the trigger. I don't hate you for it, or bear any grudge."

"Sensei..."

Aiko smiled, her gaze holding equal parts kindness and sadness. "I couldn't tell you back then, so I'd like to tell you now. Thank you so much for saving my life. And I'm sorry I forced you to kill a classmate."

"......" *Looks like you were right, Yue. She figured it out.* Hajime smiled bitterly to himself. Whether or not Aiko had realized didn't change the fact that Hajime had done something terrible.

"I just did what I wanted to. I'll accept your thanks, but I don't need an apology. Anyway, let's get out of here. The princess should be with Amanogawa and the others right now. After we've all met up, we'll decide what to do next."

"Very well. Be careful, Nagumo-kun. The Holy Church branded you a heretic. And the person who kidnapped me might be..."

"I know." Hajime nodded, his ironclad resolve evident in his gaze. "There's some stuff I need to do here once I get you to safety, so I'll probably end up fighting them sooner or later. I came here knowing that."

Aiko blushed, but she quickly snapped out of her fantasies. She needed to warn Hajime about one other thing. Before she could do so, they both heard a loud crash in the distance. The air shook.

Aiko stiffened and looked up at Hajime. He stared into the distance, his gaze fixed on a certain point. He guessed that the commotion had come from ground level, and received a report from Yue telepathically.

"Tch, this is some pretty crap timing... Wait. Actually, this might not be that bad."

Hajime clicked his tongue and turned to Aiko.

Aiko didn't know Hajime could use telepathy, but since she'd seen so many of his artifacts, she didn't doubt that he'd found out what happened somehow. She demanded an explanation with her gaze.

"Sensei, the demons have attacked. That noise was the sound of the capital's barrier being destroyed."

"Demons are attacking?! Doesn't that mean..."

"Yeah, Heiligh is under siege. My comrades told me through telepathy. The demons have a huge army of monsters with them too. They caught the human army totally by surprise."

"Impossible." Aiko paled and shook her head.

The demons shouldn't have been able to bring an army capable of invading the capital so close to the city without anyone noticing. Moreover, the barrier shielding the city was nigh invincible. It was unthinkable that the demons had, not only shattered it, but done so without being spotted.

"For now, we need to meet up with Amanogawa and the others. We'll discuss more later."

"O-okay."

Hajime scooped Aiko up and prepared to jump. She squealed and threw her arms around his neck. However, just then, a blinding light rained down from above.

"Huh?!"

It resembled moonlight; it was just more intense. Hajime's instincts told him it was dangerous, and he heeded their warning. Without a backward glance, he leaped through the hole he'd made. Aiko shrieked and clung to him even tighter, but there wasn't any time to spare.

A second after Hajime leaped from the cell, the silver light blew it to pieces.

The light made a strange noise as it slammed into the stone wall. It wasn't the sound of a physical object colliding with rock, nor the distinctive hiss of heat melting stone. It sounded as if the light simply dismantled the wall's component parts. The top of the imposing tower blew away in the wind, its stone turned into particles finer than sand.

Hajime steadied himself in the air with Aerodynamic.

"Was the tower...disintegrated?"

Although Hajime hadn't expected an answer, he got one anyway. "Correct, Irregular."

The girl who responded had a voice as pure as a bell's peal, but utterly devoid of emotion.

Hajime looked up and saw a silver-haired, blue-eyed girl gazing down at him. She floated above what had been the tower's summit. Her appearance matched Liliana's description of the nun who kidnapped Aiko.

The girl wasn't dressed in a nun's habit, though. Instead, she wore a helmet on her head, gauntlets on her arms, and greaves over her legs.

Nothing but a white sleeveless dress concealed her torso. However, metal plates covered either side of her waist. Although her garments were a bit odd, they were clearly a combat uniform. She resembled a Valkyrie from Norse mythology.

The girl soared into the sky, as if gravity had no hold over her. The moon framed her silhouette as she turned to face Hajime, glimmering silver wings unfurling from her back. They shimmered as though made of mana.

The winged figure's glorious silver hair fluttered in the breeze. She possessed a mysterious, otherworldly beauty. Unfortunately, her eyes ruined her looks.

While everything else about her shone like the moon, her eyes were ice cold. There was not even a trace of hatred in them. Only mechanical, emotionless frigidity, as though she was just a doll.

The girl met Hajime's sharp gaze and spread her arms wide. Her gauntlets shimmered, and a pair of large, hiltless swords appeared in her hands.

The two-meter longswords glimmered with the same silvery light. She swung them as though they were weightless, and addressed Hajime in an emotionless voice.

"I am Noint, an Apostle of God. My duty is to remove unwanted pieces from my lord's game board."

A clear declaration of war.

The girl standing before Hajime was a true Apostle of God, sent directly by Ehit himself. *So those so-called gods finally decided to get in my way?* Hajime had ruined too much of their fun. Now, they were going to eliminate him.

The air trembled as Noint gathered silver mana.

A wave of pressure crashed down on Hajime and Aiko like a waterfall. Aiko gritted her teeth and tried to withstand it, but she was white as a sheet. The pressure was too much. Just before she fell unconscious, however, a veil of crimson mana surrounded her. Hajime's aura blocked the pressure wave.

Aiko's eyes snapped open. She looked up at Hajime. Despite the overwhelming pressure, he didn't seem cowed. On the contrary, there was a murderous glint in his eyes, and a fearless grin on his face.

Hajime's confidence captivated Aiko as he stared Noint down, retorting, "I'd like to see you try, God's Puppet!"

Eight thousand meters in the air, far above the skies of the Divine Mountain, God's Apostle clashed with the monster who crawled out of the abyss.

⁂

Shortly before Hajime and Noint's battle, Yue, Shea, Kaori, and Liliana snuck into the palace. Liliana led them towards Kouki and the others.

Their primary goal was to find and clear the labyrinth hidden in the Divine Mountain. Normally, they wouldn't bother to help solve the kingdom's problems. To ensure Aiko's safety, though, they needed to make certain Kouki and the others weren't brainwashed. After all, they would be looking after Aiko once Hajime freed her. Furthermore, the Divine Mountain was the Holy Church's base of operations. The church's main temple was located there. To infiltrate that temple unnoticed, Hajime would need to retrieve Aiko alone. Although they could take on the Holy Church, Hajime and his comrades didn't want to start an open war.

There was nothing else for them to do in the capital, so Kaori and the others decided to join Liliana as she snuck into the palace.

Only Tio remained outside, waiting on standby in case anything happened. Yue thought it best that at least one person grasp the situation fully.

The secret passage Liliana led the girls through brought them to an unused guest room. As the last person stepped out of the passage, an antique wooden drawer slid over its entrance, hiding it from view.

"Everyone will probably be asleep. Let's start by going to Shizuku's room," Liliana whispered.

Her decision spoke volumes about who she trusted most. It wasn't Kouki, everyone's ostensible hero and leader.

The girls nodded, and filed out of the room. Shea, who had the best hearing, took the lead. The students' sleeping quarters were in another wing of the palace, so the group had to jog through a number of hallways.

They were almost there when a massive boom shook the entire castle. A second later, the sound of shattering glass rang out. All the windows in the hallway exploded, strewing the ground with glittering shards.

"Waaaaaah! What just happened?!" Shea crouched and nursed her bunny ears. They'd been perked up, listening for even the slightest sound, so the deafening boom hurt pretty bad.

"Don't tell me..." Behind her, Liliana paled and dashed to a shattered window. Yue and Kaori followed behind.

What Liliana saw confirmed her fears. "Impossible! The barrier's been...destroyed?" She brought a hand to her mouth.

The night sky was speckled with a million dots of light. However, most weren't stars, but the remnants of the now-destroyed barrier that had covered the capital. There was a brilliant flash of light, and another thunderous roar. A second barrier flared into existence and bore the brunt of another blow. Still, cracks spread across its surface.

"E-even the second layer can't... How did our defenses grow so weak?! At this rate..."

The great barrier that protected the capital actually consisted of three separate layers of defenses, created by an artifact held by the palace. Magicians worked day and night, pouring mana into it, ensuring that it never waned.

For centuries, the barrier had stood firm, protecting the capital from invasion. Never before had it been breached. That was one of the main reasons humans had been able to stand their ground against the demons.

And yet, it had been demolished in an instant.

Not only that, the second layer was nearly gone too. Each successive layer was smaller, but also more powerful. Nonetheless, it looked as though the second layer would be destroyed in a few more seconds.

The palace burst into an uproar. Hallway lamps were lit, and people ran to and fro.

"Did someone betray us? But, if that was the case, they'd only bring a small force... Isn't that an entire army at our doorstep? What's going on?"

While Liliana muttered to herself, Tio contacted the others. "Can you hear me? It's Tio. Would you like me to explain what's happening?"

Yue, Shea, and Kaori's telepathy stones began to glow. Tio's voice rang through them. It seemed she already grasped the situation outside.

"Yeah. Thanks, Tio."

"Understood. A massive army of monsters has appeared one kilometer south of the capital. The white dragon we fought at the Grand Gruen Volcano is there. That dragon's breath demolished the barrier. However, I don't see the demon who controlled it."

"So, we're really under attack? How did a monster army get here without anyone noticing? What were the scouts at the Reisen Gorge doing?!" Liliana screamed hysterically.

Yue and the others could guess how the army made it past. The demon Freid Bagwa had cleared the Grand Gruen Volcano, and could use spatial magic.

Opening a portal large enough to transport an entire army was difficult, but not outside the realm of possibility. Yue could even manage it at her skill level, with some help.

Only teleportation would have enabled an army this size to escape the notice of the Reisen Gorge's scouts, and of the villages and forts along the way to the capital. Therefore, teleportation was the only method that made sense.

Since Freid wasn't riding his white dragon, Yue guessed he must have exhausted himself by opening the gate, and was probably resting.

A second later came the sound of more shattering glass. The second layer had been pierced.

Liliana urged Yue and the others to keep going. They needed to find Shizuku as soon as possible. Yue shook her head.

"We'll part ways here. You go on ahead."

"B-but why?"

We need to rejoin the others and set up a final line of defense as soon as possible!

Yue glared out the window.

"That demon hurt Hajime. I'm going to make him regret being born."

She still held a grudge about that surprise attack. The others took an involuntary step back. Yue rarely displayed her emotions, but now, her voice burned with rage.

"Y-you're really mad, aren't you, Yue-san...?"

"Aren't you, Shea? Or did you already forget what he did?"

"Never. I won't let him die, even if he begs for it."

Shea's expression grew serious, and the warmth left her voice. When it came down to it, she was just as pissed. It was rare to see Shea, who was always cheerful, say something so violent. She, too, held quite a grudge.

"Which is why, Kaori-san, Lily-san, we'll teach that oversized lizard and its master a lesson."

"Yeah. We'll take out his army while we're at it."

Before Kaori or Liliana could say anything, Shea and Yue leaped out of the window.

Poor Freid's fate was sealed. There was no way he could hold his own against Shea and Yue. While the overpowered bunny and her vampire companion spelled doom for their enemies, they inadvertently also served as the capital's saviors.

At the very least, Yue and Shea would buy time for the humans to regroup, so Liliana didn't try to persuade them to stay. A chill breeze wafted through the shattered window, carrying the panicked screams of an entire city.

Liliana and Kaori stood still for a few seconds, exchanged glances, and resumed jogging toward Shizuku's room.

"They really love Nagumo-san, don't they?"

"Yep. When they get like that... Well, they're terrifying. I wouldn't want to be their enemy."

"Kaori... Do your best not to die. I'm rooting for you."

"I will. Thanks, Lily."

Though Shea and Yue were ostensibly helping the humans, Liliana was sure neither of them actually cared what happened to the capital. They fought only for Hajime.

"Even though I'm the princess... everyone's just forgetting about me..." Inwardly, Liliana despaired a little.

Would Lily cry if I told her I wanted to go too? Kaori wondered as she ran.

⁂

The capital was in chaos. People all over the city filled the streets to watch the barriers shatter one after another. The city guard was frantic, trying to get people back in their homes.

Some people had already packed their belongings and were trying to flee. Yet others raced to the palace and banged on its gates, begging to be let in.

Barely a few minutes had passed, but soon, there would doubtless be riots in the streets.

The palace didn't have the manpower to quell the crowds, either. Especially since the uproar in the palace was even bigger than the one outside. The kingdom's top brass awoke to learn that the demons already had a dagger pressed to the city's throat.

They did their best to organize a counterattack, but—

Smaaaaash! They didn't have time.

The final barrier shattered, and the demon army, bolstered by a horde of monsters made from ancient magic, swarmed toward the capital.

The only protection left was the city's stone walls. They were sturdily built, but everyone knew they wouldn't last a second against an army that took down their barriers.

A wave of demons cast their strongest spells at the walls. Streaks of fire, bolts of lightning, pillars of ice, and clods of earth slammed the ramparts. A massive monster the size of a cyclops smashed its mace into what remained.

A massive boar over five meters long rammed another section of wall over and over. Each collision shook the world.

A flock of Ash Dragons and black, eagle-like creatures soared overhead and began attacking the capital proper.

The soldiers on the ramparts tried to stem the tide, but there just weren't enough of them. Moreover, they'd been taken entirely by surprise. It was like trying to stop a tornado with a fan.

Tio stood atop a clock tower in the city's center and surveyed the battle. A few seconds later, Shea and Yue alighted next to her.

"Tio, did you see that disgusting demon anywhere?"

"Where's that bastard hiding, Tio-san?"

"You two... I understand how you feel, but Princess Liliana seemed quite happy when you offered to accompany her. Are you sure you should have abandoned her so casually?"

"Who cares about that?"

"There's no time to waste now!"

Yue and Shea didn't feel the tiniest bit of remorse. When it came to people they didn't care about, the pair could be quite blunt. *I suspect this is Master's influence.*

As Yue and Shea scanned the monsters, looking for Freid Bagwa, they received a telepathic transmission from Hajime.

"Hey, Tio! Get over here!"

"Whoa! Master? What's wrong?"

The urgency in Hajime's voice surprised Tio.

"I've got a really dangerous enemy to deal with. I need you to take Sensei for me. I can't fight at full strength while protecting her."

"Understood! I will head over immediately!"

If Hajime was up against an opponent who required him to go all out, there was no time to waste. Tio transformed into her dragon form and shot toward the Divine Mountain.

"Hajime, be careful!"

"Hajime-san, don't worry! Yue-san and I will take care of that stupid demon for you!"

"O-okay? Weren't you two with the princess—holy shit! Crap, I can't really talk right now! I don't know what you guys are up to, but don't die, all right?"

Although curious about what they were planning, Hajime was a bit preoccupied. He cut the transmission and focused on his own fight.

Yue and Shea hesitated. If Hajime was having a hard time, maybe they should run to his aid instead of staying in the city. Still, even if he wasn't at full strength, few enemies could match him.

"Yue-san, what do you want to do?"

"Hajime'll be fine. He has Tio with him. Let's get that demon. If we don't kill him, he might destroy other labyrinths' magic circles."

That was an additional reason Yue decided to prioritize killing Freid. She wanted revenge, but she also knew she couldn't let another ancient magic user run free.

It was possible that Freid already knew the location of the labyrinth inside the Divine Mountain. If he cleared it first, he might destroy the magic circle, like he did in Gruen.

From what they'd learned in the other labyrinths, Yue knew that each labyrinth would be restored to its former state, given time. Even the monsters in it would return. However, there was no telling how long that might take.

Yue didn't want to give Freid a chance to destroy the Divine Mountain's magic circle. The best way to make sure he couldn't do anything was to kill him.

However, revenge was still her main driving force. Keeping the labyrinth safe was maybe ten percent of the reason she was there. Two black eagles spotted Yue and Shea, and swooped over them. The birdlike creatures were three or four meters long, and quite a fearsome sight.

Shea pulled Drucken from her Treasure Trove and calmly fired an explosive slug at one eagle. Yue snapped her fingers, and a barrage of wind blades rained down on the other.

Their attacks turned the two eagles into mincemeat. Shea's bullet blew the first eagle's head off, while Yue's magic chopped the second to pieces. Their broken corpses fell to the roofs below. Chances were, the people living in those houses were awake now, if they hadn't been already.

Other flying monsters took notice and began circling. A good third had demon riders on their backs.

They kept their distance, wary of the power that had brought two eagles low in the span of a few seconds. However, when they realized they faced a little girl and a rabbitman, they scoffed. Throwing caution to the wind, they chanted spells.

Naturally, they didn't think Yue or Shea could fly. Regardless of what tricks the girls had up their sleeves, the demons doubted they could withstand a concerted barrage from above.

Yue and Shea had no interest in defending the capital. Their only target was Freid Bagwa. However, that didn't mean they would ignore anyone attacking them.

Shea tried to negotiate, just in case. "We're not your enemies! We only fought back because those things attacked us first!"

Of course, the demons simply thought Shea was mocking them. They didn't stop chanting.

Assuming that the two girls weren't worth their time, a number of demons flew off to look for other prey. A second later, they heard a loud roar and a series of screams.

"Wh-what *is* that?!"

The demons turned around to see a dragon made of lightning devouring their comrades one by one. They could hardly believe their eyes.

"H-help—!"

One demon managed to escape the slaughter and flew for dear life. Before he could reach his comrades, however, something blew him to pieces. It was Shea's explosive slug, ripping him to shreds.

The demons who'd gone ahead gazed in horror as chunks of demon and Ash Dragon rained down.

The demons stiffened and guarded themselves against the

next attack. They cast their gazes about, looking for the two girls who obliterated their comrades. They were so terrified, they forgot to even blink the sweat out of their eyes.

The demons spotted Yue and Shea relatively quickly, but the two girls weren't giving chase. In fact, Yue and Shea completely ignored them. As before, the pair scanned the horizon, looking for something.

Their demeanor made it obvious that the demons weren't even worth their time.

The demons' nervousness turned into anger. These girls had slaughtered their friends, and done so with the casual indifference of swatting an insect. That stomped on the demons' pride.

Blood boiling, they charged.

"You biiiiiitch!"

"Uwoooooooooh!"

"Dieeeeeeeee!"

Despite their rage, the demons maintained formation, which showed just how well-trained they were. They unleashed magical attacks from all four directions simultaneously. Demons were far more skilled at magic than humans. Normally, a barrage like that would be a death sentence.

Yue just sighed. Then, she waved her finger like a conductor's baton. "You should be able to tell the difference between our skill levels."

Yue's thunder dragon coiled about her, protecting her and Shea from the demons' magic.

The dragon opened its maw wide, and the demons nearby appeared to practically fling themselves in.

The demons on the other side tried to cast a barrage of piercing spells, but before they finished, a section of the dragon opened up.

Shea shot out, charging straight at them. "Tch! Flame Bullet!"

One demon cut his chanting short and cast a beginner-level spell to try and hold Shea back. Countless tiny balls of flame hurtled toward her.

Shea fired Drucken and used its knockback to adjust her trajectory, easily avoiding the barrage. Then she swung Drucken in a wide arc, aiming for three chanting demons.

"Take thiiiiiiiiiiiis!"

Shea manipulated the hammer, making it weigh over four tons at the moment of impact. Thanks to her improved body strengthening, she could still swing it easily.

The demons never stood a chance. The attack ground them to a pulp, and shattered the spines of the monsters they rode. Monsters and riders alike barely had time to scream before they died.

Shea lowered her and Drucken's combined weight to under five kilograms and used the shotgun blast's recoil to shoot up into the air.

At the same time, she switched Drucken into barrage mode and fired an explosive slug at the demon who shot the fireballs.

"Get blown to the other side of next week!"

The bullet's force sent the poor demon blasting off to the moon.

Shea poured mana into her Aerodynamic-enchanted boots and created a light blue mana platform to stand on.

She tapped Drucken against her shoulder and surveyed her surroundings. This cute bunny girl had quickly become the demons' worst nightmare.

A short distance away, Yue faced the final remaining demon.

He charged in a glorious-but-futile suicide attack. "You damn braaaaaaaaat! This is for my friends!"

Even if it meant his death, he wanted to get at least one hit on this girl.

Yue stared at him coldly. "You're 300 years too young to call me a brat."

The demon seized the moment when Yue's dragon devoured another of his comrades. He was confident the beast couldn't turn in time. He sneered, certain he'd be able to stab Yue. When the demon was mere meters away, however, a wind blade chopped his head off, and he plummeted to the ground.

Lamenting the waste of time, Yue returned to searching for Freid.

Next to Yue, Shea alighted, Drucken still resting on her shoulder.

"They totally thought we were fighting for the kingdom, didn't they?"

"Yeah. Well, whatever. If that's what they want to think, just let them."

"You really don't care about them, do you? Well, I guess I don't, either."

Despite their best efforts, Shea and Yue were unable to locate Bagwa among the horde.

Yue worried that he'd found the labyrinth's entrance and teleported there already. Just then, though...

"Huh?! Yue-san!"

"Mmm...?"

The moment Shea called out, Yue leaped off the clock tower.

A second later, an egg-shaped portal opened, unleashing a barrage of aurora-colored light.

The light enveloped the clock tower, obliterating it. It didn't stop there; it swallowed all the houses and buildings in its path.

"As I suspected, you do have some form of clairvoyance. How troublesome..."

They turned to see the foe they sought, Freid Bagwa, riding his white dragon.

He looked rather irritated that the two managed to dodge his surprise attack so easily.

As Freid emerged from the portal, a hundred demonic riders astride Ash Dragons surrounded Yue and Shea.

Part of the city's outer wall crumbled with a thunderous crash. Demons and monsters swarmed in. A number of squads broke away and started running toward Freid.

He wanted to make sure to finish the girls off for good.

"To think, you actually survived. I shouldn't have underestimated that man's tenacity... He's dangerous. To defeat him, I shall have to ensure his comrades, you girls, die first."

Yue and Shea grinned fearlessly.

Yue spoke the same words that Hajime had said a few seconds ago, 8000 meters above them. "I'd like to see you try."

"Just try and kill me!" Shea echoed.

The army of monsters and demons attacked all at once. Flaming javelins hot enough to scorch the air itself, jets of water so powerful that they could cut steel, blades of wind sharper than swords, blocks of ice larger than boulders, dark gray spheres filled with petrification magic, and bolts of crackling thunder hurtled toward the two girls.

A massive aurora trailed behind the other spells.

There were forty demons, and more than a hundred monsters. Their attacks flew in from every conceivable direction.

The spells melded into a storm of deadly magic. Still, neither Shea nor Yue seemed worried. They didn't even try to dodge. Most of the demons assumed they'd just given up. Freid, however, had an ominous premonition. He hurriedly pulled his dragon away.

"Cosmic Rift!"

Yue cast her spell.

Two shimmering portals appeared in front of the aurora. Freid narrowed his eyes. The portals were right beside each other, so even if light entered one, it'd just come out of the other and hit the girls anyway.

Freid's mistake was assuming that Yue summoned only a single pair of portals, since that was the most *he* could do.

Because Freid was distracted by the portals in front of the girls, he noticed too late that there was another portal behind him.

"Blast! Everyone, run!" Freid shouted a warning, but there was no time.

Yue and Shea disappeared inside the first gate, while the second swallowed the aurora and spat it out behind the demons.

Freid just managed to fly out of the way, but most of his army was decimated.

"How dare you make me kill my own men? I underestimated you. I should have predicted that you would be able to open multiple gates."

Through his anger, Freid felt a burgeoning fear. Yue was capable of far more impressive magical feats than he was, even with the same spells.

He was curious as to how she could cast spells without incantations or magic circles, but his priority was to find out where his opponents had disappeared to.

"Freid-sama! Over there!" One of Freid's men pointed at the outer wall. Yue and Shea stood atop it. They hadn't wanted to fight in the city, since innocent citizens might get caught up in the battle. And they knew Freid wouldn't call off the entire invasion to chase them down. This was a challenge. If he wanted them, he'd have to fight them without his army.

On the other hand, if he left them alone, he'd leave his rear vulnerable to attack.

Freid couldn't ignore them. He homed in with his Farsight and saw Yue and Shea hold out their hands and beckon, as if to say, "Bring it on."

The demons were livid. Not only were they being belittled by a bunny girl and a woman the height of a child, the two were clearly confident that the demons didn't even pose a threat.

Although the demons were few in number, they were certain they were the strongest creatures in the land. They took pride in that, and having that pride trampled enraged them.

"You little bitch!"

"You're just a filthy little beast! Don't get so full of yourself!"

The demons spat out curses and charged. Still, they didn't rush forward blindly. Wary of Yue's powerful magic, they sent the monsters first, as shields. Many monsters and demons on the ground fired off attacks as well.

Shea had stored an unbelievable quantity of explosive slugs inside her Treasure Trove, so she didn't need to hold anything in reserve. She fired off bullets one after another into the horde.

Pale blue shockwaves of mana exploded across the battlefield, bringing death to anything they touched.

All that remained were crushed corpses.

To stop Shea's mad rampage, Freid's white dragon and the Ash Dragons all fired their breath at her.

Even Shea, with her body strengthening, wouldn't come out of such a concentrated attack alive. However, she still wasn't worried.

"Spatial Severance."

Yue summoned a black sphere in front of Shea. The superdense black hole bent and absorbed the dragons' breath.

"Ngh, you used that before too. That must be ancient magic which I have yet to acquire," Freid growled. "Listen up, men! I'll take that blond mage! The rest of you must strike down that rabbit girl! Keep them split up, and don't let them coordinate attacks!"

"Yes, sir!"

It would be easier to take the girls on if he separated them. Shea tried to rush back to Yue, but a demon wrapped his black eagle in a tornado and shot straight at her.

Shea tried to swat him away, but it was difficult, since a number of other demons attempted the same maneuver. Instead, Shea used Drucken's recoil to leap aside and swung her hammer in a wide arc, blowing her foes away.

Another wave of demons came. This time, Shea wouldn't have time to dodge or counter, so she held Drucken aloft and took a defensive stance.

She pressed one of her hammer's many triggers, and a round shield popped out of the end with a metallic clunk.

"I'll kill you even if it costs me my life!" spat the blond-haired demon who rushed her. There was so much vehemence in his voice, Shea doubted it was just rage at his dead comrades.

The demon attackers pushed Shea further and further away from Yue. She toyed with the idea of increasing her weight and temporarily retreating to the ground. Before she could do so, a portal opened behind her.

Shea glanced at Freid. He ordered wave after wave of demons and monsters to keep Yue occupied, then cast another teleportation spell.

"Yue-san! I'm sorry, but I can't get back over to you!"

"Yeah. That's fine. I'll kill this guy for you."

Before Shea was pushed through the gate, she saw Yue give her a thumbs up. Shea smiled back, any worry draining from her face.

The attacking demon snarled. He hated being ignored,

especially since he was right in front of her. Shea let him push her back, and fell through the portal.

"That grinning face of yours makes me sick. I'm gonna rip your limbs off and drag your corpse in front of your friends."

That was the first thing Shea heard as she stepped into the air on the other side. This demon seemed to hold a grudge against Shea. She tilted her head as she looked at him.

"Have we met somewhere before? I don't recognize you."

"Do you remember the red-haired demon woman you killed?"

Shea didn't understand why he was suddenly bringing up a woman.

The male demon ground his teeth, thinking Shea didn't remember at all.

"The one you killed in the Great Orcus Labyrinth!" he screamed, voice dripping with venom.

"Oh! You mean her!"

"You biiiiiitch!"

Seeing that Shea had totally forgotten, the male demon roared and sent a barrage of wind blades after her. Shea dodged them without even looking.

"Hey, what was so important about her, anyway? I don't get why you're so mad."

"Her name was Cattleya... And she was my fiancée!"

"Ah! I see now. Well, that explains it."

Shea nodded. It seemed this was Mikhail; the demon they'd killed had talked about him.

Shea didn't know how Mikhail found out that Hajime killed

Cattleya, but it looked as though he'd come for revenge. That was why he wanted to kill Yue and Shea, then drag their corpses to Hajime.

"What gave you the right to kill Cattleya?! She was kind, and wise, and loyal!"

Shea dropped the playful act and gave Mikhail a look that chilled him to the bone. "Why should I care?"

"Y-you...!"

"If she didn't want to die, she shouldn't have fought us in the first place. I mean, she was the one who attacked us. Hajime-san even warned her. He gave her a chance to run. I can understand why you'd want revenge for your dead lover, but there's no point telling me. It's not like it has anything to do with me. If you killed someone I cared about, would you want to hear about what kind of person they were? No, right?"

"Sh-shut up! I'll make you pay for what you did to her! You won't die an easy death!"

Mikhail created another tornado and sent it flying.

Since it didn't surround the eagle, Shea guessed that the tornado was Mikhail's own magic. With another chant, Mikhail summoned numerous wind blades to cut off Shea's retreat.

She blew the blades away with a swing from Drucken, then made herself lighter and jumped out of the eagle's path.

However, while Shea and Mikhail spoke, many other demons appeared through the portal. Shea was outnumbered. Judging from the fact that the demons all rode black eagles, she guessed that this was Mikhail's personal squad.

The demons fired a barrage of stone needles. They fell upon Shea like a hailstorm. However, she simply diverted them with an explosive slug. Then, she jumped into the opening she'd created and closed in on an eagle-riding demon.

Shea slammed Drucken down without mercy, crushing the demon's bones and organs instantly. It sent him flying into the darkness. Shea extended Drucken's handle and pulverized another demon-eagle pair.

"Grr... Don't let her get close! We control the skies! Keep your distance, and bury her in magic and stone needles!"

Mikhail grasped the scope of Shea's close-combat strength and ordered his men to stay back. The demons once again rained spells down, but Shea lithely dodged every attack, dancing through the sky with her Aerodynamic-enchanted boots.

Every time she tried to close in on an enemy, however, they flew back, maintaining their distance. Shea was starting to get annoyed.

"Sheesh. Quit darting around like that! Fine, I'll just have to beat you all to a pulp!"

Bunny ears standing on end, Shea pulled something from her Treasure Trove.

It was a red sphere, made entirely of metal, and a good two meters in diameter. Chains hung off one section, and Shea attached Drucken's top to those chains.

Gravity took hold of the sphere, and it fell towards the ground. Shea kicked it back into the air and hit it as hard as she could with her hammer.

With a loud metallic clang, she sent the ball flying at an insane speed.

The demon in the ball's path tried to dodge out of the way, but the sphere fired a shockwave and adjusted its trajectory. The ten-ton ball crushed the eagle and its demon rider, who were unable to escape. Their shattered remains fell to the earth below.

With another swing, the sphere reversed directions and headed back to Shea's side.

In the time the ball took to return, Shea kept the demons busy with her explosive slugs. Those demons who couldn't defend in time were killed. Once the sphere returned, Shea sent it hurtling off towards a new target.

This was the newest addition Hajime had fashioned for Drucken. It was basically a massive kendama. Shea could control its weight and direction with magic, and with the recoil from the explosives Hajime had packed inside.

"Oi oi oi oi oi!"

Shea sent the sphere whizzing across the battlefield. It went out, killed someone, returned to her, then went out again. The dazzling red meteor lit up the capital's skies, spelling death for anyone in its vicinity. Before long, it was drenched in demon blood.

"Curse you and your strange techniques!" Mikhail bit his lip and barked out orders. "Everyone, retreat! Attack her from the very edge of your range!"

He circled Shea, firing restraining spells one after another to slow her down.

Shea leaped higher into the air, dodging every spell. It was as if gravity had no hold over her. Then, however, another torrent of spells came down from above.

"Hmph. Pathetic!"

Shea raised Drucken overhead and twirled it rapidly. The sphere began to spin as well. The rotating ball became a shield, deflecting the barrage of powerful spells.

"I have you now!"

Thinking Shea had her hands full, Mikhail rushed at her.

His eagle launched a deadly barrage of stone needles, which Mikhail accelerated with the wind spell Gale Sovereign.

The storm of needles pelted toward Shea. She increased her weight tremendously and allowed gravity to pull her to safety.

Mikhail smirked. He had expected that. He chanted another spell, planning to bury Shea in a storm of wind blades. That was exactly when things stopped going as planned. Shea pulled a fist-size metal ball seemingly out of thin air and let it fall.

"Here goes!" She kicked it with all her strength toward Mikhail.

Before he could finish his spell, the ball slammed into his eagle with a meaty thunk.

"Caaaaaaaaaaaaaaaaaaaaw!"

"You little...!"

The black eagle hurtled toward the ground, with Mikhail still astride it. In one last act of desperation, he fired another burst of stone needles as he fell out of sight.

Shea just barely managed to deflect the needles with Drucken. Still, a few needles punched through, piercing her arm and shoulder.

"He did it! He got her with the Cotriss' needles!"

"It's over now!"

The needles weren't large enough to cause serious damage, but the demons grinned as if they'd won.

Shea cocked her head in confusion. A second later, she realized why. The parts of her body that had been stabbed started to petrify. It appeared this Cotriss monster could fire needles that petrified anything they touched. That was quite a troublesome ability.

Normally, something as deadly as petrification could only be cured through light magic or strong healing items. Since Shea was fighting the petrification on her own, she should have been done for. There were no healers in sight, and even if she did have medicine, the demons weren't going to give her time to drink it. Before long, she'd be fully petrified.

A second later, her foes' triumphant grins turned into looks of dumbfounded despair. Shea proved to possess abilities beyond the realm of common sense.

"Grr... I let my guard down. Still, this isn't enough to stop me!"

Shea pulled the needles out of her arm and closed her eyes. The petrification stopped spreading and, like a receding tide, shrank away. Within seconds, it vanished, and the holes in Shea's arm closed.

"Wh-what the...?!"

"How did she do that?!"

Shea hadn't downed any potions, nor had her attackers seen her chant any spells. She'd just concentrated, and the petrification, along with her wounds, vanished. The demons trembled in fear. Their voices shook. They were facing something they couldn't understand.

Shea hadn't actually done anything special. She just used restoration magic.

As with other ancient magics, her aptitude for it was strikingly low. The most she could do was heal minor wounds and remove status effects. Unlike Yue's automatic restoration, Shea couldn't regenerate lost body parts, or instantly heal fatal wounds. And she definitely couldn't return objects to their former state. Still, with a little concentration, she could heal minor wounds and fractures and recover from most slow-progressing status effects. Given enough time, she could heal more serious injuries as well.

The combination of Shea's overwhelming strength and near-instant regeneration left the demons bereft of options. There was no way for them to beat someone who possessed a tank's firepower, and could fly through the sky and heal on command. Generals back on Earth would have been terrified by her overwhelming strength.

The demons' eyes were full of terror, just as Hajime's past opponents' eyes had been.

This bunny girl's a monster!

"Now then, let's get back to it."

Shea shouldered Drucken and launched herself at the stunned demons. Her fluffy bunny ears fluttered in the breeze.

Each swing of her hammer brought certain death.

The fear finally broke them. The demons charged at Shea, all thought of strategy and formation gone.

Shea calmly dealt with the rush, crushing her attackers with her kendama or obliterating them with explosive slugs.

As the last member of Mikhail's squad fell, a dark shadow covered the moon.

Shea looked up and saw clouds forming above her. Mikhail fell through them, heading straight for her. It seemed his eagle was too injured to do anything but dive.

"You may be good, but I bet even *you* can't dodge a thousand lightning bolts at once!"

At Mikhail's words, countless bolts of lightning poured down, with no discernible pattern or logic. Electricity filled the sky.

Normally, the skill Thunder Hammer fired a single massive bolt of lightning from the heavens. However, Mikhail fractured the spell, spreading its power over a much wider area. He truly was a master of magic.

The lightning bolts quickly overtook him.

It seemed Mikhail planned to take Shea down with him while the lightning distracted her. Even with the spell's power diluted, and even if Shea was a godlike monstrosity, the thunder would at least slow her down.

Moreover, the lightning was traveling a hundred miles an hour. No one could follow it with their naked eye, much less dodge.

Mikhail had watched his comrades die one after another while he chanted. No matter what, he would make sure it wasn't in vain.

What happened next, however, defied Mikhail's expectations once more.

Shea dodged the lightning. Or, more accurately, she stood where she knew the bolts wouldn't strike her.

Mikhail had underestimated her. He hadn't realized Shea possessed a skill that let her dodge things too fast to see.

Over the past few weeks, Shea had unlocked another of Future Sight's derivative skills: Prophetic Vision. It allowed her to see two seconds into the future whenever she wished. It wasn't nearly as powerful as Branching Paths, but it also required far less mana. Furthermore, because of her constant training, she could activate it quickly.

"What the hell are you?!"

"Just your average bunny girl," Shea joked as she dodged the storm.

Naturally, Mikhail also passed right by. As he did, Shea rounded on him with her kendama.

He was too close for the ball itself to hit, but the chains wrapped around him, trapping him in place.

"Nnnnnngh! Let me go!"

"As you wish!" Shea swung Drucken around, and sent Mikhail hurtling toward the ground. The centrifugal force in Shea's swing was tremendous, and Mikhail slammed into the ground with the force of a meteor. The wind barrier he put up at the last minute kept him alive, but only just. Most of his bones were shattered, and he was coughing up blood.

Shea alighted on the ground nearby. She shouldered Drucken and walked up to the broken demon.

Mikhail looked at her with empty eyes. Merely staying

conscious was an ordeal. The corners of his lips twitched upwards into a self-deprecating smirk. Even he wasn't sure whether that was because he'd failed to get revenge, or because he just watched one girl wipe out his entire squad. After what he'd seen, all he could do was smile.

In his mind, Mikhail apologized to Cattleya for not avenging her. Eyes locked on Shea, he uttered his final words. "Gah...you... *cough*...monster!"

"Hee hee! Thanks for the compliment!"

His insult only served to make Shea happy.

Ah... If there really is an afterlife, I'll need to look for Cattleya there. That was the last thought that flashed through Mikhail's mind before Shea's hammer ended his life.

Shea looked down at his battered corpse and smiled to herself.

"Looks like I'm finally strong enough to be called a monster too. Tee hee... I'm getting closer to Hajime-san."

"Now then, I should see how Yue-san is doing."

Shea looked towards the source of Yue's mana. It seemed like she'd teleported quite far.

If I hurry, I might still land a few good hits on that bastard. With that thought, Shea dashed off.

Ash Dragons filled the sky in such numbers that they blotted out the moon. There were more than a hundred. At their center was a massive white dragon with a gaping hole in its chest. Atop the dragon rode Freid Bagwa.

He watched Shea and Mikhail disappear through Freid's Cosmic Rift. Then, he turned back to Yue. "I hope you don't

consider this cowardly. Dividing your enemy's strength is one of the basics of strategy."

Although she showed no signs of using wind magic, Yue continued floating in the sky. Freid expected to see some kind of reaction after throwing her companion into a portal, but the girl just stared silently.

Like all demons, Freid considered himself superior. He was proud of his race, believed unwaveringly in his god, and was basically inflexible. Someone of a different race would never charm him.

Still, he thought it would be a waste to kill this girl, who shone as beautifully as the moon. That was the power of Yue's looks.

Of course, Freid knew he needed to kill her to weaken Hajime, and hated her for killing so many of his comrades. Still, he couldn't help but chat a while longer.

"What a waste. Woman, no matter how skilled you may be, even if you can cast spells without chanting, you have no hope of victory so long as you are a magician. What do you say? Why not join my side instead? Someone of your abilities would be treated well here."

Yue didn't even consider it.

"Hmph. Never in a million years, you ugly wretch," she sneered.

Although Yue called him ugly, Freid was more handsome than most men. His good looks, combined with his influential position, meant that demon women swooned over him. He was by no means an ugly wretch.

However, Yue had seen his expression of pure rapture when he spoke of his god. That blind devotion disgusted her.

Of course, Freid's expression was normal now, but that just made him all the more laughable. Even leaving all that aside, Yue had no intention of being with anyone but Hajime.

Freid's smile froze in place.

"So, you would choose martyrdom over me? Or is your loyalty to this country that strong? I'll tell you now, they're not worthy of your fealty. The people here are fools, deceived into blindly believing falsehoods. They are not worth your life. You would be better served learning the teachings of our god, the great Alv-sama. Once you open your eyes to the truth, you too will—wha—?!"

Yue answered his religious prattling with a barrage of wind blades. She couldn't bear any more.

A fountain of blood appeared in the night sky; Yue's blades had clipped Freid's shoulder as he tried to dodge out of the way. The fact that he reacted at all proved that he was skilled enough to conquer a labyrinth. If his senses were less finely honed, he would have lost an arm.

Yue stared coldly at Freid, and he glared back. She had nothing but contempt for this would-be demon conqueror.

"Save your pretty speeches. You hurt Hajime. For that, you will die."

Yue summoned a freezing blizzard.

It whipped around her in a tornado of snow and ice, hiding her from view. The white storm that connected heaven and earth lowered the surrounding temperature to freezing. The Ash Dragons closest to her froze in seconds.

Yue had combined the intermediate-level wind spell Tempest Flash with one of the strongest ice spells, Frost Prison.

The frozen Ash Dragons fell to the earth, shattering into a thousand pieces as they hit. It was as if Yue had brought about a localized ice age. The dragons were frozen solid. As they shattered, even their blood was icy.

"So, you refuse to even consider it. Very well. Kill her!"

Freid gritted his teeth and ordered his men to attack. He'd lost twenty Ash Dragons in one go. He didn't want to lose any more. Aurora balls closed in on Yue from all directions.

A rainbow-colored meteor shower rained down. The aurora balls easily penetrated Yue's icy tornado. In fact, they ripped the entire thing apart.

Freid expected to see Yue bloodied and beaten, but was met by the sight of her standing unhurt amidst a cluster of black spheres.

Immediately, he ordered his monsters to fire again. However, Yue's black holes sucked up the deadly aurora spheres, or redirected their trajectories completely. Yue manipulated gravity and soared higher into the sky.

Despite the deadly barrage, she was unfazed. The countless Heavenfalls and Spatial Severances surrounding her looked like miniature satellites protecting their star.

"If breath attacks won't work, we'll just hit you directly! Charge!"

The Ash Dragons obeyed immediately. Their talons were sharp enough to make mincemeat out of one tiny girl.

They came in waves, hoping to overpower her with numbers. Everywhere Yue looked, she was surrounded by gray. But even so, she wasn't worried. She simply closed her eyes and concentrated.

Thinking an unmoving target would make an easy mark, the Ash Dragons closed in, talons bared and maws open wide.

Seconds before being ripped to shreds, Yue's eyelids snapped open.

She spoke the name a single spell.

"Void Shatter."

Space itself splintered. Everything looked the way it would have through a cracked mirror. Thousands of lines streaked through the sky, and where those lines joined, the world blurred.

Any Ash Dragon caught among the lines was ripped apart. Blood rained from the sky as the lines shredded the dragons with a sickening noise.

This was Yue's new spatial spell, Void Shatter. It split space along lines she defined, mercilessly cutting anything it caught.

Because Void Shatter warped space itself, there was no defending against it. Thirty more Ash Dragons joined the list of casualties.

Freid shivered. Even he couldn't cast spatial magic on that scale, especially not that quickly.

"Such skill. Could you also be someone chosen by god? Are you, perhaps, the champion of that false god, Ehit? I see now why you refused my proposal!"

Freid nodded to himself, convinced of his own misunder-standing. Yue looked at him as if he were a particularly disgusting cockroach.

"Preposterous. I fight for Hajime and Hajime alone. Don't lump me in with the likes of you."

Freid seemed more bothered by her insults to his god than her insults to him. His expression grew dark.

Yue had angered him for real.

"Very well. Then there is nothing more to discuss. I shall slaughter you, and parade your corpse in front of your lover. I'm sure that shock will suffice to render him defenseless."

"You talk big, but can you actually do it, ugly?"

A vein pulsed in Freid's temple as Yue sneered at him again. Rising to her challenge, he attempted to back his words with action.

He barked an order to the same bird-shaped monster Yue had seen on his shoulder at the Grand Gruen Volcano. A second later, a group of the monsters invading the capital rushed over, planning to attack from the ground.

Still maintaining her gravity spells, Yue cast Draconic Thunder to deal with them.

Dark clouds formed. A second later, a shimmering golden dragon descended from the heavens. Yue fired the auroras stored inside her Spatial Severances at Freid and his dragons, holding them at bay while she focused on annihilating the enemies on the ground.

Her thunder dragon, which normally swallowed everything in its path, was blocked by a six-legged turtle monster... An Absod. It was the same creature they encountered when rescuing Kaori.

In fact, the Absod was devouring Yue's dragon.

Absods' special magic enabled them to absorb other spells and store them in their shell. And this Absod was far bigger than the one they fought in the Great Orcus Labyrinth. Yue guessed that Freid had refined its design.

Still, Yue's Draconic Thunder was nothing to sneeze at. Even as the Absod sucked in the dragon's thunder, it was lifted off the ground. Its shell creaked from the strain of defending itself.

Even improved, the Absod seemed incapable of dealing with composite magic made of multiple spells. Although it could absorb the lightning, it couldn't absorb the gravity magic as well.

Before the pressure crushed its shell, another Absod showed up to help.

Draconic Thunder couldn't withstand two powered-up Absods, and was dismantled.

The Absods fired the absorbed magic back at Yue. Two beams of light—one yellow, the other black—headed straight for her.

"How annoying."

Yue's gravity spheres were fully engaged in absorbing the Ash Dragons' auroras, so she adjusted her gravity to fall upward instead.

"I already know how to deal with that strange lightning spell of yours. So long as my Absods are here, your magic is useless!" Freid grinned triumphantly.

Yue didn't bother responding. She looked down at the Absods for a few seconds, then closed her eyes and concentrated.

"Planning to twist space again? I won't let you!"

Freid's white dragon and the Ash Dragons fired their most concentrated barrage yet. At the same time, monsters resembling black panthers leaped toward Yue.

~~Even if she could keep the auroras at bay,~~ casting impeded Yue's movements. Freid was confident the panthers would get her.

The panthers unleashed a storm of tentacles, weaving between her black spheres.

They inflicted countless wounds on Yue, leaving her a bloody mess. As bad as the injuries looked, however, none were deep.

Even if they had been, Yue's ultimate defense lay not in her barriers or gravity magic, but in her automatic regeneration ability.

When her comrades were with her, she used barriers to protect them and even dodged attacks because she didn't like getting her clothes ripped. However, Yue's original fighting style was to ignore all damage and focus entirely on attacking.

Freid watched in satisfaction as his panthers flayed her. However, a second later, his jaw dropped in surprise as her wounds vanished.

"Is that ancient magic as well? Just how many labyrinths have you conquered?!"

It was true that they all possessed restoration magic, but that wasn't what Yue was using. Freid knew his only hope was to annihilate her before she had a chance to recover. He ordered his monsters to commit to an all-out attack. Then, he began chanting another spatial spell.

Unfortunately for him, Yue finished first. Her eyes flew open, and her beautiful voice rang across the battlefield.

"Five Heavenly Dragons."

Another wave of dark clouds obscured the sky.

A raging tornado whipped up next to them.

Streams of water rushed together and froze into one solid mass.

Gray dust coalesced into a monstrous dragon.

Blue flames burning hotter than hell coiled around her.

Five enormous elemental dragons appeared in the night sky above the capital.

Each was comprised of a different element, held together by gravity magic.

The air crackled in the five heavenly beasts' presence, and the Ash Dragons screeched in fear. They instinctively realized that these divine creatures were far more powerful.

Freid's creations were no longer interested in killing Yue. Their only thoughts were of escape. They looked pleadingly up at their master.

"How...?"

Freid stared blankly at the dragons. They were so far beyond his understanding of magic that he couldn't comprehend it.

"You hope to seal my magic? Know your place."

Yue glared haughtily down at him. She looked every bit the empress she'd once been as she pointed a single slender finger at the ground.

The heavenly dragons obeyed their sovereign's will and descended on her enemies.

The lightning dragon went straight for the Absod, eager for a rematch.

The Absod started absorbing again, but this time, Yue's fire dragon was right behind. While the Absod was busy with one dragon, the other melted its shell with blistering heat.

"Aaaaaaaaaaaaaaaaaaaaaaaaaaaaaaaaaaah!"

The Absod screamed in pain as it was liquified alive. Freed once more, the lightning dragon sped on to find other targets. Namely, the other Absod, who was trying to absorb Yue's storm dragon. The thunder dragon swallowed the Absod whole, leaving only ash.

Meanwhile, the frost dragon froze another Absod solid, while the earth dragon petrified everything it touched.

Once freed, the storm dragon rushed off to slice through the other monsters Freid had summoned.

Strong as she was, Yue had difficulty controlling five dragons at once. Sweat beaded on her forehead as she directed them.

Seeing an opportunity, Freid commanded his Ash Dragons to attack.

Yue called her five elemental dragons back, and the primal forces of nature collided with Freid's devastating Ash Dragons.

The difference in strength was clear. Freid's poor dragons were slaughtered one after another.

Only now did Freid realize that he was up against a monster far beyond his own abilities. That boy he'd managed to take by surprise at the Grand Gruen Volcano wasn't the only person Freid needed to worry about. Hajime's companions were just as deadly.

How arrogant he'd been to ask Yue to join the demons as his subordinate.

Freid's only chance was to go all out.

"Shake the foundations of this world, which neither a dragon's roar, nor a giant's hammer, nor the marching of a thousand armies can hope to touch. Only the gods' sighs may cause the earth to scream out thus! Lament and despair at your inevitable destruction—Void Fissure!"

The space around Yue warped. There was a low rumbling that sounded like the screams of the planet itself.

Yue knew this kind of spell, and instantly switched to defense. Void Fissure's scope was too large for her to avoid. Normal magic had no chance against it either.

Yue dispelled her dragons and gravity spheres, then cast spatial magic of her own. She wouldn't survive if her concentration was divided.

She raised her spatial barrier just in time to catch the explosions.

They weren't normal explosions; it was as if space itself had ruptured. They wiped out the remaining Ash Dragons and monsters instantly, tearing the ground underneath Yue apart, and shredding the clouds above her to bits.

Void Fissure was a spell that forcibly contracted, then rapidly expanded, the space within a certain area. The resulting shockwaves caused explosions that were unblockable by normal means.

"Hmm... So this is the power of ancient magic."

Although everything else was destroyed, Yue was still alive.

Her clothes were tattered, and a dribble of blood spilled from her mouth, but she was relatively unscathed. Considering how destructive Freid's spell was, that was amazing. Even her slight wounds healed instantly.

Yue should have been obliterated. But, just before Freid's spell hit, she cast Illusion Cage—a spatial spell that locked a small area. It was a versatile spell that could serve both as a barrier, and as a means of capturing a target. However, its mana cost was insane.

Since she was so rushed, Yue wasn't able to completely fix the space around her. That was the only reason she took any damage. Of course, she healed instantly thanks to automatic regeneration. She cast restoration magic on her clothes, until it looked as though she'd never been hit.

Yue stood amidst the destruction, basking in the moonlight. To Freid, she looked almost divine. This time, he didn't underestimate her. Instead, he fired off another attack from her blind spot.

"I knew you'd survive that, you little monster!"

Even as he cast Void Fissure, Freid opened a Cosmic Rift behind her. He passed through, and his white dragon fired an aurora attack.

Yue was able to dodge by falling to the right. The white dragon bit her arm as it passed; a gush of blood filled its mouth. Despite the softness of Yue's skin, the dragon didn't bite all the way through. It kept Yue's arm trapped in its mouth and fired another aurora point-blank.

Freid was exhausted from casting high-level spells in quick succession. Still, he was confident that, this time, he had her.

When he saw Yue's expression, however, Freid's confidence melted away, to be replaced by complete and utter despair.

Yue was smiling. It was faint, but her lips definitely curled upward. Freid could not look away.

Yue no longer looked like a divine being. If anything, she looked like a devil. The moonlight had emphasized her solemnity before, but now it cast dark shadows over her face.

Her crimson eyes, framed by her golden-blond hair, glowed in the night.

You dare bare your fangs at me?

Yue whispered the name of the spell she had prepared.

"Revival Reversal."

The river of time can flow backward too.

Yue didn't say the words aloud, but Freid knew he was in trouble.

He and his dragon felt the spell hit at the same time.

"Gaaaaaaaaaaaaaaaah!"

"Graaaaaaaaaaaaaaaaaaaah!"

The dragon bit Yue's arm off as it writhed in pain, but she didn't seem to mind. Once her body was free, she flew upward.

Seconds later, her arm grew back.

Yue looked down at Freid, who was bleeding from multiple deep wounds.

"How does it feel? Those are the wounds Hajime gave you before. They hurt just as much now, right?"

"Gaaah! You bitch, how did—"

Freid gritted his teeth against the pain and looked up at the girl smiling sweetly at him.

They were both covered in blood.

The wound in the white dragon's chest looked raw and inflamed, as if fresh. The beast clawed at its injuries, struggling to stay in the air.

Freid's left arm had been crushed, and there was a massive gash in his chest. He coughed up blood.

Both the dragon and Freid appeared to be on the verge of death.

Their injuries were the same ones Hajime and the others had inflicted on them in the Grand Gruen Volcano.

The restoration spell Revival Reversal restored the injuries its target had suffered in the past. It was a terrifying spell that could reopen scars that should have been fully healed.

Yue had wanted to defeat Freid with this spell from the beginning.

It was her way of getting revenge. Back in the volcano, she was forced to retreat without landing a single blow on the man who hurt her precious Hajime. She swore that, the next time they saw Freid, she would beat him to a pulp.

Once they'd cleared the Sunken Ruins of Melusine and learned restoration magic, she'd discovered the perfect spell to do so. Getting Freid back by making him relive his defeat just seemed too perfect.

One problem made the spell difficult, though.

Revival Reversal required the caster to be within three meters of the target, and touching some part of their body. Moreover, it could only replicate as much damage as the caster used mana. Close combat was Yue's Achilles' heel. She honestly doubted she would have an opportunity to close in on Freid, especially since he was riding a dragon. Her plan had been to batter Freid down and get close once he was too weak to fight back. But he came to her of his own accord. When the dragon bit her arm, Yue was so happy. The creature had given her the perfect chance for revenge.

"It seems...I lack the ability to defeat you as I am. At this point, my only option is to—"

"You're not running away."

Yue raised her hand. Before she could deliver the final blow, a barrage of magic came at her from beneath.

"Freid-sama! Please retreat!"

"We'll buy time for your escape!"

The demons invading the capital had turned back to help their lord. When they saw him struggling, they called off the assault.

"You guys! Ngh... Forgive me!"

Furious at Yue's actions, the demons attacked with no regard for their own lives.

Naturally, their pitiful barrage couldn't harm Yue. Still, they bought just enough time for Freid to slip away through a Cosmic Rift.

He vanished just before Yue's flaming javelin hit.

Yue stared coldly at the demons shouting curses at her. With a wave of her hand, she cast Void Fissure, the same spell Freid had used on her.

"Die."

Twisting explosions rocked the ground. Yue had packed more mana into the spell than usual. It irked her that these pests interrupted her revenge.

"Tch... He's like a cockroach." Yue clicked her tongue.

Next time, she would make sure to kill him.

She took a deep breath to calm herself. Just then, a cheerful voice rang out across the battlefield.

"Yue-saaaaaan! Is that bastard still alive? If so, let me get a few good hits on him too... Whoa! What happened here? Did you cause an earthquake?"

Shea bounded over, leaping from one mana platform to the next.

"He ran away."

From those words, Shea could more or less guess what happened. Freid's resilience surprised her. Shea smiled bitterly and comforted Yue.

The two exchanged information and replenished their mana. As they described their fights, they saw a flash of rainbow-colored light above the palace, followed by a red streak.

They watched as pillars of light descended to the ground, shattering the city's walls and vaporizing tens of thousands of monsters.

Silence followed. The pair looked at each other and said a single word in unison.

"Hajime."

"Hajime-san."

No one else could have caused that. The two girls were of one mind.

"Let's go to the palace."

"Yeah."

Yue and Shea looked one last time at the wasteland that had once been the capital's outskirts. With weary smiles, they flew off toward the palace.

ARIFURETA:
ARIFURETA SHOKUGYOU DE SEKAISAIKYOU

FROM COMMONPLACE
TO WORLD'S STRONGEST

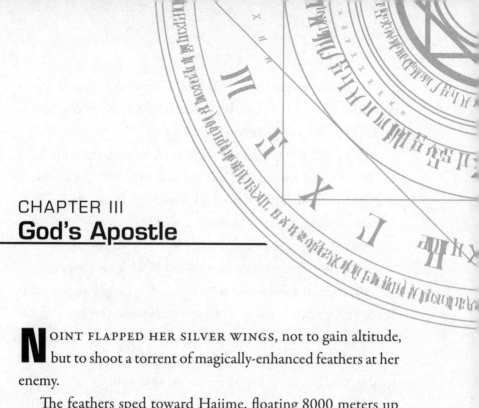

CHAPTER III
God's Apostle

NOINT FLAPPED HER SILVER WINGS, not to gain altitude, but to shoot a torrent of magically-enhanced feathers at her enemy.

The feathers sped toward Hajime, floating 8000 meters up in the air.

He raised his revolver, the legendary artifact he'd created. It had ended the lives of countless powerful foes. He fired, and Schlag let out a roar.

Hajime's bullet powered through Noint's feathers, shredding them. He had angled his single shot to cut through a swathe of the projectiles. He stepped into the hole the shot had created, letting the rest of Noint's feathers pass by.

To truly avoid your opponent's attacks, you needed the courage to step forward.

"Hyaaah!"

A cute voice interrupted Hajime and Noint's deathmatch. It seemed starkly out of place on this battlefield, where two powerful enemies put their lives on the line.

It was, of course, Aiko who screamed so unceremoniously.

For the first time in her life, she was experiencing a mid-air dogfight. Although Noint fired feathers at the same rate Hajime's Metzelei spat out bullets, he dodged each deluge.

"Sensei! Stop screaming! You'll just bite your tongue!"

"I can't just stop screaming on—ahh! I-I bit my tongue..."

Aiko ignored Hajime's warning and instantly regretted it. Tears sprang to her eyes, and not just because she bit her tongue.

Hajime knew Aiko, who wasn't particularly strong physically, couldn't handle sudden movements. Thus, he used Riftwalk, and tried to dodge with as little movement as possible.

Unfortunately, even that required him to move faster than a rollercoaster. Aiko was already dizzy.

But there weren't any alternatives. Hajime could hardly just dump his teacher. He couldn't ignore Noint's attacks for one second, and even if he could, she would target Aiko. As inconvenient as it was, holding Aiko was the only way to keep her safe.

Fortunately, Hajime wouldn't have to keep this up much longer. A trustworthy ally was on her way.

Hajime shot down another wave of feathers with Schlag, then looked at Aiko. She clung to him for dear life, eyes shut tight.

"Sensei, just hang on a little longer. One of my comrades is coming. She'll take you down to safety."

"O-okay! B-but what about you, Nagumo-kun?!"

"I still need to kill this emotionless puppet!"

"I'm sorry... I'm just a burden..." Dragging her student down frustrated Aiko.

Hajime didn't have time to reply. He hugged Aiko tight and backflipped in mid-air.

He watched a blast of silver light pass overhead. It was the same mysterious skill that had disintegrated the tower.

Aiko did her best not to scream as Hajime swung her about. As she pressed against his chest, she noticed his steady heartbeat. The fact that he was calm, even in this situation, helped ease her worries.

This isn't the time to think about that! Aiko mentally berated herself, clinging tighter to Hajime.

"Don't worry about it. I expected to run into trouble when I came here."

"Y-you didn't...have to go so far for me..."

Of course, Hajime knew that, if he wanted to obtain all the ancient magic, he needed to fight the Holy Church eventually. This wasn't entirely for Aiko's sake. However, Aiko had apparently misunderstood his intentions.

It probably didn't help that Hajime was practically hugging her as he fought. *I'm probably gonna have to resolve this misunderstanding soon.*

"I see you still aren't taking me seriously." Noint's mechanical voice was right next to him.

Hajime started. "Whoa!"

He lifted his prosthetic arm and fired a shotgun blast from his elbow. Using the recoil, he gained some distance as well. Noint raised one of her swords to block, sweeping the other in a wide arc.

Her glimmering silver swords were two meters long and thirty centimeters wide. Not only did they look intimidating, they had a very sinister ability. Anything wrapped in Noint's mana was affected by Disintegrate, her special magic. A single touch would inflict a fatal wound.

Hajime couldn't move too quickly without injuring Aiko, which forced him to use Schlag to redirect the blade while he fell back.

Noint's sword passed inches above Hajime's face, cutting off the tips of his hair.

The only reason Schlag hadn't disintegrated was because Hajime had hardened the azantium coating with Steel Skin. Even that, however, couldn't strengthen his weapons or artificial arm enough to stay in contact with Noint's swords for more than a few seconds.

Blocking the blow shaved a few centimeters off Schlag's coating. If Hajime kept this up, his weapons would be destroyed.

Noint let the force of her slash swing her around, her glimmering hair fanning out like a halo. As she completed her turn, she swung her second sword.

It was so fast that Aiko's eyes couldn't even follow it. She just saw a silver flash.

Hajime dodged to the side, using the recoil from a second shotgun blast. Once he was clear, he took aim with Schlag and fired three times.

Three streaks of red light headed straight for Noint. One went for her head, another her heart, and the last her stomach.

But Noint's reaction time was inhuman. The moment Hajime fired, she held her sword vertically, blocking all three bullets.

Hajime pulled back even further and sent out his Cross Bits. They fired powerful explosive slugs, creating huge red shockwaves. Noint dissipated those with a beat of her wings, but doing so gave Hajime more time to flee.

"Aaaaaahhhh aha ha! I can't even tell what's..."

"Sensei, could you stop making those cute noises in the middle of a duel? It's kinda killing the mood."

"C-cute?! Nagumo-kun, that's not something you can say to your teach—"

The request was more serious than Hajime made it seem. Aiko's screams sapped his concentration. In a fight between two people of his caliber, even a millisecond's distraction could get you killed. Noint was right when she said he wasn't taking this seriously. Of course, a cute woman hanging around his neck didn't fluster Hajime, but Aiko's noises were distracting.

"To think you could defend so well against my attacks while guarding that dead weight...You are far too strong. Strong people like you are unfit to be my lord's pawns."

"Thanks. Can't say I'd want to be the pawn of some shitty NEET who throws a tantrum every time things don't go his way. I'm happy to hear I'm not wanted."

"There is no point trying to taunt me. I have no emotions."

"Hm? I'm not trying to taunt you, that's just what I think."

"......"

Noint silently spread her wings and crossed her swords in front of her.

Is she really emotionless? It looks like she's trying to shake off her anger and prove that this isn't bothering her. Hajime quickly discarded the thought. There was no point worrying about it.

After all, he'd kill her either way. Regardless of what she thought, regardless of what she felt, she would die by his hands.

Noint flapped her wings and unleashed another barrage of feathers. This time, they weren't aimed at Hajime. They gathered in front of Noint and arranged themselves into an odd formation. As they overlapped, Hajime realized she was making a magic circle. Noint glared coldly through the shining silver ring. Once it was complete, she cast her spell.

"Hellfire Tsunami."

Noint summoned a burning tsunami that scorched the very atmosphere.

So, she can use elemental magic too. She simply hadn't cast her elemental spells because she believed her feathers would be enough.

Noint hadn't been fighting seriously, either.

Crimson hellfire bore down on them, and all Aiko could see was red. The tsunami was large enough to blot out the horizon.

Aiko looked up at Hajime, expecting a solution. Sweat rolled down his cheek as he peered desperately through the tsunami, searching for the spell's core. If he could shoot it, the flames would disperse.

Of course, that would require an ungodly amount of

precision, but Hajime was more than up to the task. He had trained his sharpshooting skills extensively.

However, Noint's spell was on a far larger scale than anything he'd faced before. Anyone on the Divine Mountain would have thought noon had come, the flames were so bright and all-encompassing. It was like searching for a needle in a haystack.

Time ran out before Hajime could find the core.

The massive tsunami swallowed them. Anyone watching would be sure that Hajime and Aiko were dead.

The tsunami should not have left so much as their ashes behind, but Noint continued staring at it.

"So, you can withstand even this," she muttered as the flames dispersed.

At the spell's center, Hajime's Cross Bits surrounded him and Aiko, both unharmed.

The Cross Bits formed a pyramid, connected by wires. Screens of crimson light filled the space between them and Noint.

"This is still a prototype, so I was a little worried." Hajime sighed in relief. "Thank god it worked."

This was his latest weapon enhancement. He had used creation magic to enchant wires with spatial magic, then worked them into his Cross Bits. He'd also covered the Cross Bits with spatial magic-enchanted ore. Unlike physical shields, barriers made by partitioning space were theoretically unbreakable.

However, the prototype was still in the experimental phase. Hajime hadn't tested the upgraded Cross Bits against a proper attack, so he'd had no idea how much they could take.

"Y-you..." Aiko looked blankly from the barrier to Noint. The apostle was already preparing her next attack.

This time, she sent a few feathers at Hajime and crafted over a hundred magic circles at once.

She was determined to bury him in an avalanche of magic.

Hajime guessed that his new barriers might be able to take the onslaught, but staying on the defensive would put him at a disadvantage... Especially because he wasn't certain that they could survive Noint's disintegrating light.

Furthermore, his barrier's greatest strength was also its biggest weakness. Since it partitioned space, Hajime couldn't attack through it.

Hajime dismissed his barrier and prepared to flee. He needed to keep his distance until Tio arrived.

Just as he was about to leap back, he heard singing rise from the Divine Mountain.

Hajime avoided Noint's barrage and looked down. Ishtar stood on the mountain, surrounded by an army of bishops and templar knights. The bishops held hands in a big circle and sang prayers.

Seeing a hundred-odd bishops chanting solemnly reminded Hajime of the time he'd heard a choir singing hymns back on Earth.

But what on Earth is the point of all that singing?

"Ahh! What the...? My body's—"

"Nagumo-kun?! Ah... Wh-what is this...?"

Hajime and Aiko felt a strange sensation. Their strength left them, and their mana began to disperse. It was as if something was draining their energy. Motes of light stuck to them, making it hard to move.

"Ngh... This must be some kind of debuff magic. So, this is the Holy Church's strength. Looks like they've got their defensive countermeasures all set up."

Hajime's guess was spot-on.

When Ishtar realized that one of God's Apostles was fighting, he gathered his followers. To support Noint, Ishtar instructed them to sing the Hymn of Ruin.

The Hymn of Ruin was a powerful spell that impeded a target's movements and sapped their strength. Unlike most spells, it didn't require a magic circle. It could only be activated by bishops singing together. It was the Holy Church's trump card.

"Ishtar? Unlike you, he fully understands his role. A good pawn."

Ishtar gazed up at Noint with an expression full of rapture, and she reciprocated with her cold, unfeeling eyes.

He seemed ecstatic simply to know he was helping her fight, as if there were no greater pleasure in life. Indeed, he was a convenient pawn.

Pawns or not, those guys just made this fight that much harder. This is going to be a pain.

Hajime bolstered his flagging strength with his vast reserves of mana and continued dodging. However, his movements weren't nearly as sharp as before. Noint's attacks were too strong to fend off in his weakened state.

A flood of lightning bolts shot out of Noint's circles, each tracing an erratic path toward Hajime.

Hajime shot them down with Schlag, but he wasn't able to dodge them all. One bolt grazed him. It wasn't terribly powerful, and the shock only made him stiffen for a moment.

~~However, that moment was all Noint needed.~~

"Wh—?!"

She closed in on Hajime and swung her swords in a cross shape. His reaction delayed, Hajime could only block the downward swing. The sideways blade grazed his neck, drawing blood.

"Gaaah!"

If the cut was a few millimeters deeper, it would have severed his carotid artery. Cold sweat poured down his back.

He couldn't let the fear get to him. Even as he screamed in pain, Hajime fired his elbow shotgun and used Aerodynamic to try and get out of Noint's range.

Noint followed, and he fired his Cross Bits wildly in her direction, keeping her on the defensive long enough to put space between them.

"Nagumo-kun?!"

Blood dripped from Hajime's neck onto Aiko's cheek. He'd protected her from the shockwaves with Diamond Skin, but she still took quite a beating. She was barely conscious, but was more worried for her student than herself.

Hajime had no time to reassure her. "I'm fine, just shut up!"

Even as he gave a curt reply, Noint fired another feather barrage.

Hajime shot some of the feathers down with Schlag and shredded others with his Gale Claw. The few that got past, he endured with Diamond Skin. The motes of light, coupled with his exhaustion, meant that he couldn't dodge them all.

Noint rushed forward, pulling up just in front of Hajime. She spread her wings, emitting a dazzling light. For a second, Hajime was blinded.

But his perception skills were top-notch, even without sight. He could tell that Noint had circled behind him, and he turned to fire a barrage of bullets.

His ammunition shot right through the clone Noint had created from feathers, destroying it.

A fake version of herself, made as bait.

"Wha...?!" Hajime shivered. His instincts screamed to run. He wouldn't make it in time, though. There wasn't even time to curse.

He snapped his arm back and pulled the trigger. Luckily, he'd aimed straight for Noint's head. Unluckily, all she had to do to dodge was tilt her head to one side.

She raised a sword, and cut diagonally downward into Hajime's back.

Hajime used Diamond Skin's derivative skill, Focused Strengthening, to guard, and steeled himself to take a decent amount of damage.

For a short moment, his Diamond Skin held, then the disintegration magic in her sword destroyed his barrier. The tip of her blade dug into his flesh.

"Gaaah!" His back was burning.

Worried, Aiko opened her eyes and looked up. "Nagumo-kun!"

Even as Noint cut him, Hajime planned his next move. He used the force of the blow to somersault forward. Then, he turned around to see Noint closing in. His weakened body wouldn't move in time, so he covered a Cross Bit in Diamond Skin and used it as a shield. The other Cross Bits flanked Noint and attacked her from both sides.

Noint twirled without losing speed, knocking down the explosive slugs with her wings. She slammed her first sword into the Cross Bit shield. It stuck fast in the metal, so she slammed her second sword down on top, splitting the shield in half.

Hajime's eyes went wide with surprise. Noint looked at him coldly. Her chilling gaze made it clear that this would be the end.

But Hajime hadn't given up. He'd have to make some sacrifices if he wanted to keep Aiko alive, so he was prepared to get hurt.

If I'd known Noint was this tough, I would have used Limit Break earlier. I thought I could save it until Tio got here.

Hajime raised his prosthetic arm, planning to sacrificing it for survival.

As Noint raised her swords, a thunderous roar split the air.

"Graaaaaaaaah!"

A second later, a beam of black light closed on Noint.

It was Tio's dragon breath, the all-encompassing black light which could burn through anything. Noint had no time to dodge. She cut short her attack and wrapped her wings around herself.

Tio's breath disintegrated as it hit those wings. Despite that, it shoved Noint backwards. Black and silver mana warred as Tio's breath pushed Noint against the cathedral tower. The impact's force shattered the tower, and chunks of broken masonry fell to the ground.

Ishtar's bishops and templar knights cried out in despair. Seeing their beloved apostle beaten back shook their confidence.

Hajime pulled Orkan from his Treasure Trove and fired all twelve rockets at Ishtar and his men.

This time they screamed for a different reason. Finally, Hajime heard the voice of someone he was eager to see.

"Master! Are you all right?"

Although Hajime didn't let his guard down, he smiled in relief.

At long last, Tio had arrived.

"Thanks, Tio. You saved my hide. Things got pretty dicey at the end."

Tio smiled briefly, but then, her expression grew grim again. If Hajime was hard-pressed, this enemy required her full attention. She flew to Hajime and stared at the tower.

"It is heartening to know I made it on time. As a reward, may I ask for a thorough spanking?"

"If you can get Sensei to safety, I'll think about it."

"Truly?! I will hold you to that, Master! Come, Sensei-dono. Climb onto my back."

Even now, she puts her desires first, huh? Well, I guess Yue, Shea, and Kaori are like that too. Hajime sighed and put Aiko onto Tio's back.

Aiko was pretty sure she'd overheard some rather immoral things during that conversation, but she obediently let Hajime deposit her atop Tio. She didn't want to be a burden any longer.

"Umm, Tio-san? I'm in your hands."

"Indeed. Fear not. I shall not let any harm come to you. You are important to my master."

Naturally, Tio meant that she was a teacher Hajime respected a great deal, but Aiko misinterpreted her words.

Aiko looked worriedly over at Hajime. Anyone could tell that her eyes weren't those of a teacher worried about her student, but of a girl worried about the boy she loved.

Just then, the collapsed tower burst apart. Noint emerged from the rubble, completely unharmed. She flapped her silver wings, soaring once more into the sky. Even Tio's breath couldn't pierce Noint's defenses.

"Go, Tio."

"As you wish. But allow me to assist you once I deliver Sensei-dono to safety. Even if I can't hurt your opponent, I can definitely do something about those meddlesome priests."

Tio had already guessed who had weakened Hajime. She glared angrily at the surviving clergy while Hajime stared Noint down. The murderous glint in his eyes was back. Tio wanted to make sure he could focus without interruption.

Hajime grinned and nodded, glad to have such a reliable comrade. This time, he took the fight to Noint.

"Be careful, Nagumo-kun! I don't want you to get hurt anymore!"

Tio watched as Aiko clasped her hands and prayed for Hajime's safety. "Hm? Ah, I see now. How fascinating..."

She could tell the teacher was in love with her student.

In an amused voice, Tio spoke to her. "Sensei-dono, I

understand your concern, but we must hurry. Once I deliver you to the palace, I need to eliminate those pests for Master. I cannot allow them to interfere with his duel."

Tio turned towards the ground, but Aiko stopped her. Tio glanced over her shoulder to see the teacher looking resolute.

"Tio-san. Won't it take too long to get me down and come back? We're 8000 meters up. It will waste too much time..."

"Hm? You do have a point, but... Wait, you couldn't possibly mean to—"

"If you're going to help Nagumo-kun fight, then let me fight with you. We have to do something about Ishtar-san quickly, or Nagumo-kun won't be able to win. You can't afford to waste time."

Aiko had a point, but it still didn't sit well with Tio.

Hajime's missiles had injured a number of bishops, but the clergymen were regrouping. They worked together to erect a barrier and prepared to resume their hymn. Tio wanted to stop them before they had a chance to start again, but if she let Aiko come to harm, that would break her promise to Hajime.

"I don't mean to be rude, but what exactly can you do, Sensei-dono? You have no battle experience, correct? Nor do you have any magic circles. How do you propose to fight those bishops and knights?"

Aiko gritted her teeth. Tio was right, but an idea suddenly dawned on her. She closed her eyes, put her finger in her mouth, and bit down hard. She dripped some blood on the back of her other hand and quickly sketched a magic circle.

"Despite my looks, my magic is as strong as Amanogawa-kun's.

I may not have any combat experience, but...I can at least support you! Honestly...I'm terrified of fighting human beings. Still, at this point, there's no other choice. Empty idealism will get me no-where! If I want to bring everyone back to Japan safely, then I can't run away. I have to stand before my students and fight for them!"

The kingdom had been invaded, and the bishops had turned into religious fanatics. At this point, relying on Ishtar's god to send the class home was pointless. Aiko and the other students had to carve their own path in this world.

In that case, Aiko would no longer hesitate. If there was dirty work that needed to be done, she would do it. She resolved never to let someone else pull the trigger for her again.

Tio hesitated at the determination in Aiko's eyes. Eventually, however, she gave in.

"If you're committed to this path, then I suppose I have no choice. I'm sure Master won't mind if this is truly what you want. Very well. Let us slaughter those fools together!"

"Thank you!"

Aiko was nervous, but her newfound resolve was stronger. Together, she and Tio headed for the Holy Church's great cathedral.

They were facing hundreds of knights and bishops, but that didn't seem to frighten them. Their odd tag-team combo was about to take on the strongest religious group in the world.

⁘ ⁘ ⁘ ⁘ ⁘ ⁘ ⁘ ⁘ ⁘ ⁘ ⁘ ⁘ ⁘

The first thing Hajime did was pull out Schlagen and let loose on Noint.

Sparks ran down the barrel as he accelerated the bullet. It shot out faster than the eye could follow, leaving a red streak in its wake.

Schlagen possessed enough firepower to pierce even Tio's breath. Noint's wings wouldn't be able to disintegrate the bullets easily. Noint seemed to notice that as well, and chose to dodge rather than block.

Noint flew under Hajime's shot, and charged toward him, but Hajime was ready. His Cross Bits fired explosive slugs at near point-blank range.

"Wah!"

Noint couldn't cocoon herself in her wings in time, so she slashed at the bullets with her sword.

The blade cut through the slugs like a hot knife, slicing them in half.

Although Noint's sword dissolved some of the bullets' mana, it couldn't completely negate the shockwaves.

Pulses of mana assailed Noint from all sides, slowing her down for a moment.

Hajime took advantage of that opening and rushed in. He leaped off his mid-air platform and transferred his momentum into his left arm. At the same time, he activated Steel Arms and the oscillating vibrator in his prosthetic limb.

"Haaah!" He fired another shotgun blast from his elbow to further accelerate his attack.

"Huh?!" Noint raised her second sword to block. She barely got it up in time. Hajime's fist crashed into it.

There was a deafening clash of metal against metal. Although she blocked the blow itself, the force of Hajime's punch sent Noint flying.

He couldn't let her rest, so he unholstered Donner and Schlag and fired a follow-up barrage.

There were two loud explosions. Although Noint only saw two red streaks shoot towards her, twelve bullets slammed into the swords she raised to guard.

"Gaaah!"

Hajime fired so quickly and accurately that each bullet followed the same path almost simultaneously, which was why Noint only detected two shots.

For the first time, the supposedly invincible angel's beautiful face twisted in pain. Her swords cracked as they took the brunt of the bullets.

Hajime was amazed that the blades didn't shatter. Not many weapons could withstand a fully-powered punch along with a railgun barrage.

Noint sailed through the air and crashed into another of the Holy Church's buildings, pulverizing it.

Refusing to let up, Hajime pulled Orkan from his Treasure Trove and fired a barrage of missiles. They trailed a cloud of sparks as they flew through the building, decimating what little remained.

The rockets exploded, unleashing their payload of superheated tar. The tar ignited instantly, coating the building in sticky, 3000 degree flames.

Hajime watched the flames dye the sky red as he prepared his next attack. He reloaded Orkan with missiles from his Treasure Trove and took aim at the burning rubble.

Just before he fired, he noticed his quarry was no longer there.

"Tch. Below, huh?" Hajime looked down in time to see the ground erupt below him. Noint appeared within the explosion, flapping her wings to chase him down.

She'd escaped his rockets by tunneling into the mountainside. Noint beat her wings and fired another barrage of silver feathers.

Hajime swayed from side to side, like a leaf blown in the wind, weaving between the feathers. As Noint passed him, she swung down with her greatswords. Hajime somersaulted in mid-air, dodging out of the way. At the same time, he fired Orkan's missiles.

Noint had tasted their power once already, and wasn't eager to do so again. She flattened her wings and sped forward like a meteor, outpacing the missiles. She continued firing feathers as she retreated, while also bombarding Hajime with magic from the hundreds of circles she'd created.

Magic and missiles clashed, annihilating each other in a magnificent explosion. Hajime dropped Orkan back into his Treasure Trove and drew his revolvers. He shot down the remaining spells, blowing the core of each one apart.

For a few seconds, there was silence. Hajime and Noint stared each other down.

"Hey, are you sure you should waste your time with me?"

"What do you mean?"

There's no way someone from the Holy Church doesn't know about the invasion. Hajime and Noint had been fighting nonstop, so Hajime hadn't had a chance to talk. Since there was finally a pause, he figured he should ask.

"I'm talking about what's happening below. If things keep going like this, the kingdom will fall. And once that happens, you know the Divine Mountain's going to be next. Shouldn't you be stopping the demons taking over your city instead of fighting up here?"

Hajime thought it was a perfectly logical question, but Noint looked at him as if he'd said something ridiculous.

"If that does happen, then that is how this age is fated to end."

"That's it, huh? So, in the end, Ehit doesn't see people as anything more than playthings. He just took their side this time, but in the next era, maybe he'll side with someone else? Is the demons' god one of Ehit's lackeys or something, too? Or is he just Ehit himself, in disguise?"

"And if he is?"

"I was just wondering whether the Liberators told the truth. If you ask me, you're both shady as hell."

Noint's eyebrows twitched. It seemed being called "shady" didn't sit well with her. Hajime grinned despite her obvious displeasure.

"Hey, if you really think I'm a nuisance, just send me back to my own world. If the kingdom falls, the heroes will have proven that they're not very useful pawns, so you may as well send them back too."

"I refuse, Irregular."

"Mind telling me why?"

"Because my master wishes for your deaths. Yours especially. You survived hardships that would have broken normal people, obtained unimaginable power, and found trustworthy comrades to aid you in your journey... Now, all that's left is for you to fall before achieving your goal. That is the fate my master wishes upon you. So, I kindly request that you die in a blaze of agony, suffering, and despair. That shall please my master most. The hero and his friends, on the other hand, appear to be up to something my master finds interesting. He is content to leave them alone. As long as they continue to entertain, he shall not remove them from the game board."

Hajime expected that answer, and wasn't terribly surprised. He shrugged, thinking back to what Miledi Reisen had said.

She was right, the gods really are conniving little bastards.

But one thing Noint mentioned stuck out in Hajime's mind.

"You said the others are up to something?"

"You are about to die, so there is no need for you to know."

Noint unleashed another barrage of feathers and magic, putting an end to their conversation. Her assault was far more ferocious than before. Her feathers flew as fast as Hajime's bullets, and the spells were all high-level. A silver aura coated Noint's body, and she seemed to grow in size. She looked as though she was using Limit Break.

"Ah!"

Hajime faced the torrent of magic and feathers, Metzelei in his right hand and Schlagen in his left. He mowed down Noint's attacks with Metzelei, a machine gun that fired 12,000 bullets a minute. At the same time, he sniped at Noint with Schlagen.

She reacted much faster than before.

~~The instant before the bullet hit her,~~ Noint blurred, vanished, and reappeared a few meters away.

She charged at Hajime, right through the hail of bullets, moving so quickly that she left afterimages in her wake.

Hajime tracked her movements with Foresight and tried to intercept her with his Cross Bits. However, his explosive slugs hit only air as they passed through her afterimages.

A second later, Noint appeared behind him, still trailing echoes in her wake. She spun like a top, swinging her twin blades.

"Tch!"

Not even Rift Walk had allowed Hajime to keep up with her.

He managed to duck out of the way, but Noint's swords passed through Metzelei, cutting it cleanly in half. That made the energy from Hajime's Lightning Field discharge. A huge explosion blossomed between the two.

Noint hesitated at the explosion, allowing Hajime to counterattack.

Crimson streaks of mana wrapped his body as he activated Limit Break. He rushed forward at the same time as Noint. He was no longer holding Metzelei, but had drawn Donner and Schlag.

The opponents traded blows at point-blank range.

"Taaaaaah!"

"Haaaaaah!"

Hajime twisted to avoid Noint's downward swing. Before the first sword passed, her second blade came in from the side. Still, Hajime managed to get Schlag underneath. He fired upward, pushing her sword out of the way. At the same time, he fired Donner directly at her heart.

Noint circled away, and Hajime's bullet passed harmlessly through an echo. She cut diagonally upward with her first blade.

Hajime enhanced Schlag with Diamond Skin and Focused Strengthening. He concentrated the magic on the section of the barrel that had blocked Noint's sword, allowing him to multiply the effects. Noint's sword pushed Schlag out of the way, but didn't break it.

Hajime blocked Noint's second blade with Donner's muzzle. He fired just as the sword made contact. The bullet knocked the blade aside.

Noint and Hajime danced around each other, dodging and trading blows. They fought to the utmost limits of their abilities. Their concentration was so absolute that both forgot to breathe or blink.

"Uwooooooooooooh!"

"Haaaaaaaaaaaaaaaaaaaaaah!"

They screamed at each other, and charged again.

A single mistake, a single lapse in concentration, meant instant death.

They moved so fast that there was no time to think. They simply relied on instinct, trusting their abilities, experience, and reflexes.

Streaks of silver and crimson light appeared in the sky as Noint's swords and Hajime's guns clashed over and over.

The storm of blows unleashed energy pulses like solar flares. The two sped up, each trying to gain an edge over the other.

Before long, they were drenched in blood and covered in a dozen small wounds. Hajime had shallow cuts all over his body, while Noint had bullet holes everywhere.

They were evenly matched. Hajime knew that the longer this continued, the harder it would get for him.

Since the start of the fight, Noint's mana reserves hadn't gone down.

Hajime's Limit Break, on the other hand, would not last forever. Its failure would forcibly cancel out the spell, leaving Hajime in a weakened state. Although Hajime's own mana reserves were vast, they weren't infinite.

Noint, however, seemed to receive unlimited mana from somewhere. She could maintain this state indefinitely.

Hajime examined her with his Demon Eye, trying to find the source of her mana. He noticed a brilliant glowing mana crystal where her heart should be.

Hajime knew a protracted fight would mean his end, so he bet everything on an all-or-nothing attack.

"Take this!"

Hajime brought forth all of his Cross Bits, and fired a full-powered barrage of explosive slugs. He knew the shockwaves would hit him too at this range, but he was prepared for that.

"Have you lost your mind?"

Surprise colored Noint's normally emotionless eyes. Hajime's actions seemed suicidal.

Dozens of explosive slugs shot out of Hajime's six Cross Bits, enveloping both him and Noint in a whirlwind of shockwaves.

Noint wrapped her wings around herself, and Hajime activated Diamond Skin.

A massive crimson flower blossomed in the sky.

Dozens of shockwaves mercilessly pummeled their bodies. They punched through Hajime's Diamond Skin, severely damaging his organs. He gasped in pain and coughed up blood. The attack left him devastated.

Noint, too, suffered greatly. Her wings didn't protect her completely. She coughed blood, her bullet wounds bleeding more than before. Her innards were hit just as hard.

"Were you planning on dying with me?"

"Haaah... haaah... Give me a break. Who'd want a double suicide with you? Try asking that again when you're at least half the woman my girlfriend is."

Hajime panted with exhaustion, but his tone was light, as if he wasn't worried. He scoffed at Noint. *Who the hell would waste their life trying to kill you?*

Hajime pulled another weapon from his Treasure Trove. It was small enough to fit between his fingers. He flung it at Noint as if throwing a playing card.

The object made no sound as it sliced through the air, and was barely visible in the night sky, yet Noint casually batted it aside.

The fifteen-centimeter donut-shaped object spun away into the darkness. It resembled the chakrams Hajime had seen back on earth.

"Did you honestly believe something like that would work? Have you finally run out of idea—ah!"

Noint thought Hajime's attack was simply the final, futile struggle of someone who'd already lost. Then, Hajime pulled out his revolvers and started firing them from his sides.

Although Noint was directly in front of him, bullets suddenly appeared to her left and right, all aimed for her head.

She raised her swords to either side, using them as shields. Twelve bullets slammed into the blades in a burst of sparks. Like before, they all struck the same point.

Somehow, Hajime's bullets had gone right for Noint, despite the fact that he'd fired in a different direction.

The secret was in the chakrams. They were enchanted with Hide Presence and Gale Claw, making them useful assassination tools, but that wasn't all they were capable of. Hajime also enchanted them with spatial magic. They functioned as the same kind of warp gate that he created to kill the sea angel in the Sunken Ruins of Melusine.

If Hajime shot something through one of the chakrams, it would appear out of the other. Furthermore, he'd made them from spirit stone, so he could control them as freely as his Cross Bits.

Hajime had calculated everything, from Noint's reaction time, to her position, to the approximate direction in which she'd knock his chakrams. Now, his bullet barrage hit her swords exactly where he wanted. *Crack! Crack!* Both blades snapped in half.

"Wha?! How...? They shouldn't be that powerful..."

For someone who said they have no emotions, she's sure surprised a lot.

Noint hadn't noticed, but Hajime was focusing his attacks on a certain point on her swords. During their entire close-combat fight, he made sure to aim his attacks there.

He knew his abilities were approximately equal to Noint's, and tried to tip the scales by going for her weapons.

Hajime took advantage of the opening, pulled more artifacts from his Treasure Trove, and sent them hurtling toward Noint.

She couldn't dodge the ten or so objects, and tried to knock them down with her shattered blades.

It was the worst possible move she could make. Hajime had thrown wire bolas, weighed down by ore on each side.

Naturally, they weren't ordinary bolas. Normally, you had to wind the bolas up before throwing them. As these were made of spirit stone, however, Hajime controlled their flight directly.

"Ah! I can't move!"

The bolas wrapped around Noint's swords, arms, and legs, then stopped. The spheres attached to the ends pulsed with energy. Like everything else, they were enhanced with creation magic. Hajime had used spatial magic, too, so that the bolas would be fixed in place. Anything they captured would be trapped.

Since Noint could disintegrate objects, even the bolas wouldn't hold her for long. And it was impossible to seal her wings. Even if Hajime trapped them with his bolas, Noint could make them vanish and reappear at will. With her skills, she could buy enough time to do that.

Still, Hajime only needed to hold Noint in place for a few seconds. That would be enough to hit her with his finishing move.

He wouldn't let this fight go on any longer. Hajime pulled a massive, two-meter long cannon from his Treasure Trove.

It was his railgun-enhanced pile bunker. Sparks ran down the barrel as it charged. A high-pitched mechanical whirr prickled Hajime's ears. He dashed forward, cannon in hand.

"Ngh...!"

Noint wrapped her wings around herself like a cocoon. The light they emanated intensified, and she glowed like a moon.

Hajime rammed his pile bunker into her beautiful barrier. The four arms attached themselves to Noint's wings, fixing the cannon in place. The arms were enchanted with spatial magic, so Noint couldn't dissolve them easily. Red sparks danced around the cannon. The bunker was nearly charged.

"Let's see you block this one."

Hajime's lips twisted into a feral grin, murder in his eyes.

He was wreathed in a blinding crimson aura, the light of his Limit Break eclipsing Noint's silver glow.

A tiny, invisible shockwave ran across the pile bunker's muzzle as it shot forward.

Hajime had added even more features to his ultimate weapon. He'd enchanted the stake with a compact version of Void Fissure. The spell's vibrations decimated the defenses of anything it touched.

Furthermore, gravity magic increased the stake's weight to

over twenty tons. The charged energy drove it down with a thunderous bang.

The atmosphere trembled as the pile bunker slammed Noint's wings.

Powered by blastrock, Hajime's Lightning Field, and the force of Hajime's mana, the spinning Azantium stake bore through her defenses.

It shredded her wings, and punched straight through her heart. The stake's tip shot through her back where her wings sprouted, and kept going.

It flew off into the horizon like a meteorite, trailing red sparks.

"Ah—!"

"……"

There was a gaping hole where Noint's crystal heart—the source of her mana—had been. Lightning Field had cauterized the wound, so no blood dripped from the hole. The last remnants of Noint's wings dissipated, leaving her looking smaller than before. Even now, there was no trace of emotion in her eyes, although Hajime couldn't help but feel that there was a hint of reproach in her expression.

The light slowly left Noint's pupils, and she fell lifelessly to the mountainside below.

Her glowing silver figure was easy to spot on the dark ground.

Hajime lowered himself to where she'd landed, and pointed Donner at her head. His Demon Eye and Sense Presence skill both told him she was dead, but he wouldn't rest easily until he blew her head off. That had become something of a bad habit.

"Looks like this 'Irregular' was more than you could handle."

Hajime wrapped his finger around the trigger. However, before he could pull it, he was interrupted...

Booooooooooooooooooom!

By an explosion so powerful it shook the entire mountain.

Hajime turned around to see a mushroom cloud rising where the Holy Church's main cathedral had been.

"No way."

Hajime's muttered words melted into the night.

He stared, slack-jawed, as the Holy Church crumbled to nothing. It looked like something from an old war documentary back on Earth. Just then, he received a telepathic message.

"M-Master... Are you all right?"

"Huh? Oh, Tio. Yeah, I managed to finish off my opponent..."

"I see. Wonderful. I expected no less from you. We've finished up here as well. Can you meet up with us?"

"I don't mind, but...uhh...I think I just witnessed something amazing."

"We can explain that. Or rather, we caused it..."

"What?"

"For now, let's rendezvous."

"Gotcha. Works for me."

Hajime hurried over. Apparently, Tio knew what had obliterated the Holy Church's main temple and its core followers.

As he flew into the air, he spotted Tio in her dragon form, flying a short distance from the mushroom cloud.

Aiko rode on her back, seemingly panicking over something.

What's Sensei doing here? Actually, knowing her, I think I can guess. She must have asked Tio to let her help. She'd never run while others were fighting.

What interested Hajime more was why Aiko was acting like she'd done something wrong.

"Sensei. Tio. Looks like you're both all right."

"Th-thank goodness you're all right, Nagumo-kun! I was really worried."

"Master. For a moment back there, I thought we might be done for, but we somehow made it out alive. I suppose I should have known your teacher would be just as dangerous as you. I did not expect my breath to become so powerful with her help. I must say, I'm impressed."

Hajime blinked in confusion. Then, with an incredulous look, he turned to Aiko.

"Sensei, what on Earth did you do?"

"Ha ha ha ha ha! I-It's not what you think! I didn't mean for it to end up like this. It's just, the pope's barrier was really strong, so...I thought maybe, if I amplified the strength of Tio-san's breath, she'd be able to break through..."

Aiko started panicking again, her relief at seeing Hajime safe forgotten. Although her explanation was a little haphazard, Hajime got the gist.

Aiko had decided to help Tio fight Ishtar and the other bishops to prevent them from weakening Hajime.

However, Aiko had no magic circles handy. So, even though she was an outstanding magician, she couldn't offer offensive support. Moreover, the main cathedral was apparently an artifact that deployed a barrier around itself. The barrier was quite powerful, and not even Tio's breath could breach it.

Unless Aiko did something, Ishtar and the others could cast their spell without interruption. While Tio dodged the Templar Knights, Aiko racked her brains. Eventually, she realized that she had just the skill for this situation.

These were her current stats:

AIKO HATAYAMA		Age: 25	Female
Job:	Farmer	Level:	56
Strength:	190	Agility:	310 NPNI
Vitality:	380	Magic:	820
Defense:	190	M. Defense:	280
Skills:	Soil Management • Soil Restoration [+Automatic Restoration] • Large-scale Cultivation [+Improved Scale] [+Contamination Conversion] • Enhanced Fertilization • Selective Breeding • Plant Appraisal • Fertilizer Production • Mixed Breeding • Auto Harvesting • Fermentation Proficiency [+Fermentation Acceleration] [+Large-scale Fermentation] • Wide-area Temperature Control [+Temperature Optimization] [+Weather Barrier] • Farming Barrier • Fertile Rain • Language Comprehension.		

Aiko used Fermentation.

Although the mountain was made of rock, it was inhabited

by people. That meant there were plenty of things lying around to ferment. Although this was Tortus, not Earth, most organic materials still emitted a methane-like gas when they fermented.

So, Aiko fermented everything she could reach, filling the church with flammable gas. Since Fermentation wasn't an offensive spell, the cathedral's barrier didn't block it. It had to let gas and air through, or the people inside would suffocate. Tio used wind magic to control the atmosphere around the building, making sure the gas didn't disperse.

Once Aiko had created enough flammable gas, Tio fired her breath, hoping the combination would be enough to destroy the barrier. But it did a lot more than that.

"So, that's what happened."

"Indeed. The explosion blew us away. I truly thought I was about to die. Not only did it destroy the barrier, it took the entire church along with it... I have never seen such a strange fight. Your mentor is fearsome, Master. I am in awe."

"It's not like that! I really didn't think the explosion would be that big! I just wanted to make sure it would destroy the barrier! Really! Wait! What happened to the bishops and knights?!"

Aiko turned her gaze back to the church in a panic, as if she'd only just remembered. Hajime and Tio followed her gaze, examining the rubble.

"Well, they were probably blown to pieces."

The cathedral was so utterly demolished, you couldn't tell what it had been. *There's no way any of them survived.*

"They put too much faith in their barrier. I am certain they had no contingency measures in place. And I suspect they could not have survived an explosion like that."

"B-but, then... I mean, I was prepared for a battle, but..."

~~Aiko paled as she realized she was responsible for killing the~~ Holy Church's leadership. She'd been ready to fight, and perhaps even to kill, but not like this.

Aiko doubled over and vomited. Hajime scratched his head, lost for words. He drew close and grabbed Aiko's vomit-stained hands. If nothing else, maybe some human warmth would do her good.

The warmth of Hajime's hands was the only thing that kept Aiko from sinking into the depths of despair. Forgetting that they were still student and teacher, Aiko flung herself into Hajime's arms and bawled her eyes out.

"My poor back," Tio grumbled about Aiko's infirmity as she cast Restoration. "Well, I suppose it's not such a big deal."

She would have liked to let Aiko stand up on her own. Tio was the one who actually shot the breath, so there was no need for Aiko to blame herself. But they didn't have time for a long discussion, so Tio used restoration magic to stabilize Aiko's sanity.

Her spirits somewhat lifted, Aiko looked up at Hajime. Although tears, snot and vomit covered her face, he didn't seem to mind. He pulled a towel out of his Treasure Trove and wiped her cheek. Embarrassed, Aiko let him.

"Have you finally calmed down, Sensei?"

"Y-yes. I-I'm fine now. Nagumo-kun..."

Aiko flushed. A hint of longing entered her voice when she

said his name. It was clear from the way she looked at Hajime that her tone wasn't just embarrassed.

Until now, Hajime had only seen Aiko as his teacher. When she looked at him like that, it forced him to consider that she might be in love with him. *You're kidding, right? This isn't really happening, is it?* Hajime thought with a stiff expression.

He quickly averted his gaze, just as Tio called out a warning.

"Master. There's someone here. They don't appear normal..."

"What?"

Did someone actually manage to survive that explosion? Hajime followed Tio's gaze, incredulous. A bald, white-robed man stood in the ruins of the church. He stared directly at Hajime. As Tio said, there was something off about him. For one thing, he was translucent. For another, he swayed back and forth like a stalk in the breeze.

The moment the man sensed Hajime's gaze, he silently turned around and floated across the mountain. He didn't seem to be walking, nor to be affected by gravity.

Just before the man vanished, he turned and looked at Hajime once more.

"Does he want us to follow him?"

"So it seems. What should we do, Master?"

"Hmm. Honestly, I want to meet back up with Yue and Shea, but... Supposedly, ancient magic is located here. It's possible this ghost dude has something to do with that. We better not let any leads slip past."

"Hrm. Very well, let us follow him."

Tio flew to the top of the rubble pile, let Hajime and Aiko get down, and transformed back into her human form. She frowned as she noticed the stain on her back, and pulled a change of clothes from her Treasure Trove. Hajime, too, changed out of his bloodied, vomit-stained clothes into something clean.

"Ugh, I'm sorry... I got your clothes dirty..."

Aiko seemed to shrink into herself. Vomiting all over someone was one of the most embarrassing things.

Although neither Hajime nor Tio seemed bothered, Aiko couldn't get over her shame... Especially because she was coming to terms with the fact that she might be in love with Hajime. Throwing up on someone was bad enough without that.

Hajime didn't have time to wait for Aiko to get over it, so he changed the topic.

"Sorry, Sensei, but you're gonna have to come with us. There's no telling what might happen up ahead, but we can't let this chance go. I wanna find out what that bald guy is."

"O-okay. I understand. I'll come with you."

She put an awful lot of emphasis onto that last word. Hajime pretended he hadn't noticed.

The translucent man stayed ahead of them, guiding Hajime and the others through the maze of rubble. After about five minutes of walking, they arrived at their destination. The man silently turned back and stood in place.

"What exactly are you? And what do you want with us?"

"......"

The bald man didn't reply. Instead, he lifted a finger and pointed deeper into the ruins. Hajime couldn't see anything special there, but clearly, that was where the man wanted him to go.

Realizing he wouldn't get anywhere with questions, Hajime nodded to Tio. As he arrived at the indicated location, the rubble around him started to float. The ground glowed. He looked down to see one of the labyrinth's crests carved there.

"Are you one of the Liberators?"

As Hajime finished his question, the light enveloped him.

A second later, he, Tio, and Aiko stood in an unfamiliar room. It wasn't very big. The walls were painted black, and there was a magic circle in the center. Next to the circle was an old pedestal, and atop that pedestal was a book. It seemed they'd teleported straight to the end of the labyrinth.

They walked up to the circle. Aiko looked around, obviously confused. Hajime took her hand and looked at Tio. The two nodded and stepped into the circle, Aiko following behind.

Hajime braced for the usual memory-reading. However, this time, it was different. It felt as though the memory probe reached far deeper into his brain, and he groaned in pain. He worried that he might have walked into a trap, but that worry vanished a second later. The memory probe verified that he had conquered this labyrinth, and imprinted its Liberator's ancient magic on his mind.

"Spirit magic?"

"Hrm. This magic seems to let you interfere directly with others' souls."

"I get it now. So, this is how Miledi transferred her soul into that golem..."

Aiko crouched and cradled her head. It was her first time receiving ancient magic, and having something engrave itself into her memories was disconcerting. Hajime watched her for a few seconds before walking to the nearby pedestal and picking up the book.

He flipped through the pages. It appeared to be a memorandum left by Laus Barn, this labyrinth's creator. It was similar to Oscar Orcus' journal; the memorandum detailed Laus' life with the Liberators.

Hajime had little interest in the Liberators' lives, and skimmed over the pages. Laus Barn's legacy didn't intrigue him. The volume mentioned why Laus Barn hadn't left his soul behind like Miledi, and what he had to repent for, but Hajime skipped through that too.

At the very end, the tome explained the conditions for clearing Laus Barn's labyrinth. First, you needed to have cleared at least two labyrinths already. Second, you needed to have disavowed this world's gods. Third, you needed to have defeated someone under a god's direct influence. Only then would Laus' ghost appear and guide challengers to this room. In other words, this labyrinth's theme was testing one's resolve. Challengers needed to prove their desire to overthrow the gods.

Hajime guessed that, if they had taken the normal route through the mountain, they would have faced a number of trials testing their determination. Although Aiko hadn't officially disavowed the gods, she always prioritized her students. On top of that, she'd contributed to the main cathedral's destruction. That was enough for Laus to consider her an official conqueror of this labyrinth.

Most of this world's residents would be hard-pressed to fulfill Laus' conditions, but for Hajime and the others, it was easy.

Hajime took Laus' ring and his book. Aiko recovered from the shock of having her mind probed and, since their business here had concluded, the three walked back to the magic circle that brought them there. Laus Barn's crest glowed, and they returned to the mountain.

"You all right, Sensei?"

"Ugh, yes. I think I can manage." Aiko rubbed her temples and nodded to herself. "I'm amazed that such magic exists, though. If something like this is out there, maybe there really is magic that can take us back to Japan, too."

"All right, we know where the labyrinth is now," said Hajime. "Let's go meet Yue and Shea and bring them here."

The past few days' events had taken their toll, but Aiko was excited at the prospect of finding an alternative way home. "I almost forgot! The capital is under attack, isn't it? I hope everyone's all right..."

At Hajime's prompting, the three descended the mountain. Time was short, so they jumped off the cliffside where the lift usually was. That section was carved smooth, so there was no danger of hitting jutting rocks.

Aiko screamed the whole way down, but Hajime and Tio ignored her.

They landed safely, although Hajime had to support Aiko. The capital was awash in flames, but Hajime's first priority was getting Aiko to safety. So, he ignored the screams coming from the streets and headed to the palace, planning to reunite with Kaori and Liliana.

When he arrived at the meeting point, he found Kaori lying dead on the ground, a sword sticking out of her chest.

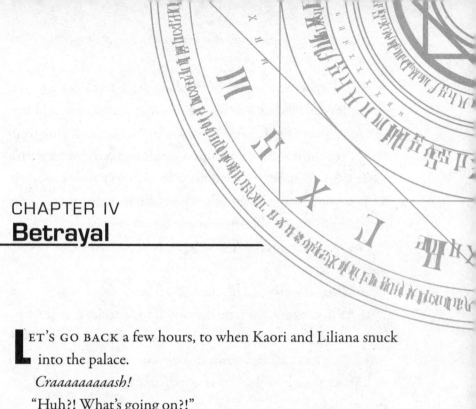

CHAPTER IV
Betrayal

LET'S GO BACK a few hours, to when Kaori and Liliana snuck into the palace.

Craaaaaaaaash!

"Huh?! What's going on?!"

Shizuku jolted awake at the sound of shattering glass. She threw off her sheets, grabbed her katana, and jumped to her feet. She was always on guard, even when she slept.

"......"

She tensed and held her breath, ready for an attack. She only relaxed when she was sure no one else was in her room.

She had been even more vigilant than usual these past few days. People had started vanishing from the palace.

The disappearances began a few weeks after they were saved from the Great Orcus Labyrinth, and after Kaori went off with Hajime.

Shizuku had worried about the disappearances since day one. She couldn't tell what was wrong, but her sixth sense told her *something* wasn't right.

~~At first, she just chalked it up to stress.~~ Her best friend wasn't by her side anymore, the demons were stronger than expected, and everyone was struggling over whether or not they could really kill. It was possible she was just on edge.

But her senses weren't deceiving her. Something was definitely wrong.

She hadn't found proof until today.

Three days ago, Aiko returned and told Shizuku that she had something important to tell everyone. Right after that, Aiko disappeared. Dinner came and went, and she was nowhere to be found.

Liliana vanished that same day. The palace guards and servants panicked.

Two people Shizuku knew well had disappeared without a trace. Yuka and the rest of Ai-chan's guard started searching frantically. Kouki and the others helped as well.

Then, Ishtar showed up and told them that Aiko had gone to the Divine Mountain to argue against Hajime being declared a heretic.

Naturally, Shizuku and the others demanded that Ishtar let them join Aiko, but he refused. The lift to the main cathedral wasn't working, and there was no alternate route.

They took their complaints to King Eliheid, but he simply told them that Aiko would return in three days and they should wait. Reluctantly, the students backed down.

Shizuku's worries continued to grow. She still had no proof, but she was certain that something was happening. Worse, Captain Meld went missing too, so she couldn't ask him for advice.

Three days. If we just sit tight for three days...

Three days passed, and the morning of the invasion dawned.

Neither Aiko nor Liliana returned.

Ishtar and the other priests vanished as well. Furthermore, the guards they'd assigned Aiko, David, and his squad disappeared too. The lift to the main cathedral still wasn't working.

Both the king and the prime minister refused to meet with the students. Soon, it would be four days since Aiko and Liliana disappeared.

However, only Yuka and Shizuku seemed to be worried.

Although Kouki did find it odd that Aiko hadn't returned, he couldn't accept that something dangerous might be going on within the palace itself. He thought the discussion about Hajime's heresy was just dragging on.

Shizuku could tell Kouki's feelings regarding Hajime were clouding his judgment. Moreover, his mind was too preoccupied with Kaori, and whether he could really kill, to think about much else.

Since most of the other students still looked up to Kouki, the fact that he wasn't worried was enough to reassure them. If Kouki said Aiko was okay, she was okay.

So Shizuku decided to consult Yuka and her friends. They were the only students who shared Shizuku's sense of unease.

They decided that, if Aiko hadn't returned by that night, they'd scale the mountain, lift or no lift.

After finishing her preparations, Shizuku climbed into bed ~~fully alert. Aiko hadn't returned, and Shizuku was growing suspi~~cious of everyone in the castle.

Which brings us back to the present.

Shizuku put on her equipment and slipped out of her room.

She silently cursed as her door squeaked slightly.

Down the hallway, Yuka, Taeko, and Nana were standing outside their rooms. They stood stock still, timidly examining their surroundings.

"Ah, Shizucchi!"

Nana spotted Shizuku and called out without thinking. Shizuku put one hand on her sword. Yuka and Taeko bopped Nana on the head.

"Idiot! What if that was an intruder?!"

"Don't be so careless, dummy!"

Nana apologized tearfully. Shizuku waved her hand to let them know the coast was clear.

Yuka and the others stepped into the hallway while Shizuku jogged to Kouki's room and knocked.

The door swung open immediately. Kouki stood there, fully dressed. Behind him, Ryutarou was in the process of getting up. The sound had woken them as well.

Shizuku sighed, and looked at Kouki with a pained expression.

"Kouki, you really need to be more careful. Don't just open the door for anyone who knocks... Look, you should at least make sure the person outside is a friend. What if I'd been an enemy?"

"But we're in the palace. Why would there be enemies here?"

Kouki tilted his head in confusion. Although he'd heard the noise, he still believed the palace was completely safe.

Judging from his bleary eyes, he wasn't fully awake yet.

"Well, something's not right, so stay on your guard," Ryutarou called out from behind him.

"All right, all right. But I think you're just overthinking things, Shizuku."

Neither of them made any move to get ready.

"Anyway, Shizuku, what was that noise? It sounded like something shattering..."

"I'm not sure. I'll go wake the others up and see if anyone knows. I have a bad feeling about this..."

Shizuku turned back to Yuka. Yuka nodded, and she and her friends split up to wake the others.

Unsurprisingly, those used to fighting on the front lines were already up and ready. Jugo Nakayama, Kentarou Nomura, Kousuke Endou, Ayako Tsuji, Mao Yoshino, Daisuke Hiyama, Reichi Kondou, Shinji Nakano, and Yoshiki Saitou answered Shizuku's summons immediately.

The rest of Aiko's bodyguards were out before Shizuku even reached their rooms.

Sadly, the other students weren't so prepared. Those who hadn't fought in months were extremely slow to respond, and some were still asleep. Shizuku had to beat a few of them awake.

Others, she coaxed out of their rooms, because they were too scared to come out.

"I'm sorry for waking you up in the middle of the night, guys. But most of you heard that noise, right? It's probably safe inside the palace, but I think we should still go see what's happening. It might be dangerous, so let's go together."

Kouki's words breathed life into the students, and those who were still drowsy finally woke up.

The students nodded nervously, wondering what could possibly have happened while they slept.

Just then, footsteps approached from the end of the hallway.

The students turned and saw Nia, Shizuku's personal maid, running toward them. She was the one who'd reprimanded them earlier for relying too much on Shizuku.

"Nia!"

"Shizuku-sama..." Nia's tone was forlorn.

It was surprising to see her so openly depressed. Nia was from a family of knights, and normally, she was much more composed.

Shizuku opened her mouth to ask what was wrong, but before she could say anything, the words spilled from Nia's mouth.

"The barrier's first layer has been destroyed."

"Wh-what?!"

The reason for Nia's unusual solemnity quickly became clear.

"The demons launched an assault. They have an army outside the gates, and they've already broken the first barrier."

"How did they...?!" Nia's report was so shocking that even Shizuku couldn't stay calm.

The other students broke into an uproar. None had believed the demons would ever reach the capital, which lay on the continent's northern tip. Everyone assumed the demons would need to conquer other human cities and forts before they could assault here.

Even if the demons did reach the capital, the students had believed the barrier would hold. After all, nothing had breached it for centuries.

Their shocked reactions were only natural.

"Nia, there's a total of three barriers protecting the capital, right?" Kouki asked with a grim expression.

There was. Each barrier was smaller and sturdier than the last.

"That is correct, Kouki-sama. The demons destroyed the outermost layer with a single attack. It's only a matter of time before they break through the rest..."

Kouki nodded and considered his options. After a few moments of deliberation, he decided to strike.

"We'll go out and try to buy some time. In the meantime, evacuate the residents. If we can just hold out long enough for the soldiers and knights to get into formation..."

Only a few students looked as though they agreed—just the other frontliners, and Aiko's guards.

The others looked away, ashamed. They had lost the will to fight. That day in the Great Orcus Labyrinth had crushed their spirits.

Even if it was just a defensive battle to buy time, they didn't have the confidence to face an army.

Kouki realized he couldn't force the other students, and closed his eyes in resignation. *We'll just have to do what we can with the few people we have.* Before he could say as much, Eri interjected.

"Wait, Kouki-kun. Rather than rushing out without preparing, I think we should find Meld-san and his knights first."

"But...Eri..."

Eri turned from Kouki to Nia. "Nia-san. You said they had an army, but do you know their exact numbers?"

"I'm not sure, but they looked a hundred thousand strong."

Everyone gulped. This was no small raid. This was a full-scale invasion.

"Kouki-kun. There's no way we can take on an army that large. We need more people. We're the strongest resource the humans have; we can't just waste ourselves recklessly. I think it would be smarter to find Meld-san first."

Although Eri spoke softly, her words were resolute. She was still a member of the hero party, after all. Moreover, her suggestion was logical.

"Yeah, I agree with Eririn. That's the smart thing to do. I knew those glasses weren't just for show!"

"G-glasses don't automatically make people smart, Suzu."

"Hee hee! I agree with Eri as well. She seems to be the only one thinking rationally. What do you say, Kouki?"

Kouki hesitated, but in the end, he gave in. Like the rest of the party, he trusted Eri's judgment.

"You're right. In times like these, we need to stay calm. Let's link up with Meld-san and his knights."

Nagayama, Hiyama, and Yuka agreed. And thus, the search for Captain Meld began.

First, the students headed for the staging area, where they figured the knights would be.

In their haste, no one noticed a member of their party grinning evilly.

⁕⁕ ⁕⁕ ⁕⁕ ⁕⁕ ⁕⁕ ⁕⁕ ⁕⁕ ⁕⁕ ⁕⁕ ⁕⁕ ⁕⁕ ⁕⁕ ⁕⁕

Plenty of soldiers and knights were gathered at the training grounds. It was the designated staging area during emergencies, so that wasn't surprising.

Jose Rancaid, the vice-captain of Heiligh's knights, was explaining the situation to everyone. Most of the soldiers were pale-faced. Hearing that the barrier had broken must have shaken them.

Kouki despaired when he saw how low the soldiers' morale was. Jose spotted Kouki walking into the courtyard, and stopped explaining to address him.

"I'm glad you're here. Have you heard what happened?"

"Yeah, Nia told us. Umm, where's Meld-san?"

Kouki looked around the courtyard, trying to spot Meld in the press of bodies.

"The Captain's busy right now. More importantly, come, join me. You're our leader, so you should stand in the center."

Jose ushered Kouki and the others to the middle of the courtyard.

The students who'd given up fighting seemed reluctant to join, as they weren't doing anything to help. However, they couldn't resist the tide of soldiers pushing them onward, and were jostled along with Kouki.

Shizuku didn't like how silent and emotionless the knights and soldiers looked. Something was off about them. In fact, something was off about this whole situation. Her unease grew stronger. She gripped the hilt of her katana.

"Hey, Shizuku. Is it just me, or...?"

"It's not just you. Don't let your guard down. Something strange is happening."

Yuka did her best to stamp down her mounting dread. Although Shizuku didn't want to go deeper into the crowd, she couldn't do anything about it. Fighting the crowd was inadvisable.

Something's not right.

The other frontliners felt it too, but no one said it aloud.

Finally, the crowd shoved Kouki and the others into the center of the courtyard. Jose continued his speech. Shizuku grew more worried.

"Comrades, the situation is dire. However, there is no need to fear. No one can match us. No one can defeat us. Death will take none of you today, for we have the hero on our side. Remember, men, today is the day we've trained for all our lives. Draw your swords, comrades!"

As one, the soldiers and knights unsheathed their weapons.

"Wha... Whoa," someone stammered in the midst of it all.

Shizuku and the others turned towards the noise. Kousuke had been casually muscled out of his spot next to Jugo.

"U-umm..."

Another confused voice. This time, Yuka was separated.

They weren't the only two, either. Before long, many other students, mostly those who fought at the front lines or belonged to Aiko's guard, were split up. Each was surrounded by a platoon of soldiers and knights. Goosebumps rose on Shizuku's arms. Her instincts screamed to get out.

"Everyone, run—"

Before Shizuku could finish her warning, Jose pulled something out of his pocket and raised it high above his head.

"Behold, this marks the beginning of a new age!"

At his words, the soldiers turned to him as one. Confused, the students followed suit.

There was a bright flash.

Whatever Jose held emitted a burst of light as intense as Hajime's flash grenades.

The students screamed as the flash pierced their eyes. They turned away, but were already blinded.

A second later, there were a number of meaty thuds.

They were followed by a series of screams.

Not screams of surprise, but of pain.

"Agh?!"

"Gah!"

"Gwaaah?!"

After that, people fell to the ground with loud thumps.

Amidst the chaos, Shizuku drew her weapon and readied herself.

She just barely managed to block the sword thrust that came for her.

Like the others, Shizuku had been blinded. But thanks to her years of training, months of experience, and excellent senses, she was able to fight back.

~~Finally, her sight began to return, and~~ Shizuku examined her surroundings. A nightmare greeted her.

Her classmates had been stabbed in the back, and lay on the ground. She was prepared for something terrible, but this was beyond her expectations.

What on Earth is happening? Why are they doing this? Shizuku's voice caught in her throat. "Wha...?"

Her classmates' wails pierced her ears. The scene in front of her was so shocking that her brain shut down.

Don't tell me they're all dead!

Although Kouki, Ryutarou, Suzu, and Yuka all lay in pools of their own blood, however, they were breathing.

Knowing that her friends still lived brought Shizuku some small measure of comfort, but the other frontliners were too gravely injured to move. Cold sweat poured down her back.

Kousuke was the most badly hurt. Swords weren't sticking out of just his back, but his limbs, too. He twitched weakly on the ground.

Worse, the rest of Shizuku's classmates had been cuffed with mana-sealing shackles.

No one would be able to heal them.

What do I do? What do I do? Shizuku desperately cast her gaze about, looking for a solution. Then she noticed something strange.

"Oh, my. I guess I should've expected you to come out of that unscathed, Shizuku."

A single classmate wasn't on the ground in a puddle of their own blood, or pinned down by a cluster of soldiers. And right now, they sounded nothing like their normal self.

"Huh? What? Wh-why? What are you—" Shizuku trailed off, stunned. She'd opened her mouth more out of reflex than anything.

A second later, a knight charged from behind.

"Ngh?!"

Despite her shock, Shizuku managed to dodge. Her betrayer looked down at her, exasperated.

"I can't believe you dodged that too... Of course, *you'd* be the one to make things difficult."

"Seriously, what are you—"

A storm of steel cut Shizuku off. All the soldiers around her attacked at once. Their movements were unusually sharp, as if they were powered up.

Still, Shizuku managed to dodge somehow. While she wove between swords, she heard someone call out to her, and turned around.

"Shizuku, help me!"

"Nia!"

Nia lay on the ground, a knight straddling her. She was seconds away from being pierced by his sword.

Shizuku dashed to Nia, ducking through the horde of soldiers using a combination of No Tempo and Supersonic Step. She bashed the knight away with her sheath, sending him flying.

"Nia, are you all right?"

"Shizuku-sama..."

Shizuku helped Nia to her feet, warily observing the nearby troops.

Nia hugged Shizuku, seemingly terrified.

A second later, she drove a dagger into Shizuku's back.

"N-Nia? Wh-why?"

"......"

Shizuku's mouth twisted into a pained grimace as she looked down at her friend.

Nia's eyes were devoid of their usual warmth. She appeared expressionless, as if she were an unthinking doll.

It was then that Shizuku realized.

Nia wasn't acting odd because the capital's barrier was destroyed. Her subdued demeanor and empty eyes were exactly like those of the knights and soldiers.

In other words, Nia was under the influence of whatever had driven them all crazy.

Unfortunately, Shizuku came to this realization too late. Nia pinned her to the ground, twisted Shizuku's arms behind her back, and shackled her with the same magic-sealing cuffs the soldiers had put on the others.

"Aha ha ha ha! I guess even you couldn't predict *she'd* stab you, huh? Yeah, see, that's why I waited until the last minute to put her under my control."

The burning sensation in Shizuku's back contrasted starkly with the cold ground at her cheek. The soldiers weren't acting strange because of demons; it was this student's work.

The truth stung. Shizuku couldn't accept it.

No, she didn't want to accept it... That someone she trusted had betrayed her.

They'd gone through so many crises together. It was inconceivable that she would betray them, but Shizuku couldn't deny her eyes.

"What is the meaning of this, Eri?!"

Eri, the quiet, thoughtful, kindhearted girl who always put others first, who had fought with Shizuku for the past few months, was actually a traitor.

She'd purposely missed the students' vitals, so they lay there in pain, gazing at her in shock, while she gloated.

Eri's soldiers made no move to attack further. They stood at attention, lifeless eyes trained on their new master.

Eri walked past the students, examining each in turn. Jugo lay on the ground, twitching. Kousuke had lost so much blood he'd nearly fallen unconscious. Yuka stared wide-eyed at her, disbelief written across her face. The only noise that broke the silence was Eri's footsteps echoing off the cobblestones.

Eri ignored Shizuku's question and stopped before Kouki.

With a maniacal grin, she whipped off her glasses, grabbed his mana-sealing collar, and dragged him to his feet.

"E-Eri... Why...gah...would you..."

Although he wasn't as close to Eri as Kaori and Shizuku were, Kouki still considered her a good friend. He couldn't understand why she would betray them. Gritting his teeth against the pain, he forced his question out.

Eri didn't answer. Her expression didn't look entirely sane.

"Caaaught you, Kouki-kuuun," she said in a singsong voice, leaning over him.

"Mmmf?!"

She pressed her lips against Kouki's in a passionate kiss.

The sound of their mouths carried surprisingly far across the empty courtyard. Eri lost herself in the act, savoring the kiss as if she'd desired it her whole life.

Stunned, Kouki tried to shake her off, but the nearby soldiers pinned him in place. In his weakened state, bereft of magic, Kouki couldn't overpower them.

Eri finally pulled away, satisfied. A silver thread of drool connected them. She licked her lips seductively, then turned to the other students.

They stared at her, their expressions a mixture of confusion and pain.

Eri nodded in satisfaction and focused her attention on Shizuku.

"Well, that's how it is, Shizuku."

"What do you mean, 'That's how it is...?' Gah!" Shizuku glared at Eri, blood dribbling from her mouth.

Eri shook her head in an exaggerated motion, as if talking to a particularly slow child. "Still haven't figured it out? You see, I've always wanted Kouki-kun to myself. I just did what it took to make him mine. Make sense now?"

"If you loved Kouki...all you had to do was confess! You didn't need to go this far..."

Eri's face went blank for a moment.

But then, her grin returned.

"No, no, no, no. That wouldn't work. Kouki-kun's too kind to play favorites. Even though you're all trash, he's too nice to ignore you. The only way to make Kouki-kun mine and mine alone was to clean up the trash lying around him."

Eri shrugged her shoulders, as if her motives were the most obvious thing in the world.

Everyone was too shocked to be angry with her disparaging remarks. Her entire personality had changed, and Shizuku doubted that the girl in front of her was really Eri at all.

"Tee hee! I'm so glad we came to this world. Getting rid of all of you would've been difficult back in Japan. Which is why, of course, I can't let you guys go back home. Because Kouki-kun's going to spend the rest of his days here, with me. Forever." Suddenly, everything clicked.

"Don't tell me..." Shizuku said hesitantly. "The reason they broke the barrier so easily...was because..."

"Ah ha ha! You noticed? Yep, I did that... I smashed the artifact that powered the barrier."

Shizuku's guess was spot-on. That was one mystery solved, although it still didn't explain how the demon army reached the capital unnoticed. Eri nodded to a platoon of soldiers standing silently beside her, like reanimated corpses. Shizuku guessed they were the ones who actually carried out the deed.

"I mean, if I killed you guys, there's no way I'd be able to stay in the kingdom. So, I went to the demons and made a deal. I'd let them into the capital and take care of you guys and the soldiers, and they'd leave me and Kouki-kun alone."

"When...did you get the chance to..." Kouki muttered in disbelief.

Eri had trained with them in the palace all along. It should have been impossible for a demon to get past the barrier and contact her. Kouki still half-hoped that this was all some big misunderstanding.

Sadly, even that hope was dashed.

"Remember that woman we fought in the Great Orcus Labyrinth? Before we left, I used necromancy on her. I commanded her to deliver a message to the demons who retrieved her body. To be honest, I was scared it wouldn't work. I needed to get in touch with them without getting killed, so I used necromancy... But I wanted to keep those skills hidden, so they wouldn't seem suspicious. It turned out all right in the end, though."

Eri had reanimated Cattleya's corpse to deliver a message to the demons who retrieved it. That was also how they'd discovered who'd killed her.

The demons delivered their reply by reanimating a human corpse and sending it to Eri. The barrier was primed only to keep out demons, so the corpse made it past.

Shizuku, already pale from blood loss, paled even further when she realized the implications.

Necromancy utilized the lingering regrets people left behind when they died. Although she'd hidden her abilities, Eri had long since mastered the skills needed to reanimate people. In other words, the soldiers in the courtyard, and even Nia, weren't acting strange because they were under some kind of mental control, but because they were dead.

"Then...that means everyone here is..."

"Only moving because of my necromancy, of course. They all died ages ago. Aha ha ha ha!"

Shizuku gritted her teeth, her mind refusing to accept it.

"Y-you're lying! There's no way a dead person should...gah... be able to talk!"

"I'm just that good. I can give my corpses a portion of the personality and memories they had in life, so they're able to hold a conversation. It's an original spell I came up with: Spirit Binding."

Normal necromancy could only read the last thoughts of the deceased, or animate dead bodies by injecting mana into the lingering regrets they left behind. Skilled practitioners could reanimate corpses, but those corpses were mindless.

Their abilities would be inferior to their living versions. And, as the corpses were incapable of thought, they needed to be controlled directly. Of course, a simple command like "attack" didn't require constant management, so a necromancer could set a horde of corpses on someone without having to micromanage them all.

But holding a full conversation, as Nia and Jose had, should have been impossible for a corpse.

With Spirit Binding, Eri ripped her victims' memories and personalities from their souls, and implanted them into their corpses.

She interfered directly with her targets' souls. With just her own skills, Eri had managed to create an inferior version of ancient magic.

That was how overpowered her necromancy abilities were. Despite claiming that she was bad at necromancy, Eri was actually a genius. Furthermore, she'd devoted all her free time to secretly honing her art. The warped motives driving her growth were truly terrifying.

The only reason Eri hadn't killed the students right away was that she could only use Spirit Binding on one person at a time.

Still, Shizuku found it hard to believe that no one noticed Eri slowly taking over the army. Spirit Binding took time, and the first cases appeared days ago.

A terrible thought ran through Shizuku's mind.

"Don't tell me...you killed Ai-chan and Lily too...?"

"Hm? Nah, I didn't touch them. I've got nothing to do with that."

Shizuku breathed a sigh of relief. She'd been worried Eri had eliminated the teacher and princess because they caught on to her plan.

Eri saw some of the tension drain from Shizuku and grinned wickedly. "It's too early to relax."

"Huh?"

"The girl who took Ai-chan is pretty scary. She knew what I was up to, and actually decided to cooperate. All the most important people in the kingdom are under her control, you know. Remember how the king and his nobles started acting weird?"

"Ah!"

Shizuku wasn't the only one who gasped. Yuka and the others had spent the past few days searching everywhere for Aiko, only to discover she'd been kidnapped.

Thinking back, the king and his ministers certainly were acting odd.

But none of the students had suspected that the kingdom's rulers were brainwashed.

"You know, I was pretty worried when she told me she knew my plans. I thought I might have to kill her."

Eri wiped imaginary sweat off her brow. Obviously, a lot more must have happened during that encounter, but Eri didn't explain.

"Anyway, it's thanks to her that everything went so smoothly. I was able to speed up my plans by months. Heaven itself is on my side! Everything I do has god's blessing! Don't worry, everyone, your deaths won't have been in vain! I'll put your corpses to good use as vanguards in the demon army!"

Eri danced in the moonlight, flitting between her former classmates and the soldiers' reanimated corpses.

Arms spread wide, she spun in a circle. She truly believed that her actions were ordained by god.

Finally realizing that Eri was serious, Kouki interrupted her deranged cackling.

"Ngh... Stop this, Eri! If you keep going like this, I really..."

"You won't forgive me? Ah ha ha... I knew you'd say that. You're so kind, Kouki-kun. That's why all this trash gravitates to you. So I'll have to Spirit Bind *you* too. That way, you'll look only at me, and only say what I want you to! You'll be mine and mine alone! Aaaah... It's going to be so wonderful!"

Eri wrapped her arms around herself and shivered in ecstasy. None of her classmates could believe this was the same quiet, thoughtful, bookish girl they knew.

She'd gone crazy. That was the only explanation.

Although Spirit Bind preserved some of the host's original personality and memories, the necromancer still had full control. No sane person would want an undead puppet for a lover.

"This isn't real... It can't be! The Eririn I know would...never do something like this! Somebody's...gah...somebody's controlling her! That has to be it! Open your eyes, Eri!"

Blood dripped from Suzu's mouth as she yelled. It hurt to move, even to talk, but Suzu tried to crawl towards Eri.

Eri turned to Suzu and grinned maniacally. Then she walked to the student closest to her, Kondou.

Afraid of where this was going, Kondou whimpered in pain and tried to back away. Unfortunately, he was still pinned down, his mana sealed. All he could do was squirm.

Eri stopped in front of him, that same maniacal grin on her face. Kondou shivered, knowing full well what was next. Kouki and the others yelled at Eri to stop.

"St-sto—gaaaaaah...!"

Kondou's pleas transformed into a garbled scream. A single sword plunged into his heart.

It wasn't a wounding blow. It was fatal.

"Reichi! Gaaah!"

"Damn you, Nakamuraaa! I'll—gah!"

Saitou and Nakano yelled out, but the knights pinning them dug their swords in deeper, cutting them off. The students could only watch.

Kondou's spasms slowly weakened, and he grew still. Tough as he was, even he couldn't survive a stab to the heart.

Eri raised a hand and began an unfamiliar incantation. Once she finished, a transparent version of Kondou appeared. The apparition overlapped with his corpse and melted into it.

The knights holding him down stepped back, freeing him.

Kouki and the others gulped as they watched Kondou's dead body rise to its feet. He had the same lifeless expression as Nia and the soldiers.

"Aaand done. That's one puppet complete."

Eri's cheerful voice rang through the silence. She didn't sound like someone who just killed her classmate and desecrated his corpse.

"E-Eri... Why...?"

Eri turned back to Suzu.

"Thanks, Suzu," she said in the same chipper tone. "It's because of you that I was able to stay by Kouki-kun's side. Both here, and in Japan."

"Huh?"

"You don't get it? All along, it was as though there was an unspoken rule that only Kaori and Shizuku could be close to Kouki-kun. If I tried to approach him, the other girls would gang up against me. Since I was powerless back in Japan, getting into that circle would've taken forever. That's why I'm so glad you were there. You were so stupid that everyone just laughed at everything you did. No one got mad at you, even when you joined Kouki's circle. Being known as your 'best friend' was the best thing that could have happened. I could be beside Kouki-kun, and no one would say anything. Once we arrived in this world, I was even in the same party. You're the most convenient best friend I could ask for! Thank you so much!"

"Ah..."

Something inside Suzu broke. Her best friend, the person she'd trusted the most, had used her. Everything Suzu knew about Eri was a lie. The light went out of Suzu's eyes, her mind shielding her from the anguish.

"Eri, how dare you!" Shizuku screamed, struggling in Nia's grip.

Nia grabbed Shizuku's hair and slammed her to the ground.

Shizuku glared at Eri through the pain. Being rendered immobile did nothing to dull her anger.

"Tee hee! Oooh, you're mad now. I love it when you make that face. You know, I've actually always hated you. You got to be by Kouki-kun's side all the time, and yet you acted like it was a chore. I couldn't stand that arrogant attitude of yours! That's why I've prepared a very special role for you."

"What...do you mean?"

"Tee hee... I wonder what your best friend will think when you kill her?"

Shizuku's eyes opened wide. "You're going to make me kill Kaori?!"

Eri clapped her hands theatrically, as if to say "good job figuring that out." The corners of her lips twitched into a smile.

Eri wanted to turn Shizuku into a puppet and use her to kill Kaori.

"To be honest, I wouldn't have minded letting her live, since Nagumo took her with him... But someone here reallllllly wants to make her his puppet. He's been a huge help, so I guess he deserves a reward. Plus, I'm a good girl who keeps her promises!"

Shizuku forced herself to move, even though she knew it would exacerbate her wounds.

"D-don't screw with—gah?!" Before she could get up, Nia stabbed her again.

"Ha ha! Does it hurt? It does, doesn't it? Don't worry, I'm a nice girl. I'll let you sleep real soon..."

Eri walked to Shizuku. It appeared she would be next.

The other students struggled against their captors. They didn't want to see anyone else end up like poor Kondou.

"Stop! Please, stop this, Eri!"

Kouki struggled especially valiantly. The five mana-sealing shackles restraining him cracked. In his attempt to activate Overload, he'd put inordinate strain on them.

However, the undead knights held Kouki in joint locks, keeping him pinned down. Since the knights' brains no longer functioned, there were no limiters to keep their muscles in check. They were stronger than they'd been while alive.

Despairing, Kouki could only watch as Eri approached Shizuku.

Shizuku did her best to remain conscious. At the very least, she wanted to face her death head-on. She refused to give Eri the satisfaction of passing out.

Eri smirked at Shizuku and took a knight's sword. She apparently wanted to do the honors herself.

"Bye, Shizuku. I gotta say, pretending to be friends with you made me want to puke," she gloated, sword held high.

Shizuku glared at Eri, but her thoughts turned toward Kaori.

She knew there was no way she could warn Kaori, but Shizuku still sent off one final message to the girl traveling the world with her crush.

I'm sorry, Kaori. But, please, don't trust me next time we meet... Live a long life...and be happy...

Silver moonlight glinted off the sword. Eri brought it straight down, like a stake towards a vampire's heart.

As she watched its approach, Shizuku prayed.

Please, let my best friend survive this ordeal.

Please let her find happiness.

I'll die before you, and I know I might end up hurting you. But still, I'm sure you'll be fine. You have Nagumo with you, after all.

Live happily, together with him. I hope...

Time slowed to a crawl, and Shizuku's entire life flashed before her eyes. *So, that really does happen when you're about to die...* Sensing the end of her existence at hand, she waited for the moment when everything would turn black.

"Huh?"

"Wha...?"

Shizuku and Eri cried out in surprise.

A palm-sized light barrier had stopped Eri's sword.

The two were startled out of their reverie by a voice that shouldn't have been there. A strained, almost panicked voice.

The voice of the girl Shizuku had just wished happiness to—the voice of Shizuku's best friend.

"Shizuku-chan!"

Ten glowing shields appeared around Shizuku, surrounding her in a dome of protection. Kaori created a few more shields and sent them at Nia and Eri. These flashed brightly and exploded in a supernova of light. Kaori overloaded her barriers with mana, making them burst. It was a makeshift way to turn her defensive skills into offensive ones.

"Huh?!"

Eri raised her arms to block the light, but the shockwave and shards of shattered shield bowled her over.

Kaori's Barrier Burst blew Nia away, too. The maid quickly recovered and moved to restrain Shizuku again, but Kaori stopped her.

"Divine Shackles!"

Chains of light slithered upwards from the ground and wrapped around Nia and Eri.

Still dumbfounded, Shizuku turned toward the sound of Kaori's voice. There was no way her best friend should be here, but there she was, standing among the zombified soldiers.

It wasn't an illusion. Kaori really was there.

Tears of happiness spilled down Kaori's cheeks. She'd made it in time. Barely, perhaps. But, this time, she'd protected the people she loved.

"K-Kaori…"

"Just sit tight, Shizuku-chan! I'll save you!"

Seeing how badly the students were injured, Kaori quickly moved to heal them. She started chanting Aetherflow, the greatest light recovery spell.

The students' wounds were serious enough that she needed to prioritize healing over everything else.

"Why are you here?! Why do you all keep getting in my way?!"

Face twisted in an insane snarl, Eri ordered her soldiers to attack. The soldiers rushed Kaori, intent on stopping her chant.

A glowing wall of light met their swords. Not a single soldier managed to break through it.

While Kaori cast her healing spell, Liliana raised a golden dome to protect her. She stood behind Kaori, trying to make sense of everything. She couldn't fathom why her soldiers and knights were attacking the students, nor why Eri seemed to be in charge.

"What happened to you all?! Why are you acting like this?! Come back to your senses! Eri, what's going on here?!"

Liliana demanded an answer, but Eri ignored her.

Although she was a princess, Liliana was also a skilled mage. In fact, she was skilled enough to single-handedly protect More's caravan from over forty bandits. It was an easy task to hold back a group of knights long enough for Kaori to finish her spell… Even knights strengthened via zombification.

Panic colored Eri's face as her plan began to crumble.

"Tch. Guess I've got no other choice."

Impatient, she looked to where her classmates lay.

She didn't have time to turn them into her puppets. Her only option was to kill them before Kaori finished casting her spell.

Before Eri could move, one of the knights banging into Liliana's barrier lost his head. His decapitated corpse slumped to the ground.

None other than Daisuke Hiyama stood over the knight's body.

"Shirasaki! Princess Liliana! Are you two all right?!"

"Hiyama-san? How can you move with such terrible wounds?!"

Liliana paled as she saw Hiyama's condition. Kaori was too disciplined to stop chanting, but her eyes opened wide in surprise.

Hiyama's shirt was blood-soaked, and still more blood spurted from the hole in his chest. He'd obviously pushed himself to the limit to break free.

Hiyama staggered and leaned against the barrier to steady himself. Liliana hurriedly opened a Hiyama-sized hole in it to let him in.

Once he was safely inside, he collapsed to the ground.

A second later, Shizuku yelled out a warning.

"Wait! Get away from him!"

Blood dripped from her mouth as she shouted. It hurt to talk, but she had to try. Eri had mentioned that one of her accomplices wanted Kaori for his own, and Hiyama had escaped his bonds when even Kouki couldn't. The connection was obvious. Hiyama knew Liliana's barrier would hold until Kaori finished her spell.

Yet he'd attempted to "save" them anyway. There could only be one reason.

Sadly, Shizuku's warning was too late.

Hiyama leaped to his feet and shoved Liliana out of the way, breaking her concentration and dissolving the barrier. "Kyaaa!"

He circled behind Kaori and stabbed her through the chest.

"Ah—!"

"Kaoriiiiiiiiiiiiiiiiiiiiiii!"

Shizuku's devastated scream echoed through the courtyard.

Hiyama pressed his face into Kaori's neck, madness in his eyes. One of his hands still held the sword hilt sticking out from Kaori's chest.

Hiyama had faked his injuries from the beginning. He only pretended to fall with the other students. In reality, he was Eri's insurance against any more of Kouki's heroic bursts of strength.

The moment Kaori appeared, Hiyama knew she'd heal everyone and ruin their plans. So, he put on an act to lower her guard.

"Heh heh heh heh... Finally! I finally did it! I knew it... I really am better than Nagumo. I am, aren't I, Shira... I mean, Kaori? Right? I'm totally better than that loser! Heh heh heh... Hey, Nakamura, hurry up and bring her back. You promised you would."

Eri shrugged noncommittally and walked over to Kaori.

Before she could start casting, Kouki interrupted her.

"Gaaaaaaaaaaaaah! How dare youuuuuuuuuu!"

He pushed so hard against his restraints that they cracked. Watching Kaori get stabbed had sent him berserk.

The cracks in Kouki's restraints grew wider, and the knights holding him down were struggling. His strength was immense. Unfortunately, it wasn't quite enough for him to break free.

Hiyama, watching everything with detachment, heard whispering next to him. Looking down, he noticed that Kaori was still breathing. Her wound was fatal, but she wasn't dead yet.

He brought his ear to her lips, trying to make out the words. "Mother...heaven...embrace...Aether...flow."

Kaori had continued chanting through the pain, and somehow managed to finish her spell.

Even at death's door, she was stubborn to a fault.

Hiyama stared at her in shock.

Kaori knew she only had seconds to live. And yet, she hadn't spent her final moments crying, lamenting her fate, or even calling out to the boy she loved. She used what little time she had left to fight.

The way she saw it, that was the best way to show Hajime her devotion. The boy she'd fallen for never gave up, no matter how tough the foe, or how unwinnable the situation. If she truly wanted to call herself a member of his party, the least she could do was keep on fighting.

And so, Kaori traded her life to cast one last spell. Her indestructible resolve held out, and she chanted to completion.

Ripples of light spread around her.

The light covered the courtyard in seconds, healing anyone who was injured. It forcibly pushed out the swords stuck inside the students. At the same time, it slowed the zombified soldiers' movements.

The light tried to heal Kaori as well. However, unlike the other students' injuries, her wound was fatal. Hiyama had sawed his sword back and forth inside of her, and the light couldn't repair such grievous damage fast enough. Hiyama had been hell-bent on making sure she died.

"Aaaaaaaaah!" Kouki let out a primal roar.

With his wounds healed, he was strong enough to shatter his weakened restraints.

A tremendous amount of white mana surrounded his body. Free of his bonds, Kouki activated Overload, Limit Break's ultimate derivative skill. It quintupled his stats.

"I'll...never forgive you monsters!"

Eri's knights tried to restrain him, but he grabbed the sword that had stabbed him and sliced them in two. Strengthened or not, the soldiers were no match.

Unperturbed by the carnage, Kouki held out his right hand, calling for his Holy Sword. Eri's soldiers had taken it, but it wrenched itself from their grasp and spun through the air toward Kouki.

"Hold him down," Eri commanded in a flat voice.

Her soldiers rushed at Kouki.

"Out of my way... Celestial Flash!"

He mowed them down with a single attack.

Kouki still hadn't overcome his aversion to murder, but right now, he was too angry to care. Besides, his opponents were technically already dead. Killing zombies wasn't the same as killing people, and Kouki acted without hesitation.

In his reckless rampage, he took out a few soldiers holding other students down, more by luck than anything.

One of the freed students fled back into the castle without anyone noticing.

The others—Ryutarou, Atsushi, and Yuka—were forced to fight off the soldiers crowding around them.

As always, no one paid attention to Kousuke. Even when his mana was sealed, no one had noticed him. But, then, Kousuke's innate talent for going unobserved didn't require magic. So long as people didn't stare directly at him, they would forget he was even there.

"Tamai! Sonobe! Here!"

Kousuke grabbed Atsushi's artifact, a powerful cutlass, and one of Yuka's artifacts, a set of twelve throwing knives. He tossed them to their owners, wanting to arm the pair before the soldiers restrained them again.

Even Kousuke's shout wasn't enough to attract attention. When the artifacts' owners saw their weapons at their feet, however, they guessed what had happened.

"Careful, Tamai! Don't cut my hands!"

"How clumsy do you think I am?"

Yuka held her hands out, and Atsushi cut through her shackles with impeccable precision. His job was Cutlassier, so he knew how to use his weapon. Freed, and able to use magic, Yuka activated her own artifact. So long as she had one knife in her hand, she could call back all the others.

The knives themselves weren't strong, but the fact that Yuka could always summon them made them quite powerful.

Yuka's remaining knives flew toward her, cutting through the soldiers holding Taeko and Nana.

In the meantime, Atsushi succeeded in freeing Akito and Noboru.

"Suzu! Put up a barrier! Protect the ones who aren't fighting!" Ryutarou barked while Atsushi, Yuka, and Kousuke freed everyone they could.

Ryutarou knew the stay-home group would be too scared to fight, so he asked Suzu to guard them.

Eri realized that turning everyone into puppets was impossible now, and changed tactics. Her soldiers began striking to kill, not to immobilize.

Ryutarou hoped Suzu could save the other students now that she was free. But, when he glanced back, he saw her sitting still.

"Huh?"

Suzu's eyes were glazed over. It looked as if she wasn't even registering the battle going on around her.

"Suzu!"

"Ah... S-sorry!"

Her usual cheeriness was nowhere to be seen. From her expression, she was obviously in no state to fight.

Cursing Eri for whatever she had done to the girl, Ryutarou scooped Suzu up and went to defend the remaining students.

Most of the rearguard were still shackled, and couldn't help him.

Jugo, Atsushi, and the others formed a protective circle around the remaining students. Ryutarou muscled his way into the ring and began punching. It was a fight to protect his comrades, so it was natural that he joined in.

No matter how many zombie soldiers the group defeated, however, more rose to take their place. *Just how many damn people did she zombify?!*

"Crap!"

"Calm down, Sakagami!"

Jugo tried to keep Ryutarou in check. The two of them were the students' living shield. Yuka and the others could only attack because Ryutarou and Jugo were taking the brunt of the blows.

Without Ryutarou, the students would be overwhelmed.

Jugo knew how much Kaori's death pained Ryutarou, but if he leapt into the fray, everything would be over.

"Get out of my way! Kaoriiiiiiiii!"

Shizuku tried to claw her way over to Kaori, tears in her eyes. But the waves of knights held her back. She was too distraught to fight effectively, and her blows missed more often than not. Seeing how badly she was fighting only distressed her more, which, in turn, dulled her blade further.

Then, Kouki used brute force to punch a hole in the wall of soldiers and create an opening.

Pure hatred oozed from him as he charged forward, wrapped in an aura of blazing white light.

"Eri, Hiyamaaaaaa!"

"That's as far as you go, Kouki-kun."

Eri used her final trump card. She knew Kouki well enough to have charted all of his weaknesses.

A single soldier stepped between Eri and Kouki.

As Eri expected, Kouki lowered his sword.

"No... Not you too, Meld-san..." he called in a trembling voice.

Standing in front of Kouki was none other than the captain of the kingdom's knights, Meld Loggins.

"Kouki... Why are you pointing your sword at me...? I didn't teach you to fight so you could kill humans..."

"Huh? Meld-san... I'm not..."

"Kouki, don't listen to him! Meld-san's already dead!"

Shizuku's words shocked Kouki from his reverie.

By the time he returned to his senses, however, Meld's sword was bearing down on him.

Kouki hurriedly raised his own sword to block. Meld's blow was so powerful that the ground beneath Kouki cracked. Meld's internal limiter had been removed, like the other soldiers', allowing him to exert his full strength.

"Meld-san... I'm sorry!"

Face twisted in anguish, Kouki fired off a series of lightning-quick slashes. Even in death, though, Meld's swordplay was impeccable. Although Kouki used Overload, Meld was still just able to keep up.

That was partly because Kouki still hesitated. He knew that Meld was already dead, but that didn't make the fight any easier.

Still, despite that handicap, Meld had no chance. After a furious flurry of blows, his sword flew from his hand.

Kouki stepped in and swung wildly at Meld's neck.

But just before he parted Meld's head from its shoulders—

"Please don't kill me... Kouki."

"Huh...?!"

Kouki's sword stopped inches from Meld's neck. *Could it be that Captain Meld isn't dead, and he's really just being controlled? Can we still save him?*

Kouki was easily swayed by emotion, and couldn't commit. That was his greatest weakness. He should have made a decision and stuck with it. Either save Meld, or kill him. But he couldn't. He changed his priorities based on whatever new information became available. Although Kouki never doubted his own righteousness, and always interpreted things in a way that was convenient for him, he stumbled when things came down to the wire.

Meld kicked a nearby sword up into his hand and struck at Kouki. This time, it was Kouki who was pushed back.

"Wha—?! Gah! Wh-what the...? I suddenly feel weak—"

The strength drained from Kouki's limbs, and he sank to his knees. But his Overload hadn't expired; it still had a few minutes. Besides, the Overload's recoil didn't leave Kouki vomiting blood. He retched, a mouthful of blood splattering the ground.

"Phew. Looks like it's finally working. I used a potent poison, but... I guess I should've expected you'd be able to resist it, Kouki-kun. If I hadn't kept the captain handy, I might really have lost," Eri said nonchalantly.

Kouki hugged himself and looked questioningly up at her.

She ran a finger across her lips and smiled sweetly.

"Hee hee! If the prince's kiss wakes the princess up, then the princess' kiss puts the prince to sleep, and makes him hers...

permanently. Don't worry, the poison's not lethal. You'll just be paralyzed for a little bit! Fear not, I'll be sure to kill you with my own two hands, Kouki-kun!"

"So that kiss back then was...gah..."

When Eri kissed Kouki, she'd fed him poison.

She'd taken the antidote herself, so it didn't affect her. Nobody would have expected her to poison someone with a kiss, especially not the boy she ostensibly loved.

"Eri, you really are... Augh!"

Kouki was once again reminded that Eri's nice girl act was just that... An act.

The poison paralyzed Kouki's limbs, and he slumped to the ground. He lay there, spasming uncontrollably. No matter how hard he struggled, he couldn't reassert control.

"Just wait right there, Kouki-kun!" Eri smiled in satisfaction as she confirmed that Kouki was fully immobilized. Then she turned on her heel and headed to Kaori.

In another few minutes, Kaori's soul would leave her body, and Eri would no longer be able to bind it.

Hiyama urged Eri on, his face a ghastly mask. Not only had they killed Kaori, they were going to desecrate her corpse. The thought made Shizuku's blood boil. She fought through the press of soldiers, trying to reach her best friend.

As Shizuku watched, however, Eri raised her hand over Kaori's head and started to chant.

Ryutarou, Jugo, Yuka, Atsushi, Kousuke, Kentarou, and even the students who were cowering all rose up and charged, enraged.

Still, they couldn't overcome the wall of bodies, and were forced to watch as Eri continued.

In a few more seconds, Kaori would be nothing more than an undead puppet who listened to Hiyama's every command.

They wouldn't even grant Kaori the dignity of death.

Eri and Hiyama sneered as they watched the students' futile attempts to stop them. In the midst of the despairing shouts and anguished screams, a single voice rang out.

"What the hell do you think you're doing?"

Hajime Nagumo had finally arrived.

Time seemed to stand still. Everyone stopped and turned toward Hajime. He emanated an aura of intimidation so powerful it was palpable.

Since Eri's zombie soldiers had no emotions, it didn't affect them. It affected Eri, though. Her instinctive fear transmitted itself to her soldiers, and they crowded around her instead of continuing their assault.

Hajime took in the situation, ignoring the hundreds of stares.

A contingent of soldiers and knights were attacking the students, who were clumped in a corner, fending them off. Kouki lay in a pool of his own blood, and Meld stood over him. Shizuku was on her knees, the katana he'd given her still in her hands. Eri and Hiyama looked like they'd seen a ghost. And lying in Hiyama's arms was Kaori, a sword still sticking out of her chest. Her heart wasn't beating, which meant—

"Eyaaah!"

Someone screamed.

Hajime looked like a demon from hell. His expression was so terrifying that everyone's blood ran cold. It felt like he had their hearts in a vice, and a snap of his fingers would kill them. They all stood rooted to the spot, bodies frozen, as they imagined what horrific death awaited them.

A second later, Hajime vanished. He moved faster than human eyes could follow. With a thunderous boom, he appeared next to Kaori.

Hiyama flew across the courtyard and smashed right through the wall at the far end.

To avoid hurting Kaori further, Hajime held back a little, which was the only reason Hiyama wasn't dead.

"Gah...*hack*...ngh."

Half-buried in the wall, Hiyama spasmed and coughed. His internal organs were pulverized, and most of the bones in his upper body were shattered, but he still lived.

The pain was so great that it knocked Hiyama unconscious, then woke him again. He groaned, agony leaving him unable to move.

Hajime didn't even spare him a glance. He lifted Kaori in his arms, and gently brushed the hair off her face.

Then, in a loud voice, he called out orders to his comrades.

"Tio! Take care of her!"

"V-very well. Leave it to me!"

"Sh-Shirasaki-san!"

Hajime's words broke Tio out of her shocked stupor, and she hurried to take Kaori. Aiko ran over as well, her face pale.

Tio chanted the strongest healing spell she knew.

"Aha ha ha... Give it up! She's already dead. I never thought you guys would show up... Well, I guess I should have expected it, since Kaori was here. It looks like Hiyama's outlived his usefulness, so how about I give Kaori to you instead? If you promise not to fight me, I'll use my magic to resurrect her. She won't really come back to life, but she'll still look pretty, at least. It's better than letting her rot, I imagine. What do you say?"

Although Eri was smiling, beads of cold sweat dripped down her forehead. *Why'd this monster have to show up and ruin all my plans?!* Her thoughts showed clearly on her face.

Monitoring Aiko's reaction, Hajime stood up and faced Eri.

Eri knew she didn't stand a ghost of a chance. Her only hope of staying alive was to convince Hajime that she could be useful. Still, the glare in Hajime's eyes was murderous. He walked to Eri, his face a terrifying mask of rage.

"Wait, hold on! Let's talk things through, Nagumo. Look at all these soldiers. They look like they're practically alive, don't they? It's unfortunate that Kaori died, but I can make her like them, at least. Besides, this way, you can do whatever you want with her. So, if you don't want her to rot, you need to keep me ali—"

Eri backed away, desperately trying to persuade Hajime.

At the same time, someone snuck up behind him. The figure moved faster than Eri's other puppet soldiers, and thrust his spear at Hajime's unguarded back.

Eri had finished transforming poor Kondou into her puppet, and used him to attack.

Although Kondou was zombified, his overpowered strength remained. His job was Dragoon, and he had been a master of the spear. A spiral of wind surrounded Kondou's weapon as it shot straight into Hajime's heart.

"Aha ha ha... You shouldn't have let your guard down! If you let your anger control you, you'll—"

Eri began to gloat, but stopped almost immediately when she saw that Hajime was still walking towards her. He didn't seem fazed at all by the attack... Because it hadn't even hit him.

If she had stood behind him, Eri would have noticed a coin-sized bundle of crimson mana holding Kondou's spear back. Hajime had used Diamond Skin and Focused Strengthening to block the blow.

Hajime pointed his left elbow behind him and, without preamble, fired a shotgun blast.

There was a tremendous bang, and a barrage of bullets slammed into Kondou's face, pulverizing his skull. Pieces of his head fell to the ground with a series of wet plops.

"Tch... Get him." Eri frowned, ordering the rest of her soldiers—including Meld—to attack.

Although Hajime wasn't as attached to Meld as Kouki was, the captain was one of the few adults in this world that Hajime had trusted. In fact, Hajime trusted Meld enough that he'd been willing to save him with a precious Ambrosia vial in the Great Orcus Labyrinth.

Eri hoped that would cause Hajime to hesitate, like Kouki had. Meld rushed in while the other soldiers held back, looking for opportunities to strike.

The captain swung his sword at Hajime with all of his considerable might. The force would have sliced any normal sword or shield in half, but Hajime stopped the blade with the tip of his prosthetic finger.

"So, she got you too, huh? What a shame."

Kouki and the others watched, dumbfounded, as Hajime heaved a despondent sigh and pushed Meld's sword back.

Then, a miracle occurred.

"Ah... P-please..."

Hajime knew those were the words of the real Meld Loggins. Even if she seemed to be, Eri wasn't controlling him now.

There was only one response Hajime could give.

"Leave it to me."

Bang! Another barrage of shotgun shells flew from Hajime's arm and shredded Meld's corpse. Blood-red flowers blossomed all over his body. Hajime could have sworn Meld smiled at the moment of impact. Unfortunately, he didn't have time to dwell on it.

Hajime pulled his gatling gun, Metzelei, from his Treasure Trove. Red sparks ran down its length, and its barrel spun up.

Atsushi and Yuka knew what was coming next, and their faces twisted into striking impressions of The Scream.

"Everyone, get down!"

"Oh, shit. Out of the waaaaaaaaay!"

Ryutarou and Jugo pushed down anyone who was too slow to react. A second later, Metzelei spat death at 12,000 rounds a minute.

This weapon had turned a Liberator's golem army into rubble, obliterated a battalion of monsters, and even overwhelmed an

Apostle of God's deadly feather barrage. Human bodies wouldn't last a second.

Bullets ripped through Eri's soldiers and turned the courtyard into Swiss cheese. Hajime rotated in place, mowing down everyone around him.

Bloody mist filled the air, and chunks of flesh rained down.

Soldiers died by the dozen, their strength and training meaningless in the face of such destructive might.

Finally, Metzelei's rampage stopped, and silence filled the courtyard. After a few seconds, there was the sound of footsteps.

The students were too stunned to move. They could only watch as Hajime marched toward Eri.

She dropped to the ground and waited for the storm of death to descend. When she opened her eyes, the sight of Hajime's boots greeted her.

Eri raised her head timidly. Hajime stared down at her. His gaze made her feel small, as if she were nothing more than a pebble.

Metzelei was gone now. He faced her down bare-handed.

Eri stared dumbly at Hajime, the silence stretching on until he finally opened his mouth.

"So?"

"Ah..."

Hajime didn't know why Eri had done what she did. However, her actions made it clear that she was his enemy.

If that was all, Hajime would have killed her and been done with it, but Eri had also hurt someone important to him. That was the one thing Hajime would never forgive. Just killing Eri wasn't enough. He wanted her to taste despair. He wanted to prove that there was nothing she could do.

Eri realized that, and gritted her teeth in frustration. A trickle of blood dripped from her lip. A few moments ago, she was in complete control. Everyone danced to her tune, and her dominance was a simple fact. Somehow, Hajime destroyed all that in seconds. The unfairness of it all infuriated Eri. She glared daggers at Hajime, hatred overpowering her fear.

"You little—"

Before Eri could finish, she felt a cold, metallic object press into her forehead.

Hajime had drawn Donner so fast that she hadn't even seen it.

"I don't care what drove you to this, I don't care what your motives are, and I don't have time to listen to you explain. If that's all you've got to say...then die."

Hajime wrapped his finger around the trigger. Eri could tell from his eyes that he wouldn't hesitate to kill her, and didn't care that doing so meant he'd never make Kaori his puppet.

I'm going to die. That single thought filled Eri's mind.

Fortunately, she had the devil's luck.

Before Hajime could pull the trigger, a fireball came out of nowhere. It burned white-hot, and moved with quite a bit of force, but wasn't nearly powerful enough to hurt him. Hajime shot right through the spell's core, and the fireball dispersed.

"Nagumooooooooooooooooo!"

Hiyama burst from behind the fireball, charging straight for Hajime. He was covered in wounds, and didn't even seem capable of proper speech. Somehow, however, he found the strength to fight.

Hiyama had a sword in his hand, although his right shoulder was shattered and dangling limply. Blood dripped from his mouth.

The fact of the matter was, he looked utterly pathetic.

"Shut up!"

Annoyed, Hajime kicked his attacker in the chin. Hiyama rose a few inches into the air, but didn't go flying. The force of the impact was transferred entirely into his body.

Hajime raised his leg high, and brought it down in an earth-shattering axe kick.

His heel slammed Hiyama's skull and smashed it straight into the ground. The floor cracked as Hiyama's head hit, and a fountain of blood spurted from his forehead. Hiyama's eyes rolled back in his head; he fell unconscious instantly.

He was obviously at death's door, but Hajime carried on.

He kicked Hiyama's head again as it bounced back, sending him flying into the air. He held back, however, so that Hiyama would regain consciousness.

As Hiyama fell back down, Hajime grabbed the back of his collar and held him aloft. Hiyama struggled against Hajime's grip, but his weak thrashing achieved little. Hajime was beyond the realm of mortal strength, and Hiyama had lost too much blood.

"Ish all your fault! If it washn't for you, Kaori would've been mine!" Hiyama vented his deep-seated resentment.

Hajime was honestly a little impressed that anyone could sink so low. Hiyama's unabashed depravity would make normal people sick.

Hajime, however, didn't even speak. His face was an expressionless mask. Hiyama wasn't worth wasting his emotions on.

"It wouldn't have mattered whether I was here or not. Hell would freeze over before you managed to do anything worthwhile with your miserable existence."

"Ish all your fault!"

"Don't pin the blame on other people. You're the one who decided to stoop to this level. You've always been a loser, but you didn't lose to other people. You lost to yourself. You never once tried to take responsibility. All you ever did was sit on the sidelines and insult everyone, when really, you were always the failure."

"I'll kill you! No matter what ish takesh, I swear I'll kill you!"

Hiyama had gone completely insane.

Hajime gave him one last pitying glare before looking off into the distance. The demon army had made it all the way to the castle gates.

He threw Hiyama into the air once more and punched him with his artificial arm. The force of the blow spun Hiyama like a top.

"Good luck surviving out there. Knowing you, you probably won't make it."

Hajime spun around and slammed a roundhouse kick into Hiyama's chest, unconsciously holding back just enough to keep him alive.

With a rippling shockwave and a sickening crunch, Hajime's foot connected, and Hiyama flew out of the courtyard, right into the path of the oncoming demons.

Hajime made Hiyama's death a painful ordeal, not because Hiyama had knocked him into the abyss all those months ago, but because he tried to kill Kaori.

It was clear that Hajime cared for Kaori, although he was only dimly aware of it. And so, he kicked Hiyama into the horde of monsters and demons, letting them rip him apart.

Unfortunately, that meant he ran out of time to kill Eri.

Not because she ran away. But because a new pest appeared. Hajime looked up to see a beam of aurora-colored light headed straight for him.

"Tch."

He clicked his tongue, leaped to the side, and fired Donner at the light. Three red streaks shot through the deadly beam, like dragons scaling a waterfall.

A second later, the light's trajectory changed. It headed straight for Kouki, and Eri hurriedly pulled him clear.

She wanted him as her puppet, and wouldn't let the light turn him to ash.

As the light dissipated, Freid descended into the courtyard on his white dragon.

"Stay right there, boy. If you try anything funny, I'll kill your precious comrades."

Freid appeared to be under the misconception that Hajime was fighting for the kingdom.

Looking around, Hajime saw that they were surrounded by a sizable monster army. Freid had used his teleportation magic again.

Knowing he couldn't beat Hajime in a head-on duel, Freid was trying to take the students hostage. Although Hajime didn't realize it, this was Freid's last resort. Yue's spell had left him gravely injured, and he was in no condition to fight.

The white raven on Freid's shoulder was healing him, but it would be some time before he recovered fully.

"Master!" Tio called out. "I have stabilized her for now! But restoring her will take time. If possible, I would like Yue's assistance. She will not last long like this!"

Hajime glanced over his shoulder and nodded.

His classmates looked at him in confusion, not comprehending what he was trying to do.

Freid, however, stared at Tio in surprise. He could use ancient magic too.

"I see... So, you've discovered more ancient magic. Could this be the magic of the Divine Mountain? I would very much like to know its location. If you refuse to tell me, I'll—aah!"

Hajime interrupted Freid's pathetic attempts to intimidate him with a bullet from Donner.

One of the turtles put up a barrier that just barely managed to block it.

Freid narrowed his eyes, and ordered his monsters to group around him.

"What do you think you're doing? Do you not care about the lives of your countrymen? The more you resist, the more the capital's people will suffer. Or are you just too stupid to understand your position? I have over a hundred thousand monsters stationed on the outer wall, and another million waiting in reserve. You may be strong, but can you protect this city from such a large force?"

Hajime glared coldly at Freid for a few seconds before shifting his gaze to the massive army waiting near the capital's outskirts.

He pulled a fist-sized spirit stone from his Treasure Trove, and poured mana into it until it glowed with a dazzling light, far brighter than his bracelets when he manipulated the Cross Bits.

"Tch... What are you planning?!"

"Shut up and watch."

Freid had a terrible premonition. He ordered his dragon to fire its aurora. However, Hajime kept them both at bay with Donner. A few seconds later, he finished his preparations.

Divine wrath descended from the heavens. A massive pillar of light shot from the sky, obliterating all obstacles in its path.

It eradicated everything it touched, regardless of age, race, strength, or affiliation. The sky lit up, and for a few moments, it looked as though it was noon.

Kweeeeeeeeeeee!

The pillar of light was a good fifteen meters in diameter, and scorched the very air as it passed. It instantly vaporized anything it touched; even things that weren't directly in the light's path melted.

Hajime poured more mana into the spirit stone. The pillar began to move, swallowing up the monsters and demons as they fled.

Death came for them all. Inescapable, inexorable death. Unless they could teleport, no creature could outrun Hajime's laser.

Monsters and demons surged into the capital, desperately trying to find shelter.

The light zigzagged around the plains outside the city and dispersed as it reached the wall.

White smoke from blackened earth hung in the air. Wherever the light passed, it had gouged deep furrows in the ground. Hajime's attack had scarred the earth.

The few demons who managed to escape collapsed in a stunned heap. In the span of a few seconds, they'd lost almost their entire army.

Freid, Eri, Shizuku, and the other students were just as shocked. They stared at Hajime in amazement.

"You're the moron here. Did I ever say I was fighting for the kingdom? Or that these guys were my comrades? Stop jumping to conclusions. If you really want to carry on your pointless war, be my guest. Just know that, if you get in my way, I'll wipe you off the face of the earth. I don't have time to kill a million of your stupid monsters, so I'll let you go this time. Hurry up and get out of here. You're in charge, right? Order your army to retreat."

Freid's rage bubbled up. Hajime had wiped out most of his comrades, and now he took this arrogant attitude?

Still, Freid didn't want to lose the rest of his army. Sure, he could open portals to teleport them elsewhere, but so long as he didn't understand how Hajime's attack worked, there was no guarantee they'd be safe. The last thing he wanted was to get hit by another of those lights.

Truthfully, Hajime didn't want to let Freid go. But his number one priority was saving Kaori. If they took too long, she'd be beyond their powers. Worse, this would be their first time using Spirit magic. They'd have to pull everything off without a trial run.

Most importantly, however, Hajime couldn't fire that laser again. It was a prototype, and one shot had broken it. Hajime could take on a million monsters even without the laser, but that would take too much time. Killing Freid here would turn the demon army into a disorganized mob. And, right now, that was the last thing Hajime wanted.

Freid clenched his fists until his hands bled. However frustrated he was, he couldn't waste his brethren needlessly. He opened a portal and glared at Hajime.

"I swear I'll make you pay for this. I swear it by my god! You'll meet your end at my hands!" Freid spat, his words dripping with hate.

He turned on his heel and beckoned for Eri to follow.

For a moment, Eri thought of taking Kouki. But she caught sight of Hajime's bone-chilling stare and thought better of it. Cold sweat poured down her forehead. She hurried after Freid.

Before entering the portal, she shot one last crazed look at Kouki. Despite the poison, Kouki was still conscious, and her look sent shivers down his spine.

Eri didn't say anything, but clearly, she would stop at nothing to make Kouki hers. This was her declaration of war.

Eri and Freid passed through the portal, and three balls of light burst high in the sky—likely the signal for retreat.

Yue and Shea arrived just as the army was leaving.

"Mmm... Hajime, what happened to that ugly demon?"

"Hajime-san! Where'd that piece-of-trash cretin go?!"

They'd come to beat up Freid. They didn't ask about the pillar of light because they knew Hajime had caused it.

Hajime didn't answer. Something far more pressing needed their attention.

He explained what had happened to Kaori. Shocked, the two looked at her corpse. When they saw Hajime's grim expression, they quickly composed themselves.

In an almost pleading tone, Hajime begged Yue to save Kaori.

"Okay, leave it to me," Yue replied. Although she didn't fully understand the situation, she knew what took priority.

They headed over to Tio. Hajime gently took Kaori from her and began to walk out of the courtyard.

Before he could leave, Shizuku staggered over.

"Nagumo-kun! Kaori's... She's... what should I do?"

Shizuku looked more ragged than Hajime had ever seen. She was on the verge of breaking.

The earlier battle kept her from dwelling on Kaori's death, but now that the immediate threat had vanished, reality crashed into her.

When he saw Shizuku's expression, Hajime hesitated. After a moment's deliberation, he shook his head.

"Shea, take care of Kaori. Tio, show everyone where the labyrinth is. I'll be there soon."

"Kaori-san..." Shea took Kaori from Hajime's arms and held her tightly. "I promise we'll keep her safe."

"Understood. Shea, Tio, we're heading for the summit. Follow me."

The three girls flew off, using their significant abilities to reach the mountain as quickly as possible.

Everything happened so fast that no one knew how to react. Hajime walked through the crowd of silent students and knelt in front of Shizuku, who sat on the ground.

He cupped her cheeks and raised her face, forcing her to meet his gaze.

"Stay strong, Yaegashi. Trust us. I promise I'll let you see Kaori again."

"Nagumo-kun..."

A faint glimmer of light returned to Shizuku's eyes. Hajime smiled gently.

"If you're not there to look after everyone, how are these fools going to manage? Besides, Kaori wouldn't want to see you like this either... Right? We all need you. No one else is masochistic enough to take care of these guys."

"Who're you calling a masochist, you dork? Can I...really trust you?"

Hajime's smile faded, and he nodded sincerely.

Looking into his eyes, Shizuku could tell he was serious. He would find a way to bring Kaori back, even if he had to wade through hell. His unwavering determination warmed her heart.

The color returned to her face. She nodded to Hajime with newfound resolve. She would put her faith in him and his comrades.

Relieved that Shizuku no longer looked as though she was about to break, Hajime stood up. He pulled a vial out of his Treasure Trove and handed it to her.

"This is..."

"Give it to that other childhood friend of yours. He looks like he's in pretty bad shape."

Shizuku turned back to Kouki with a start, as if she'd only just remembered he was there.

After Eri left, the tension had drained from Kouki, and he fell unconscious. His breathing was shallow; he looked weak.

Shizuku remembered how this medicine had healed Meld from near-death. It was obviously extremely valuable and rare.

"Thank you, Nagumo-kun."

Shizuku clutched the vial to her chest, tears in her eyes.

Hajime nodded and turned around.

He dashed off into the sky, chasing after Yue and the others.

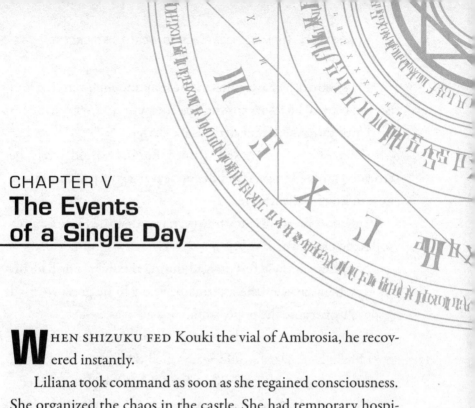

CHAPTER V
The Events
of a Single Day

WHEN SHIZUKU FED Kouki the vial of Ambrosia, he recovered instantly.

Liliana took command as soon as she regained consciousness. She organized the chaos in the castle. She had temporary hospitals set up for the injured, and dispatched people to find out what had happened.

Eri had turned close to 500 soldiers into her puppets. Excepting the few hundred Hajime riddled with bullet holes, they had all vanished without a trace. Liliana surmised that they followed Freid as he retreated, and that they were somewhere in demon territory.

Her scouts discovered magic circles made of mana crystals buried in the nearby hills, which explained how Freid transported such a massive army without being spotted. Chances were that Eri made her puppet soldiers draw the magic circles in secret.

Eri's soldiers had assassinated the king and high-ranking ministers days ago. Heiligh's throne was empty.

Until things settled, Liliana took charge.

Once the storm passed, Prince Lundel would likely be crowned king. He'd survived the upheaval in the palace and was next in line for the throne.

The most pressing issue, however, was that the Holy Church still hadn't sent word.

No priests or paladins arrived during the fight, nor had any shown themselves in the aftermath. The people grew worried, _especially because the pope, Ishtar, was gone as well.

A certain white-haired boy was morbidly curious to find out how Heiligh's citizens would react when they discovered the cathedral was destroyed, and all the highest-ranking clergy killed.

Rumors spread that Lord Ehit had saved the capital by sending the huge pillar of light, and most residents only grew more devout. The irony wasn't lost on Hajime.

He had, however, come up with a countermeasure. Liliana nearly fainted when he sent the letter detailing his plan. Aiko, too, buried her head in her hands and groaned when she read it. They couldn't even vent their frustrations at Hajime, as he hadn't come down from the Divine Mountain.

Naturally, many people advocated sending a search party up the mountain. But everyone in the capital was busy with the reconstruction, and no one could be spared to make the 8000-meter climb. The lift directly to the summit still wasn't working, so climbing was the only way up.

Hiyama's remains were discovered a short distance from the courtyard.

His body was half-devoured; clearly, he'd been eaten by monsters after Hajime had kicked him out of the courtyard. Since there were traces of a struggle, he'd likely been eaten alive.

Hiyama's left arm was completely gone. The bloodstains suggested that, after he lost it, he tried to crawl to safety, only to be caught and eaten from the feet up. The death was so gruesome and painful that no one wanted to think about it.

The more people searched through the wreckage, the more they came to understand how the demons took them so completely by surprise. Five days after the battle, they'd put most of the pieces together. Kouki and the other students helped Liliana rebuild the city, now that they'd fully recovered. Their thoughts often turned to Hajime, who hadn't reappeared.

Most of them had seen Hajime in action before, so they'd had an inkling of how strong he was. But even they hadn't expected that he could call an all-powerful laser down from the sky. It reminded them vividly of the power gap between themselves and Hajime.

His strength was shocking enough to Kouki and the others. For those who chose not to fight, it was an eye-opener.

The others had told the stay-home group of Hajime's strength, of course, but they hadn't truly understood it.

Hajime and his comrades were a hot topic among the students.

Another common subject of gossip was Shizuku.

She seemed to be doing fine, and completed every task assigned to her. But she often stopped in the middle of her work and looked off into the distance. Everyone knew she was taking Kaori's death hard, but no one knew how to comfort her.

They'd all heard what Hajime said: that he'd bring Kaori back somehow. But none of them really believed it.

A few students worried he might bring Kaori back as an undead doll, the way Eri could. That would only hurt Shizuku more, and some of the students, especially Kouki, mistrusted Hajime.

Kouki was also downhearted. He'd watched Meld die before his eyes, and Hajime had saved him twice now. Not only that, their difference in strength was obvious. Since he also believed Hajime had somehow tricked Kaori into leaving him, Kouki wasn't very fond of his former classmate at that point. That said, even Kouki realized he was directing his anger at the wrong person. However, he couldn't help it.

Kouki was too dense to recognize that his feelings stemmed from simple jealousy. Even if he had realized, he wouldn't believe it. He would just interpret the circumstances to suit his perspective... Although it was possible that the realization might have made him grow.

Regardless, both Kouki and Shizuku were stuck dealing with their own complicated feelings, and Ryutarou was too much of a musclehead for anyone to consider him reliable.

Normally, Suzu would have taken charge and kept everyone together, but she was as depressed as Kouki and Shizuku. Everyone could tell her smiles were forced, and that she was still hurting.

Eri's betrayal pained her more than anyone. After all, Suzu

thought they'd been best friends for years. Hearing that she'd just been used so Eri could get closer to Kouki stung.

All the people who could have held the group together were busy sorting through their own feelings, and a pall fell over the students.

Hiyama and Kondou's friends retreated into themselves. The others grew suspicious of each other. There was no telling who might be a traitor, and many students stayed in their rooms to avoid contact.

Eri's betrayal had lasting repercussions beyond just the loss of a friend.

Still, none of the students gave in to despair. Plenty threw themselves into the reconstruction effort to avoid thinking about what had happened. Aiko and Yuka's efforts kept them, if not optimistic, at least less depressed.

Aiko was as worried about Kaori as anyone. If she could, she would be with Hajime. But Aiko knew what they were trying to do and, with Tio and Yue there, Hajime had no need of her.

So, she prioritized taking care of the others. Aiko was a hard worker by nature, and she went to every student, listening to their worries and trying to cheer them up.

Even if they had grown suspicious of each other, the students trusted Aiko. She was their salvation.

Yuka and Aiko's other guards were also a rock for much of the class, especially those who'd lost the will to fight. The guards had been their peers, so they knew how the others felt. Without them, it was possible the non-combatants would have been lost.

Of course, the students—and many other people in the palace—asked Aiko what had happened on the Divine Mountain, but she refused to talk.

She knew they wondered about the church, but now wasn't the time.

If people climbed the mountain, that would interfere with Hajime's work. Besides, Aiko's thoughts grew dark every time she thought of what she'd done.

Her spell might have been more effective than she'd expected, but that didn't change the fact that she'd been prepared to kill.

She decided to confess her sins when Hajime returned.

What she had done was a crime, after all.

Although she acted cheerful, Aiko was terrified inside. What would her students think of her, once they found out she helped blow up the temple and everyone inside? She was responsible for the deaths of hundreds.

She'd done it because she was tired of these people treating her students like pawns, and she didn't regret it, but murder was murder.

It was possible the students wouldn't see her as their teacher anymore. However, Aiko was resolved to accept the outcome, whatever it might be.

At the very least, David and the others had survived.

They'd used their position as templar knights to request an interview with Aiko after she was kidnapped. When Ishtar denied their request, they'd looked for her on their own. Tired of the knights snooping, Ishtar ordered them back to the capital and placed them on standby. In other words, he barred them from the cathedral. Their "standby" orders actually consisted of being confined to a church prison in the capital, and no one saw them again until after the invasion.

No one knew why they hadn't been brainwashed, or turned into puppets.

Aiko suspected it was because they were also pawns of Noint's god, but there was no way to confirm that.

Like most others, David and his knights helped with the reconstruction to avoid thinking too hard about the future.

The only way everyone could keep calm was to ignore their problems and throw themselves into work. The kingdom's remaining knights were tested to see which could serve as captains.

The knights' new commander was a woman named Kuzeli Reil. She was originally part of the Royal Guard, and Liliana's personal bodyguard.

Her vice-commander was a man named Neyto Komold. He was promoted from his old post as captain of squad three.

The two of them organized a test in which everyone would fight Kouki to determine who was fit to be captain. As the battles wound to a close, Kouki wiped a bead of sweat off his brow.

"Thank you for helping out, Kouki-san."

Kouki turned to see Liliana smiling at him.

"It's no big deal. Don't worry about it. You've got it way harder. You've barely slept these past few days, Lily. It must be tough."

Kouki smiled tiredly, and Liliana let some of her own exhaustion show through.

In truth, neither had gotten much sleep, although for completely different reasons.

"There's no time for sleep. We have to toll up the casualties, contact their families, repair the destroyed buildings and homes, track down any missing people, repair the walls and barrier, send messages to the rest of the kingdom, restructure the army... It's not an easy job, but someone has to manage it. Complaining about it won't make the work go away. Mother's been helping out as well, so it's not that bad. The people who are really suffering are those who lost their homes and loved ones..."

"But you also..."

Liliana's father, the king, had been killed by Eri and transformed into a zombie. But Kouki could tell that it wasn't a good idea to bring that up, so he trailed off.

Lily guessed what he was about to say and smiled sadly.

"Really, I'm fine," she said, and changed the topic. "How's Shizuku?"

"Same as before. She's doing her best to act normal, but whenever she's not doing anything, she stares at the mountain."

Kouki looked over to Shizuku, who was discussing something with Kuzeli.

Those two were quite close, and appeared to be engrossed in a discussion about how to organize the new regiments.

Whenever there was a lull in the conversation, however, Shizuku's gaze turned upward.

"She's...waiting for them to come back, isn't she?"

"Yeah. To be honest...I don't really trust Nagumo. I'd rather Shizuku didn't talk to him again, but..."

Surprised, Liliana turned back to Kouki.

His brow furrowed, and it was clear his feelings on the matter were complicated. Jealousy, suspicion, fear, pride, gratitude, hate, and impatience warred within him, resulting in an expression that was very difficult to read.

Unable to find anything to say, Liliana looked toward the mountain.

The weather was so perfect, it was hard to believe the capital had nearly been devastated days before.

It almost felt as if the clear sky was mocking them. Liliana glared at it angrily.

Just then, she spotted a few black dots in the sky. She squinted, trying to get a better look. Before long, the dots grew. Something was falling right toward them. Panicking, Liliana called out to Kouki.

"K-Kouki-san! What's that over there?! It looks like something's falling!"

"Hm? What do you... Guys! Be careful! Something's coming!"

Kouki followed Liliana's worried gaze, and hurriedly called out a warning. It was possible that this was some kind of enemy attack.

Shizuku and the others rushed over, eager to get out of the way. As soon as they'd fled, the dots landed.

There was a tremendous crash, and a huge cloud of dust filled the courtyard. From within it emerged Hajime, Yue, Shea, and Tio.

"Nagumo-kun!"

Shizuku rushed over the moment she recognized them.

She'd waited and put her trust him. After five days, her impatience was understandable.

When she noticed Kaori wasn't among them, Shizuku ground to a halt. Her face fell, and the worry she'd shut away began nagging once more.

"Yo, Yaegashi. Glad to see you're still alive."

"Nagumo-kun... Where's Kaori? Why isn't she here?"

Shizuku couldn't hide her anxiety. Hajime's casual tone reassured her somewhat, but the fact that she didn't see Kaori still worried her. What if Hajime hadn't been able to bring her back?

Hajime looked away awkwardly.

"Oh, uh, she'll be here soon. Just, uhhh... Her appearance is a little different from before. It's totally not my fault, though, so please don't get mad at me. Okay?"

"Huh? Wait... What do you mean? What's not your fault? You're really making me worry now, you know! What did you do to Kaori? Depending on your answer, I may have to cut you down with the sword you gave me...!"

Shizuku's expression grew deadly, and she grabbed the hilt of the black katana at her waist.

Hajime tried to placate her, but a scream from above distracted them both.

"Kyaaaaaaaaah! Hajime-kuuuuuuuuun! Catch meeeeee!"

Shizuku looked up and saw a silver-haired girl falling toward them at high speed.

Shizuku's outstanding kinetic vision allowed her to get a

good look at the girl as she fell. She had beautiful blue eyes to complement her silver hair, but her tearful expression ruined the effect. She flailed around wildly as she fell, as if flapping her arms and legs would somehow slow her descent.

She fell straight toward Hajime, confident that he'd catch her.

Of course, Hajime wasn't that kind of guy.

A second before the girl crashed into him, Hajime jumped out of the way. She looked over in surprise, and slammed into the ground face-first.

Is she dead? The students thought, staring at Hajime in terror.

Lilliana and Aiko were terrified as well, but for a completely different reason. They'd never forget that face for as long as they lived. The blue-eyed, silver-haired girl groaned in pain as the dust cleared.

Liliana and Aiko hurriedly yelled out warnings.

"Wh-what are you doing here?!"

"Everyone, get out! That's the woman who kidnapped Aiko-san and helped Eri take over the castle!"

The students and knights grabbed the hilts of their weapons.

Shizuku, who reacted faster than anyone, was already in her drawing stance. Hatred glimmered in her eyes. She wouldn't forgive anyone even slightly involved in Kaori's death. The moment this newcomer showed her an opening, Shizuku would strike.

The beautiful girl, Noint, got to her feet. The fall hadn't damaged her in the slightest.

She shot Hajime a reproachful glare before turning to Shizuku. Noint spoke to her in a flustered voice, in stark contrast to the emotionless tone she possessed when Hajime fought her.

"Ah! Wait, Shizuku-chan! It's me!"

"Huh?"

Shizuku stared suspiciously. She definitely didn't recognize this girl.

"You're not gonna sound very convincing if you say it like that..." Hajime muttered, then trailed off when "Noint" glared venomously.

She and Hajime seemed too comfortable to be enemies. And although this girl looked and sounded nothing like Kaori, her mannerisms and the way she addressed Shizuku were the same.

Shizuku took her hand off her sword and stared dumbly at Kaori.

"Kao...ri? Is that...really you?"

Glad that her best friend still recognized her, Kaori's face lit up with a dazzling smile.

"Yep, it's me, Kaori! Kaori Shirasaki, your best friend. I know I look pretty different now, but...I'm alive!"

"Kaori... Aaaaaah! *Kaori!*"

After a few seconds of silence, the realization sank in. Shizuku burst into tears and hugged her friend. She had no idea what had happened. However, it was clear that, even though Kaori was in a different body, she was really, truly alive.

Kaori hugged Shizuku back.

"I'm sorry for making you worry. Everything's okay now, though."

"*Sniffle... sob...* Thank goodness you're alive!"

The two clung to each other.

The others watched in silence as the pair cried their hearts out under the noon sun.

•/• •/• •/• •/• •/• •/• •/• •/• •/• •/• •/• •/• •/•

"So, what exactly did you do?"

Eyes still red from crying, and blushing slightly in embarrassment, Shizuku rounded on Hajime.

Liliana had suggested they talk somewhere more suitable, and they'd gone into the feasting hall. Only the students, Aiko, and Liliana were present now.

All Hajime had managed to explain so far was that Kaori's soul had been transferred to Noint's body.

"Well... Put simply, we used magic to preserve Kaori's soul and transferred it to Noint's healed...remains? Corpse? Whatever you'd classify it as."

"I see. That makes absolutely no sense."

Shizuku glared at Hajime. Her gaze seemed to say, "Are you really trying to explain this properly?"

Kaori sighed, and took it upon herself to explain.

"Umm... So, Shizuku-chan... You know how the magic we use is a degraded version of the magic from the age of the gods, right?"

"Yes. I studied up a little on this world. Ancient magic is the stuff that comes up in all the old histories, right? They could control the core elements that govern this world's laws, while the elements we have are derivatives... Wait. Is that how Nagumo-kun did it? He's capable of using ancient magic that...can control people's souls? And that's how he kept your soul intact, and transferred you to a new body, even though you died?"

"Yep! You're so smart, Shizuku-chan!"

Kaori puffed her chest out proudly. Shizuku really was quick on the uptake. Hajime knew that, too, but it was still impressive.

"But then, why are you in *that* body? Was yours damaged beyond repair? I'm sure even regular healing magic should've been able to heal your wounds..."

"Oh, actually, we managed to preserve Kaori's body. At first, we actually put her soul back into it."

Of the magic they'd obtained so far, Spirit magic was the most astonishing. With Spirit magic, you could theoretically attain immortality by transferring your soul every time your body grew old.

When a person died, their soul lingered for a few minutes before dispersing. Tio had used Binding magic to tether Kaori to this realm and keep her soul from deteriorating until they found a suitable host. Had they been any later, Kaori might have been beyond saving, so it was fortunate that Tio arrived when she did.

After that, they used Adhesion magic to tie Kaori's soul to her body. Technically, Adhesion magic could tie a soul to anything, organic or not.

If you tried to attach a soul to an injured or aged body, the subject would just die again. However, if you put the soul into a healthy host, they were revived. You could also attach a soul to an inorganic object, as Miledi had, and avoid aging entirely.

Naturally, this magic wasn't so easy to use that you could pull off a perfect transfer on your first try.

Tio, an expert with hundreds of years of practice under her belt, needed assistance from Yue's magical genius to even have a chance.

Although they ultimately succeeded, it took five days of non-stop casting.

Fortunately, both Yue and Shea acquired Spirit magic without any difficulties. Neither of them had ever believed in Ehit, so clearing that condition wasn't an issue.

They hadn't destroyed any servants of the church, though, so they were forced to go through the actual labyrinth, which consisted of various attempts to brainwash them into serving Ehit, alter their subconscious minds, lead them astray with visions, and all manner of misdirection and persuasion. Once they cleared those obstacles, they had to fight illusions of past warriors from the church. Neither of those trials, however, posed much of a problem.

"Then why are you... What happened to your original body? Was something wrong with it?"

"Calm down, Shizuku-chan. I'll explain everything."

Kaori pushed Shizuku back into her seat and continued.

At first, Hajime fixed Kaori's body with Restoration magic, and they attempted to revive her in her original form.

However, Kaori herself objected to that.

With Spirit magic, it was possible to converse with souls using Soul Link, a magic similar to Telepathy.

Kaori, still in spirit form, asked Hajime to put her into a golem like Miledi. She was confident he could make one far more powerful than her former body.

Although Kaori had come to terms with her own weakness in the Sunken Ruins of Melusine, that didn't mean she wanted to remain weak.

She had no intention of leaving Hajime's side, but had been killed trying to fight with him.

It was humiliating, frustrating, and pathetic. She wanted strength at any cost, even if that meant throwing away her human body.

Once Kaori made her decision, there was no changing her mind. Hajime knew how stubborn she could be. They did try and persuade her, but she refused to listen. In the end, Hajime gave in.

Just as he was about to craft the strongest golem he could, Hajime had a flash of inspiration. *Maybe we can use her instead?*

Noint.

Her body wasn't too different from a normal human's, but her strength and abilities were far superior.

That seemed just as likely to work as putting Kaori's soul in a golem, and it would save Hajime from crafting one from scratch.

He found Noint's remains and asked Yue to restore them.

Then, they attempted to attach Kaori's soul to Noint's inhuman, apostle body. Surprisingly, it worked.

Unfortunately, the magic crystal that had served as Noint's heart no longer supplied her body with infinite mana. However, Kaori was able to use Noint's special magic, Disintegration. On top of that, she could wield Noint's twin great swords, and use her powerful wings.

At the moment, Kaori couldn't even fly properly. Once she got used to it, though, she'd be every bit as powerful as God's Apostle. All the experience and skills Noint had accumulated over the centuries were stored in her muscle memory. Kaori just needed to learn to tap into them.

She could also control mana directly, so she was every bit as powerful as the rest of Hajime's comrades.

Kaori's reaction while examining her new body was quite a sight to behold, not least because it was so strange to watch Noint frolic joyfully. Having someone who tried to kill you smile and hug you was a surreal experience, even for Hajime.

Although it wasn't actually the same person, Hajime had almost punched Kaori on reflex. He hadn't, but only because Shea grabbed his wrists.

Then Yue froze Kaori's original body to preserve it. It currently rested in Hajime's Treasure Trove.

Kaori's body looked like Sleeping Beauty, if Sleeping Beauty was encased in a block of ice. Yue was confident that she could restore Kaori's ruptured cells using restoration, so if Kaori ever wanted her original body back, Hajime was relatively certain it could be arranged.

"I see." Shizuku buried her forehead in her hands as Hajime finished his explanation. "Haaah... You've done a lot of crazy things, Kaori, but this really takes the cake."

Shizuku could feel a killer headache coming on. This was even worse than when Kaori had run into the game store's 18+ section to get one of the *eroge* Hajime said he liked. When the man at the register told her she had to be at least eighteen to purchase the game, she'd blurted out, "I'm getting it for my dad!" The episode had become legendary in that store. It was so embarrassing Shizuku had practically died.

"Hee hee! I'm sorry I made you worry, Shizuku-chan."

"It's fine... All that matters is that you're alive."

Shizuku smiled at Kaori, who still looked a little apologetic. She turned to Hajime with a serious expression and bowed her head.

"Nagumo-kun, Yue-san, Shea-san, Tio-san. Thank you for saving my best friend. You've done so much for me, and I honestly can't think of any way to repay you, but...at least know that I'll never forget this debt. If there's anything that I can do, don't hesitate to ask. I'll do it in a heartbeat."

"Uptight as always. Don't worry about it too much. We just saved one of our own."

Shizuku smiled wryly at Hajime's casual reply. He hadn't merely saved Kaori's life, but all the other students' lives, too. It was the second time he'd rescued them.

Shizuku knew that he'd probably only done it because it aligned with his goals, and that he really didn't think anything of it. His cavalier attitude still irked her, though.

She pursed her lips and glared. "So you say, but didn't you also console me and give Kouki that rare medicine?"

"Dealing with Kaori would've been a pain if you'd broken down, Yaegashi, so..."

"Th-that's a horrible way of putting it, Hajime-kun."

Hajime met Shizuku's gaze. "But more importantly... A certain teacher told me that I shouldn't live my life in such a lonely way. I'm not sure I can always follow that advice, but I figure I can at least try..."

Aiko listened quietly to their conversation. She turned to Hajime, teary-eyed. "Nagumo-kun..."

Most of the students were impressed that Aiko's words had reached Hajime, who barely listened to anyone anymore. They suspected that fact was what had moved Aiko. However, Yue, Shea, Tio, Kaori, Aiko's personal guard, and Shizuku could tell that a different emotion was packed into Aiko's gaze.

Unable to believe it, Kaori turned to Yue, who nodded sharply, confirming her suspicions. Then she looked over to Shizuku, who averted her gaze and looked up at the ceiling. Atsushi ground his teeth while Yuka smiled drily.

Realizing the atmosphere was starting to grow awkward, Shizuku changed the subject. There was still a mountain of things she wanted to ask.

"By the way, Sensei. What did you want to tell us the day you were kidnapped? Is it related to why Nagumo-kun is going around acquiring ancient magic?"

Hajime silently turned to Aiko. "Go on," his gaze seemed to say.

Aiko cleared her throat and began explaining how the gods were crazy, why Hajime was traveling the world looking for ancient magic, the details of her kidnapping, and the subsequent destruction of the Holy Church's temple.

The first to speak after she finished was Kouki.

"What the hell? So, we've just been dancing to their god's tune this whole time? Why didn't you tell us sooner, then?! You could've said something when you saved us back in Orcus!"

He glared at Hajime, who just watched silently.

Infuriated, Kouki leaped out of his chair and stalked over.

"Say something! Why didn't you tell us?!"

"Calm down, Kouki!"

Kouki was too angry to listen to Shizuku. Hajime furrowed his brow and heaved a weary sigh. Annoyed, he finally turned to Kouki.

"If I'd told you, would you have believed me?"

"What?"

"We're talking about *you* here. The guy who only believes evidence that fits his worldview. If I told you that the god everyone believed in was crazy, and what you were doing was completely pointless, you wouldn't have bought it. Hell, you probably would've gotten mad instead."

"B-but if you'd explained it enough times, maybe..."

"Moron. Why do I have to go out of my way to make you listen? Just because we're classmates doesn't mean I have to bend over backwards to help you. If you keep spouting crap like that, you'll end up like Hiyama."

The other students looked away, unable to meet Hajime's cold eyes. Only Kouki continued glaring. That explanation wasn't good enough.

Yue looked disparagingly down at Kouki, but he was too angry to notice.

"But if we're going to fight the gods together from here on out, then..."

"Wait, wait, wait. When did I ever say I was going to fight the gods? Don't just jump to conclusions, hero! If they come after me, yeah, I'll probably kill them. But I have no intention of looking for them. Once I've cleared all the labyrinths, I'm going back to Japan."

Kouki's jaw dropped open.

"Wha... You mean, you don't care what happens to the people of this world?! If we don't do something, the gods will toy with them forever! How can you just abandon them like that?!"

"I'm not so strong that I can just save everyone by snapping my fingers, dude."

"Why...why won't you help?! You're way stronger than I am! You could pull it off somehow, if you really wanted to! If you have power, shouldn't you use it for the sake of justice?!" Kouki yelled. As always, his single-minded adherence to justice reared its head.

But when someone as indecisive as Kouki spoke those words, they weren't persuasive. At least, not to Hajime. He gave Kouki a withering look.

"If I have power, I should use it for justice? That's why you always mess up when it really matters. Personally, I think power should be wielded with clear intent. You don't do something because you have the power to. It's *because* you want to do something that you obtain the power to achieve it. If you really think you're obligated to do things just because you have the strength, then for you, strength is nothing more than a curse. You lack resolve, Kouki. Anyway, I'm not going to argue about the path I've chosen. If you keep pissing me off, I'll send you flying out of here, like Hiyama."

Once he said his piece, Hajime lost all interest.

Kouki finally realized that Hajime didn't hate his classmates, or this world. He really just didn't care.

Furthermore, having his biggest weakness thrust before him left Kouki too shaken to argue. He wanted to say that Hajime was wrong, that he had enough resolve, but he couldn't get the words out.

The rest of Hajime's classmates realized that it was too much to hope that Hajime had come back to help them. The other frontliners already knew he wasn't going to rejoin their party. In fact, they were a little terrified of Hajime. They knew they really would end up like Hiyama if they crossed him.

After all, Hajime hadn't hesitated to kill Meld, Kondou, and the other knights. Sure, they were undead zombies, but normally, you'd have a few reservations about killing people you knew.

Moreover, most of the students who stayed in the castle after Hajime's fall had bullied him at some point, so they couldn't even meet his gaze.

"Is there nothing I can do to convince you to stay? If not permanently, at least until the capital's defenses work again?" Liliana pleaded.

The capital was still reeling from the battle, and although Liliana had made sure all the teleportation circles were destroyed, there was no telling when and where the demons would attack next. Hajime was her sole trump card against them. The demons' general had only retreated because of Hajime and his comrades. Their mere presence was enough to deter another invasion.

"Now that we've killed one of God's Apostles, we need to hurry. It took five days just to bring Kaori back. I was planning on leaving tomorrow."

Liliana's shoulders slumped, but she couldn't afford to give up. There was no telling when Freid might attack. If Hajime wasn't there to help, humanity would almost certainly lose.

"In that case... The beam of light that destroyed the demon army came from your artifact, right? Could you perhaps leave that behind to protect the capital? In return, I'll do anything in my power as princess to aid you in your journey."

"Oh, you mean Hyperion? Sorry, can't. Actually, it was just a prototype... And that one shot busted it completely. I'm gonna need to improve its design before I can use it again."

Hajime's newest weapon, Hyperion, was effectively a massive laser that focused sunlight. He had launched it into the atmosphere before descending from the Divine Mountain.

Inside Hyperion, a series of lenses focused light and funneled heat into a partitioned space in Hajime's Treasure Trove. Once it charged, Hyperion enchanted the light with gravity magic and fired it through a focused lens toward the ground.

Hyperion's greatest strength was that it could charge up even at night, because Hajime had linked his Treasure Trove to the artificial sun in Oscar Orcus' hidden chamber. That artificial sun was created through a combination of spatial magic, restoration, and likely some other ancient magic Hajime had yet to acquire.

It was the joint product of multiple Liberators, and from what Hajime had seen, was probably their best work.

With his current skills, Hajime knew there was no way he'd be able to duplicate the artificial sun. Moreover, Hyperion was still a prototype. It couldn't withstand its own heat, and had shattered after one shot.

Still, Hajime had created a few other anti-army weapons, so he could leave one of those behind. He was reluctant to do so, however.

"I see..." Liliana's shoulders slumped.

Kaori, Shizuku, and Aiko glared at Hajime. The three of them knew what he was like. Although he had softened around the edges, his fundamental stance of not giving a shit about people hadn't changed. He'd only helped at all because he didn't want to make Yue and the others unhappy.

Which was why none of the three said anything. They didn't have to; their disapproving glares were enough.

Hajime sipped his tea and tried to ignore them, but they didn't give up. Eventually, he grimaced and gave in.

"Fine. I'll repair the capital's barrier before I go."

"Nagumo-san! Thank you so much!"

Hajime ignored Liliana and turned to Kaori and the others. *This good enough for you?* The trio beamed.

Both Yue and Shea thought Hajime had gone soft, but that wasn't a bad thing. They gave him knowing smiles. *Well, I guess doing a good deed every once in a while isn't too bad,* Hajime thought, smiling faintly.

"By the way, where do you plan on going next, Nagumo-kun? If you're seeking ancient magic, then your goal would be to conquer the remaining labyrinths, correct? And since you're heading east... I suppose your current destination is the sea of trees?"

"Yeah, that's the plan. I was gonna pass through Fuhren first, but I'd have to go out of my way to get there now, so I think I'll just skip it."

An idea suddenly came to Liliana. "In that case, you would pass through the empire, would you not?"

"Yeah, I guess so..."

"Would you be willing to take me along?"

"Hmm? Why?"

"I need to tell the emperor many things. I dispatched an official envoy, but I would like to get this information to him as fast as possible. That mobile artifact of yours can take me there far faster than anyone traveling on horseback, can it not? I was thinking of going to the empire in person to deliver my report."

Hajime was taken aback by Liliana's boldness. *For a princess, heading into a foreign country alone was a rather dangerous endeavor. Although, now that I think about it, she snuck out of the castle all alone and joined up with a traveling caravan just to find help. I guess I should have seen this coming.*

It wouldn't be any extra work for Hajime to drop Liliana off, since the empire's capital lay directly in his path. He didn't mind granting a simple request like that, although he made his intentions clear first.

"I don't mind taking you there, but I won't be staying in the capital. Don't expect me to stick around for your talks."

"Hee hee!" Liliana chuckled at Hajime's wary attitude. "I wouldn't dream of imposing. So long as you can take me there, that's good enough."

Kouki had remained silent since Hajime raked him over the coals, but now he butted back in. "Then take us, too. There's no way we can leave Liliana in the care of a guy who says he doesn't care about this world. We'll be her guards. And if you won't do anything to save this world, Nagumo, I will! But first, I need strength. I need the same ancient magic you have! If I travel with you, I'll be able to obtain it too, right?!"

"Uhh... I'll tell you where the labyrinths are, so just go there yourself. The last thing I want is you following me around."

Stop making these decisions on your own, seriously. It was pretty brazen of Kouki to beg Hajime for help right after complaining about his methods.

Aiko spoke up timidly, remembering what Hajime said about the labyrinths.

"But, Nagumo-kun, didn't you say before that if we went into the labyrinths with our current skill level, we'd just be killed?"

"Err... Well, you know... Look, if even an incompetent guy like me could do it, I'm sure you guys can. It'll be fine, really. You just need determination and grit."

I can't believe she remembered that. Hajime looked around nervously.

"We won't be able to do it, will we?"

Hajime couldn't meet Aiko's eyes.

As far as he was concerned, offering the rest of his classmates a ride back to Japan once he found a way to travel between worlds was helpful enough.

He had absolutely no desire to babysit them as they tried to conquer the labyrinths. It would be a waste of time.

Shizuku looked up at Hajime, regret and frustration written all over her face. Their recent defeats clearly weighed heavily on her.

"Nagumo-kun, please. Just one labyrinth. If we can obtain even a single one of the ancient magics, we'll have a solid chance at tackling the others. Won't you help us with just one?"

"You do realize you guys can't just leech off me in there, right? You have to prove you contributed enough to clearing the labyrinth, or when the magic circle reads your memories, you'll be denied."

"I understand. But, leaving aside the talk of fighting the gods, all of us want to go home. We're determined enough to risk our lives fighting, if that's what we have to do. So...please. I know you've already done so much, and I don't want to ask another favor after saying I'd repay my debt, but you're the only person we can rely on. Won't you lend us your strength one more time?"

Shizuku trusted Hajime's judgement. If he thought they didn't stand a chance in the labyrinth, she knew they needed his help. It was clear from her expression how much it pained her to ask.

Inspired by Shizuku's dedication, Suzu lowered her head. "Please, I'm begging you, Nagumo-kun. I want to get stronger, so I can talk to Eri again. Please! I swear we'll pay you back somehow. Take us with you!"

There were a lot of things Suzu wanted to say to Eri, and she wouldn't be able to unless she became stronger. Hajime could sense her desperation.

"Come on, Nagumo. Just one. I wanna get strong enough to protect my friends. I don't ever wanna be forced to watch them die again."

Even Ryutarou prostrated himself. This was the first time Hajime had seen him bow to anyone.

He probably blames himself for being unable to do anything in the Great Orcus Labyrinth, or in the recent fight with Eri. Ryutarou clenched his fists so hard his nails drew blood.

Hajime deliberated for a few moments. Normally, he'd never agree to something so burdensome. Babysitting Kouki and the others in the Haltina Woods was the last thing he wanted to do. He was on the verge of telling them to try the Great Orcus Labyrinth or the Reisen Gorge and leave him alone.

But then he thought of his fight with Noint, and wavered. In the visions they'd seen at the Sunken Ruins of Melusine, there was a girl who looked exactly like Noint. She'd taken control of kings and emperors, and done the gods' dirty work behind the scenes.

Could Hajime really be sure Noint was God's only Apostle? That seemed far too naive.

Noint herself said Hajime was an anomaly, and that it was her god's wish that he die an agonizing death. It stood to reason that if one apostle failed, Ehit would send an army. Wouldn't it be better to help Kouki and the others grow stronger? That way, they'd make good fodder for the inevitable clash.

Hajime was seriously considering using other people as meat shields against his enemies. Even for him, that was a new low.

Had anyone challenged his motives, he would have countered with, "I mean, weren't you heroes planning on fighting the gods anyway? What's the problem here?" And so, for completely selfish reasons, Hajime decided to let Kouki and the others join him. He sent a questioning glance to Yue and the others to make sure they had no objections. As usual, they didn't.

Shizuku and the rest sighed in relief. They thanked Hajime profusely, not realizing what he intended for them.

"Hajime's a terrifying man."

"That's Master for you. He really is a monster."

Both Yue and Tio saw through Hajime's plan. They kept their voices low enough that no one else heard.

Hajime ignored their muttered comments and started thinking about the future. His journey was drawing to a close. No matter who stood in his way, no matter how dangerous things got, he'd fight his way through and get home, together with everyone he cared about.

Once again, he reaffirmed his resolve, steeling himself for what was to come.

⁕⁕ ⁕⁕ ⁕⁕ ⁕⁕ ⁕⁕ ⁕⁕ ⁕⁕ ⁕⁕ ⁕⁕ ⁕⁕ ⁕⁕ ⁕⁕ ⁕⁕

After they hashed out the details, Hajime, Yue, and Shizuku headed into the city.

The main street was noisier than usual.

Normally, that would indicate a bustling, lively city. But most of the voices today sounded subdued. The capital had seen too much tragedy.

Only five days had passed since the battle, and most of the citizens were still grieving for their homes and loved ones.

Despite their despair, they worked diligently to repair the city. They worked through the pain of their loss, repairing homes and clearing streets. That, more than anything, spoke to how strong the capital's residents were.

Hajime observed the restoration efforts as he walked down the street, a large bag of pseudo-hot dogs in his arms. Tortus's version of the popular street food used some unfamiliar meat to fill the buns.

Hajime, Yue, and Shizuku all stuffed their faces as they headed to the Adventurer's Guild. Once they finished their business there, Hajime would repair the city's barrier. Since he needed someone to guide him, Shizuku tagged along.

Shea, Kaori, Aiko, and Tio waited inside the castle. Shea had realized non-humans wouldn't be very welcome in the city right now, and chose to remain indoors.

Even if the people knew that demons had attacked them, right now, any non-human was a fair target.

Since the capital was the seat of the church's power, not many non-humans lived there to begin with. Even possessing beastmen slaves was frowned upon. Hajime had to admit, Kaori and the others made the right choice.

Although Kaori's current body looked passably human, no one would mistake her for one. Aiko could have tagged along, but she'd decided to help Liliana with her mounting workload. Tio could easily pass as human, but she was exhausted from five days casting Spirit magic, and was taking a well-deserved rest.

"So... What exactly are we going to the adventurer's guild for?" Shizuku took another bite of her cheese-coated pseudo-hot dog.

"I need to let them know I've completed a quest. To be honest, I wanted to go to Fuhren to tell the quest's issuer, but that's too much of a pain. Besides, I'm sure headquarters will pass the report along."

"Is this...about that Myu girl? Come to think of it, I haven't seen her around anywhere..."

Hajime explained how he'd returned Myu to her mother.

"I wish I could have hugged her," Shizuku muttered sadly.

Although Shizuku hadn't known Myu long, the girl's cuteness had won her over.

Shizuku certainly didn't expect Yue's reply. "Don't worry, you'll be able to see her again. Hajime's taking her to Japan."

"To Japan? Nagumo-kun, what's that supposed to mean?"

"Exactly what it sounds like. I promised Myu that I'd show her my home."

"Wait, but...Myu's a Dagon."

Hajime shrugged, as if that wasn't an issue.

"I get what you're trying to say, but that's not a problem. There are plenty of ways to help her blend in on earth, and if that doesn't work, I'll think of something else. You know what they say: it's not about whether you can or can't, it's about whether you do or don't."

"I suppose you have a point, but..."

"Besides, it's a bit late to worry about this now. Shea's got bunny ears... Hell, even Yue doesn't look that normal. She's paler than anyone on earth, and her teeth are pointed. It's not like I can change how they look. You didn't think I'd leave them behind?"

I suppose that's true. Shizuku smiled to herself. Next to her, Yue smiled faintly as well. She tugged Hajime's sleeve.

Is it just me, or did it suddenly get hotter around here? Shizuku finished her hot dog and fanned herself.

She left Hajime and Yue to their flirting and thought back to Kaori. At this point, she was confident Hajime could do anything he put his mind to. Still, she couldn't deny that Kaori had chosen a difficult path.

"You've been taking care of Kaori, right?" Shizuku said in a worried voice.

"Hm? Well, you should probably ask her that. It's how she feels that matters, right? At the very least, I'd like to think I've been keeping my promise. I haven't done anything terrible, anyway."

Kaori seemed so happy, Hajime probably was treating her well, but Shizuku couldn't help but ask. Hajime shot her a look that clearly said "You're being really overprotective, you know that?" and Shizuku turned away in embarrassment.

Yue sighed, and dropped a bombshell. "It's because you're so soft that she tries to assault you. You need to be sterner with her, Hajime."

"O-okay."

"Wait, what? Hold on a second. Hajime's getting assaulted? By who?"

"By Kaori. She already managed to sneak in a kiss. Curse her."

"I-I see." Shizuku gazed off into the distance, marveling at how far Kaori had come. In more ways than one. It left Shizuku feeling a little lonely. "You've climbed the stairs to adulthood before me, Kaori..."

"Watch out for Aiko too, Hajime. She's dangerous."

"You don't seriously think she's in love with me?" Hajime muttered, averting his gaze from Yue's sharp stare.

Their conversation snapped Shizuku out of her reverie.

"I see you're aware of the possibility. What did you do to her, Nagumo-kun?"

"Hey, don't automatically assume that this is my fault."

"You know, Ai-chan was acting pretty weird when she came back from Ur. She blushed whenever your name came up... I get the feeling you did more than just kill a monster army over there. Now hurry up and confess. This is important! I need to know whether Kaori has more rivals!"

"Look, I really didn't..." Hajime desperately racked his brains for anything he could have done.

Before he could figure it out, Yue spilled the beans. "He kissed her. Passionately."

"Nagumo-kun! How could you?! She's your teacher!"

"Wait, calm down. There's a perfectly good explanation for this. Stop shaking me!"

You damn harem protagonist! Shizuku thought, as she grabbed Hajime by the collar and rattled him back and forth. Hajime hurriedly explained that Aiko had been poisoned, and that he'd needed to feed her Ambrosia directly, or she would have died.

Naturally, Yue added that he'd shot Shimizu to spare Aiko's mental anguish, and rescued her from the church's clutches as well.

Now I'm certain... Ai-chan's fallen for him.

"Well, I get that you weren't doing it on purpose... But surely you must have noticed Ai-chan's feelings, Nagumo-kun. When did you first suspect it?"

"Probably after she blew up Ishtar and the others. She looked at me kinda...longingly, I guess? I wasn't sure, but I started to think, maybe... So, she really is in love with me?"

"Yep. She is."

"She definitely is."

Yue and Shizuku nodded without hesitating. Hajime looked up at the sky, exhausted. He couldn't believe it.

"What are you going to do about it?" Yue and Shizuku asked, their gazes piercing.

Hajime agonized for a few seconds before coming to a simple, if inelegant, solution.

"I'll just pretend I never noticed."

"Well, I doubt Ai-chan's going to come on to you. I suppose it's better than trying to address it and making a mess of everything..."

"Hmm...? Oh, I get what you mean. She definitely cares about being our teacher. So, as long as she still thinks of me as her student, pretending I haven't noticed is the best course of action."

I really just thought that was the easiest way of dealing with it.
Of course, Hajime didn't say that aloud, but Shizuku's penetrating stare told him she'd guessed.

~~Hajime ignored her and ate another hot dog. By the time~~ they reached the guild, the three had eaten their way through the entire bag.

The capital's Adventurer's Guild was even more impressive than Fuhren's. The grand double doors sat open, throngs of adventurers coming in and out. After the invasion, the number of requests had increased exponentially.

The three got in line at a counter. There were ten counters total, and all were busy. However, the receptionists were consummate professionals, and the line moved forward at a steady pace.

For some reason, the receptionists were all beautiful women. Beautiful, and cute. Very, very cute.

However, their looks didn't stir Hajime's desire. As far as he was concerned, no one was cuter or more beautiful than Yue. Plus, she was holding his hand. There was no way he'd let his gaze wander.

Which was why he really wished Yue would stop trying to crush his fingers. *No, really, I don't care about any of those other girls!* Hajime lamented to himself.

Shizuku breathed an exasperated sigh, which Hajime ignored. Walking to the now-free receptionist's desk, he passed over his Status Plate, and the documents proving that he had fulfilled the request.

"By the way, is it possible to report this quest's completion to Ilwa, Fuhren's branch chief, from here?"

"I believe so. Was this...a personal request? Please excuse me for a moment, sir." The receptionist tilted her head.

Branch chiefs rarely made requests of mere adventurers, so her confusion was genuine.

The adventurers at the adjacent desks stared slack-jawed at him.

When the receptionist saw the details printed on Hajime's Status Plate, her jaw dropped open too.

She looked from the Status Plate to Hajime, then back down to the plate.

"Y-you are Hajime Nagumo, correct?"

"Hm? Yeah, that's me. Says so on the Status Plate, doesn't it?"

"My sincerest apologies, but could you head to the guild office? I was given instructions to take you there if you ever appeared, Nagumo-sama... Please wait just a short while, and I'll bring the guild master out right away."

"Uh, all I want to do is let Branch Chief Ilwa know that I completed his request. I need to go repair the capital's barrier after this, so I really don't want to waste too much time."

"U-umm, but I really can't... I promise I'll bring him out right away, so please, just wait a few seconds!" The receptionist sprinted away with Hajime's Status Plate and documents.

Hajime slumped and looked glumly at the floor. Yue and Shizuku patted his shoulders, attempting to comfort him.

Just as Hajime started to think that it wasn't worth the trouble to update Ilwa, the receptionist returned. An old man with shrewd eyes and an impressively long beard accompanied her.

From the man's bulging muscles, Hajime was certain that he was one of those buff old-dude types in anime and manga. This was probably the guild master.

The moment the old man appeared, muttered conversation broke out in the main hall. The news spread through the rest of the guild, and before long, it was all they talked about.

The guild master's name was Balse Laputa. The mere mention of his name could bring down floating castles. Fortunately, Balse didn't seem to have a request for Hajime. He had simply heard about him from Ilwa, and wanted to meet Hajime in person.

So far, every visit to an Adventurer's Guild ended with Hajime getting mixed up in something he wanted no part of, so he breathed a sigh of relief. Unfortunately, nothing Hajime did could end without some kind of incident.

"Balse-dono, would you be so kind as to introduce me to your guests? If you hold them in high esteem, they must be admirable adventurers indeed. I would love to get to know them better, especially those two pretty ladies. A gentleman like myself simply cannot leave without learning their names."

A handsome, blond-haired man sauntered up to Hajime and the others. Four beautiful women followed him. The other adventurers whispered to each other.

Apparently, the blond man's name was Abel, and he was a gold-ranked adventurer. He'd earned the nickname "Blade Lord" among the others.

Balse introduced Abel to Hajime. When he mentioned that Hajime was also a gold-ranked adventurer, the others in the guild hall whispered even more furiously. Hajime didn't like where this was going. He tried to usher Yue and Shizuku out of the Guild, but Abel wouldn't let them leave so easily. His interest in Yue and Shizuku was anything but pure.

Shouldn't this guy know that Shizuku's part of the hero party?

Abel flashed Hajime a dazzling smile.

"Oh, so you're also gold-ranked. You look rather young... How did you gain such a prestigious rank so quickly? Let me guess, you cheated your way into gold...? Oops, I probably shouldn't have said that in public. My bad." His perfect smile didn't waver.

Abel wasn't even worth Hajime's time. Nothing good would come of talking to him. Yue and Shizuku wholeheartedly agreed, and they tried to leave again.

"Now, now. No need to run away because you're up against a real gold-ranker." Abel blocked Hajime's way. "I promise I won't bite. Well, if you're too embarrassed to show your face, I don't mind if you leave... But what about you two beautiful ladies? Could I entice you to join me for a meal? Let me show you what a *real* gold-ranker is like."

It was obvious from Abel's attitude that he couldn't dream of any woman turning him down.

His arrogance might have impressed some, but Yue, Hajime, and Shizuku were far stronger. They found his posturing laughable.

Balse, who had heard of Hajime's power, struggled to hide his chortling.

"Hey, Yaegashi. Dealing with handsome losers like this is your specialty, right? I'll let you handle him. This guy's like Amanogawa-lite."

"Excuse me? What do you mean, that's my 'specialty'? Also, that's an insult to my childhood friend. Kouki might be bad, but he's not this bad... Is he? I don't think so. Actually, at this point, he's more pitiful than anything."

"You're harsh, Shizuku. But I agree."

The three walked around Abel. He frowned. No one had ever treated him with such disrespect. The girls around him glared at Yue and Shizuku.

Of course, this had to turn into a fight. Resigned, Hajime decided that, if he was doing this, he'd beat up Balse too. The guild master was roaring with laughter as he watched from the sidelines. Before Hajime could make a move, a very deep yet girlish voice called out to him.

"Oh, my. If it isn't Hajime-san and Yue-oneesama!"

Chills ran down Hajime's spine. He gripped Donner and fell into a battle stance. Everyone turned around at once.

"I-It's a monster!" Abel screamed.

"And just whooo do you think you're calling a grotesque, vulgar monster who drives people insane just by glancing their way?!"

The walking bundle of muscles glared at Abel.

His face looked like something out of a *juju* manga, and his muscles were bulkier than plate armor. At two meters tall, he towered over everyone. Yet his red hair was braided in twin tails with cute ribbons at the ends. Not only that, he wore a cute yukata, with fluttering frills. His musclebound legs were on full display.

For a second, Hajime thought it was Crystabel, the clothing

store clerk they met in Brooke. But on closer inspection, he realized this was someone else.

Assuming Crystabel isn't using camouflage magic or something...

"Eek... G-get away from me! I'll have you know I'm Abel the Blade Lord, a gold-ranked adventurer! If you take one more step toward me, I'll cut you down where you stand!"

"How cruel! First you call me a monster, now you say you'll kill me... And we've only just met! The other gold-ranked adventurer I know is much more courteous. Although...you're more my type. ♡"

While Hajime recovered from the shock of meeting another of Crystabel's kind, Abel retreated into a corner. *That guy...or would it be girl...? Anyway, they're driving Abel crazy just by standing there.*

The guy/girl sighed as Abel backed away, screaming. Still, Abel was right in their strike zone, so they continued closing in on him. They licked their lips in anticipation and pounced on their prey.

"Get away from me, you monster!"

Terrified, Abel drew his sword.

He might have been a pompous jerk, but he was still a gold-ranked adventurer. Everyone assumed a single blow from him would suffice to end the fight. What happened next was beyond their expectations.

Abel thrust his blade so fast he left afterimages. Yet the muscle maiden batted it aside with one hand, grabbing Abel in a wrestling hold.

Abel's bones creaked from the force. He struggled desperately against the muscle maiden, but couldn't escape. Then the real horror began.

"Tee hee. Naughty kids need to be punished! ♡"

"Stop! Let me—mmmf!"

Abel spasmed uncontrollably.

After a few seconds, his body went limp, and his sword dropped from his hands. He almost looked dead.

The women around him turned pale and ran. Silence blanketed the guild. Finally, the muscle maiden released Abel, who fell to the ground with a dull thud.

At this point, he was clearly the victim.

However, Abel's gold rank wasn't just for show.

He had somehow stayed conscious through the ordeal, and used the last of his strength to glare at the muscle maiden. A second later, his facade crumbled, He turned to Hajime for help.

"H-hey, you! You're a gold-ranker too, aren't you?! Help me out here! You probably just cheated your way up, anyhow. Help me, and I'll give you a legit recommendation! You have the honor of helping *the* Blade Lord! So hurry up and beat this crazy muscle monster for me, you loser!"

Hajime looked pityingly at him. It took a certain kind of scumbag to insult a person while begging them for help. *Actually, if this is the best the Adventurer's Guild has to offer, aren't they kind of screwed?* Hajime shot a questioning look at Balse.

The old man shook his head sadly, as if denying that Abel

should ever have received his gold rank. It was possible *Abel* was the one who obtained his status through illicit means.

Tired of hearing Abel insult Hajime, Yue stepped forward. Abel misunderstood and thought she was coming to his rescue.

"Oh... You're really going to help me? In that case, I promise to set aside my evening for..."

"Shut your mouth."

Although Yue's tone was still neutral, Hajime and Shizuku could tell she was pissed. Abel had gone too far. She held out her hand, and a tiny black sphere appeared in her palm.

"If you don't have the balls to fight on your own, then you don't need them."

"Huh? What do you mean?! Wait, sto—aaaaaaaaah!"

And so, yet another man vanished from Tortus, and was reborn as a "maiden."

After crushing Abel's testicles, Yue returned to Hajime with a satisfied look on her face.

Every male adventurer in the room grimaced, hands covering their family jewels. A few were weeping. Just watching had traumatized them.

The silence was broken as the adventurers whispered to each other.

"H-hey, do you think that blond-haired girl and that white-haired boy with the eyepatch are actually..."

"Wait... Y-you really think she's the Ball Crusher?!"

"No way... So, then, those two are the Love Smashers..."

"What kind of nickname is that?"

"You haven't heard of them? They're adventurers who came out of nowhere a few months ago. They say that blond-haired, red-eyed girl is like a rose. If you let her beauty fool you, you'll find yourself stung by her thorns. She might look like a goddess, but she's actually a demon who goes around crushing men's balls. That white-haired boy with the eyepatch is her companion. He's the very embodiment of irrationality. Words can't get through to him. Don't meet his gaze. Don't talk to him. Don't even let him know you exist. If you value your life, you'll never go near those two. A bard from Brooke told me those stories. Apparently, a bunch of guys in Fuhren and Horaud have had their manhoods crushed."

"That's terrifying!"

It appeared that traveling bards had carried rumors about Hajime and Yue all the way to the capital.

The adventurers shivered in fear and averted their gazes. They were convinced that Hajime would kill them if they looked at him. They edged away, balls tucked behind their legs.

"What...did you guys do?"

Shizuku turned to Hajime and Yue, amazed.

Yue didn't mind the rumors, but Hajime's lips twitched at the nicknames.

Before either could reply, the muscle maiden interrupted.

"It's been ages since I last saw you two. I'm glad you're still the same as always," they said with a wink.

"Seriously, who the hell are you? Are you a friend of Crystabel's?" Hajime asked warily. The things Crystabel did to him still appeared in his nightmares.

Shizuku, who was normally so tactful, was at a loss for words. Her face spasmed, and she hid behind Hajime, using him as a shield.

"Oh, my... Not even a greeting? Where are your manners...? Although I suppose you wouldn't recognize me like this. I confessed to Yue-oneesama long ago, and she crushed my balls... Do you remember now?"

"Oh... Is that really you?" Surprised, Yue looked up at the muscle maiden's face.

They smiled, glad that Yue still remembered them.

It was a former adventurer who'd confessed to Yue in Brooke. They'd been so persistent that Yue crushed their balls. After that, they'd come under Crystabel's wing, and learned the ways of a muscle maiden.

Their name was Mariabel now (as you might have guessed, Crystabel named them).

"I understand now how inappropriate my actions were before. I'm sorry, Yue-oneesama."

"Mmm... You've learned well. You can enjoy your new life with your head held high."

"Tee hee! I thought you'd say that, oneesama. By the way, plenty of other people have come to Crystabel to be her disciples. We had some former black-ranked adventurers, some former gangsters, and a few mercenaries who used to operate out of Horaud..."

There are so many that Crystabel's thinking of expanding. I actually came here today to find a suitable place to open a branch."

Shivers ran down Hajime's spine as he imagined an army of Crystabels. Thanks to his and Yue's actions, this world had received an influx of muscle maidens.

The strangest thing was that, before, Mariabel had been of middling height. Yet in the span of a few months, she grew to her current hulking size. Whatever methods Crystabel used to rear her disciples weren't normal.

Moreover, as Mariabel let slip, Crystabel was a gold-ranked adventurer herself. That was why her disciples were such skilled fighters. Mariabel proved as much when she incapacitated Abel.

A massive army of muscle maidens was the most terrifying thing Hajime could envision.

We really need to get back to our own world, fast, Hajime thought.

"You reap what you sow..." Shizuku muttered behind him.

Annoyed, Hajime pushed Shizuku closer to Mariabel.

Mariabel took quite a liking to Shizuku, and hugged her until she was blue in the face. After they left, Shizuku and Hajime got into a shouting match. A lot of people wondered whether the two were lovers... But that is a tale for another time.

Hajime did his best to avoid thinking about the new threat he'd unleashed onto this world as he headed towards the barrier generator.

The many soldiers guarding the building glared warily at Hajime. Their expressions only softened when they saw Shizuku with him.

No one challenged them, so Shizuku led them inside, to a

spacious marble hall. At its center stood a cylindrical artifact engraved with magic circles.

The artifact would have been two meters tall at its full height, but something had smashed it. Its top half lay in ruins a short distance away.

A number of men and women milled about the artifact, scratching their heads and muttering. They were probably charged with repairing it.

"Oh, if it isn't Shizuku-dono. What brings you here?"

An old man with an impressive mustache walked over to Shizuku. He appeared to be in his mid-sixties, and had the look of a veteran craftsman. Judging from his tone, he and Shizuku knew each other relatively well.

"Good afternoon, Volpen-san. I've brought a Synergist who might be able to repair the artifact."

"Truly? You mean that boy standing next to you?"

Volpen turned his gaze to Hajime and examined him. Although he didn't say so to Shizuku's face, he doubted this young boy could restore the barrier.

Volpen was the head of Heiligh's Synergists, and the best craftsman in the country. The barrier-generator was a relic from the age of the gods, and even someone with Volpen's considerable skill was having trouble repairing it. Volpen found it difficult to believe a teenage boy could accomplish the task.

Hajime ignored him and wove between the other craftsmen. He reached the ruins of the artifact, placed his hand on the pillar, and cast Ore Appraisal.

"Huh, I see now... No wonder it's such a tough barrier."

"Hmph, what can a brat like you accomplish?" Volpen said dismissively. However, Hajime already understood the principle behind the artifact.

He placed both hands on the stone and transmuted it. Red sparks ran down the pillar, and the pieces knitted themselves back together. The speed and accuracy of Hajime's transmutation left Volpen and the other Synergists stunned.

"It's beautiful..." Shizuku murmured, entranced by the red sparks dancing through the air. This was the first time she'd seen Hajime work.

"Well, there you go."

Less than a minute later, the artifact was perfectly repaired. Hajime fed it a little mana to reactivate the barrier. Particles of white light rose from the cylinder, diffusing into the air.

A soldier ran into the artifact chamber and reported that the barrier's third layer was functioning again.

"Unbelievable... You repaired an ancient artifact so easily..."

Shizuku smiled wryly and explained to Volpen that Hajime was, like her, summoned from another world.

"No wonder..." Volpen muttered.

When Shizuku mentioned that Hajime had made her katana, a predatory gleam appeared in Volpen's eyes. Hajime ignored him and walked toward the room with the next artifact.

But Volpen and the others weren't going to let him leave so easily. Not after such an enviable display of skill.

"Please wait! Take me as your disciple! I'll do anything!" Volpen begged, and his disciples decided to join in.

"Whoa! Wh-where the heck did that come from? Stop clinging to my legs! You're creeping me out!"

The disciples clung to Hajime's legs, rooting him place. Disgusted by the horde of old bearded men rubbing their faces on him, Hajime tried to kick them off. Still, they were surprisingly stubborn, and held on with all their might.

In the end, Hajime was forced to use Lightning Field to shock them off. Even then, they crawled after him with every last ounce of their strength.

Finally, Hajime told them directly. "Look, guys, I'm leaving the capital tomorrow, and I have no idea when I might come back. The last thing I want is a disciple, and honestly, I probably couldn't even teach you anything."

"But you repaired that artifact so easily. Not only that, you created Shizuku-dono's weapon. I couldn't even begin to guess how to construct such a thing. If you would just teach me your secrets..."

"That's because I used creation magic along with Transmutation. You guys can't use magic like that, so..."

"No way...!" Volpen's shoulders slumped in disappointment.

The artifact protecting the capital was enchanted with spatial magic, which was what made the barrier so powerful. However, that also meant that normal transmutation had little effect. With enough people working at it, it could be restored well enough to function, but never fully repaired.

Thinking he was finally free, Hajime turned to leave. Although Volpen looked defeated, however, he hadn't given up.

"That doesn't change the fact that your Transmutation skills are beyond anything I've ever seen! Please, teach me all you know!"

"God, you're persistent!"

A craftsmen's dedication to his art was not to be underestimated. Volpen was the kind of person who'd go to any lengths to improve his skills.

In the end, Hajime repaired the other artifacts while listening to the pleading of the kingdom's finest Synergists. It felt surreal to have a train of wailing old men following him.

Somehow, the news spread beyond that building, and more and more craftsmen trickled in to beg Hajime for apprenticeships. He got so fed up that he threw them beyond the city walls, but they just kept coming back, like zombies.

It was probably a bad idea to send the capital's craftsmen to the hospital while they were still repairing the city, so Hajime attempted to flee. However, the Synergists' information network tracked his every move. No matter where he ran, Volpen and the others were there. They piled on question after question, and clearly wouldn't leave him alone until he answered.

Hajime spent the better part of the afternoon playing an impromptu game of hide-and-seek.

"Damn, how are you guys still finding me? I'm using Hide Presence and everything!"

"Ha ha ha! Such skills are meaningless against a craftsman's intuition!"

"Your passion for your art betrays your location, Nagumo-donoooooo!"

"Haaah...haaah... We sense your skills' supremacy miles away!"

When it came to honing in on like-minded people, the Synergists were even better than Hajime.

He seriously considered using Donner and Schlag. The men were creeping him out, and he'd almost rather kill them then let them touch him.

Eventually, the commotion reached the castle. All the Synergists left their posts at once, and the city devolved into chaos. Liliana personally headed out to restore order, convincing the craftsmen to give up.

⁂ ⁂ ⁂ ⁂ ⁂ ⁂ ⁂ ⁂ ⁂ ⁂ ⁂ ⁂ ⁂ ⁂

"Yaegashi... You could've helped, you know. They're your friends, aren't they?" Hajime trudged back to the palace and glared at Shizuku, who was enjoying a cup of tea.

Yue, who sat next to Shizuku, rose to pour Hajime a cup. She really was devoted.

So devoted that when a horde of bloodthirsty craftsmen started chasing him around the city, she'd surreptitiously left with Shizuku.

"Don't ask for the impossible. It's true that I got to know them, since they worked on the katana, but there's no way I could've stopped them."

"You must be tired, Hajime." Yue tenderly took his head in her arms. He hugged her back, then carried her over to his seat.

"Now, that's just unfair. Yue left you too, so how come..."

"What are you talking about? There's no way I'd treat you and Yue equally. A lot of things would piss me off if you did them, but with Yue, I wouldn't care."

"Well, seeing as she is your girlfriend, I can understand that... But I still want to punch you in the face."

Just because Shizuku understood the difference didn't mean she liked it. Even if it was natural for a couple to flirt, it irked her to see them do it in front of her face.

Hajime sat Yue on his lap and fed her tea cakes. *I'm just a third wheel here, aren't I?* Shizuku thought. Just as she was about to flee to Kaori's room, someone flung Hajime's door open with a bang.

They all turned to see a young, blond-haired, blue-eyed boy standing in the corridor. He couldn't have been more than ten.

The boy glared at Hajime, and it got worse when he saw Yue sitting on Hajime's lap. Their intimacy seemed to bother him.

"You monster! How dare you do that to Kaori! A-and why are you off playing with other girls when you have her...? Unforgivable!"

The prince, Lundel S. B. Heiligh, stalked into the room.

He balled his hands into fists and rushed at Hajime with a primal roar. He wouldn't be satisfied until he punched him.

Hajime casually plucked a sugar cube from the tea tray and flung it at Lundel. It flew faster than Lundel could follow and smacked him squarely in the forehead. He fell to the ground, the back of his head slamming the floor. Lundel cradled his head in his hands and rolled around in pain.

Eventually, he recovered enough to stand up and charge Hajime again. Hajime fired another cube. This one hit Lundel with such force his head snapped back. It bounced back up in the air while Lundel crashed into the floor.

"Y-your Highness!" Lundel's bodyguards poured in. "How dare you do that to the crown prince?!"

"I'll kill you for that!"

"Men, protect the prince!"

They rushed at Hajime.

Thunk! Thunk! Thunk! A sugar cube sent each guard flying in a beautiful somersault.

Lundel and his guards were tougher than Hajime expected, however, and they got back up. Impressed by their persistence, Hajime grabbed a giant handful of sugar cubes and shot them off.

Thunk! Thunk! Thunk! Thunk! Thunk! Thunk! Thunk! Sugar cubes slammed into the guards at the speed of machine gun fire. Lundel and his guards spasmed on the ground, as though having seizures.

Although Hajime made sure not to use too much force, the cubes still hurt.

Shizuku watched in shock as Hajime tormented the prince and his guards. By the time she finally returned to her senses and tried to stop him, Hajime's attackers were writhing in pain.

Hajime ran out of sugar cubes and surveyed the damage. Lundel lay on the ground, bawling his eyes out.

He wasn't seriously injured, but the barrage had broken his soul.

His guards rushed up, trying to reassure him.

"Don't worry, Your Highness, the wounds aren't too deep!"

Liliana stepped into the room and analyzed the scene. Shizuku scolded Hajime for overreacting, while Hajime continued sipping tea. Yue sat on his lap, stuffing herself full of cakes. Lundel cried on the floor while his attendants tried to console him.

Liliana massaged her forehead, more or less understanding the situation. "It looks like I was too late."

"Princess, I think your brother's a little unstable. Could you take care of him for us?"

"Unstable?" Whose fault is that?! Liliana wanted to yell at Hajime, but Lundel had started things, so she just heaved a heavy sigh and went to comfort him.

Kaori's fate was the source of Lundel's anger.

When he'd seen how different Kaori looked, he demanded to know what had happened.

The answers basically pointed to Hajime. That alone had made Lundel angry, but his rage reached a fever pitch when he saw Kaori's fondness for Hajime.

When Lundel found Hajime—the man who forced Kaori into a new body (or so Lundel convinced himself), the man Kaori loved more than anyone—Hajime was wrapped in another girl's arms. Lundel completely lost it and rushed at him.

Lundel fully believed himself the brave knight rescuing the poor princess from the demon lord's clutches. Sadly, the demon lord was far stronger than the knight.

Lundel hadn't even gotten close. Hajime beat him with one hand and a tray of sugar cubes. The shame of such a humiliating defeat left the prince in tears.

He sobbed into Liliana's chest, crying her name over and over.

Maybe I really did go too far, Hajime thought, scratching his cheek awkwardly as *Shizuku shot him another angry glare. Yeah, that was probably really immature.*

Sadly, Lundel's travails were far from over, for it was then that Kaori walked into their room.

"Oh, Prince Lundel! And Lily, you're here too...? Wait, is Lundel crying?! What's wrong?!"

"K-Kaori?! Uh, I-I wasn't crying or anything..."

Lundel quickly extricated himself and wiped his tears. No man wanted the girl he loved to catch him crying in his sister's arms.

Kaori could tell what had happened from Hajime, Shizuku, and Liliana's expressions. The way she rebuked Hajime, however, did more damage to Lundel.

"Jeez... Hajime-kun! Don't go making the prince cry. You shouldn't bully little kids."

"Hey, he came at me. I just punished him a little for it."

Lundel was shocked that Hajime hadn't taken him seriously, but the way Kaori talked about him hurt even more. The boy clutched his chest and groaned in pain.

"'Punished him...'? Did you at least go easy on him? Remember, the prince is still a child!"

The searing pain in Lundel's chest grew tenfold. Being treated like a child by the woman you loved was the greatest shame a man could suffer.

"Of course. I just flung a few sugar cubes at him. Look, he's not even badly hurt. You don't really think I'd pull my gun on a kid, do you?"

"But he was crying in Lily's arms... Plus, look how red his forehead is. How could you ruin his cute little face? I know he's prone to misunderstanding things and rushing in without thinking, but Lundel's a good kid at heart. You should be nice to him..."

Now Kaori was pointing out how "cute" Lundel looked. Furthermore, she clearly realized that he'd been crying. The prince fell to all fours and hung his head in despair.

"Uh oh..." Lily muttered.

Shizuku and Lundel's bodyguards begged Kaori to stop. Any more inadvertent verbal barbs, and they were nervous she might really kill him.

Unfortunately, Kaori wasn't done. She went over to Lundel.

"Are you okay?" she asked, full of worry. "See, Hajime-kun, you were too hard on him..."

"No, really, I'm fine. More importantly, Kaori... What do you think of me?" Although covered in bruises, Lundel worked up the courage to ask the question burning in his heart.

"What do I think of you? Let's see... I'm kind of jealous of Lily, I guess. I wish I had a rambunctious little brother like you."

Kaori delivered those words with a smile, but they were poison to Lundel's ears. "Gah...! L-Little brother..."

Why do you have to rub salt in the poor kid's wound?! Shizuku stared at Lundel, imploring him to quit before he hurt himself further.

Lundel, unfortunately, had too much foolhardy courage to stop. His father died only a few days ago, and until recently, he'd cried into Liliana and his mother's arms every night. He made a promise at his father's grave that he'd be strong, however, and he wasn't going back on his word. He would be king one day. He couldn't let himself be weak.

"So, then... You'd rather be with *him*? What's so good about that guy anyway?!"

Lundel glared daggers at Hajime. The prince obviously thought himself the better man. Even now, Yue nestled in Hajime's lap. You couldn't blame Lundel for considering Hajime a terrible womanizer.

Sadly, Kaori had set her heart on Hajime, and Hajime alone.

"Huh? Wh-what's this, all of a sudden? Jeez, that's so embarrassing. But... Hee hee...! Yes, I suppose I would. He's the man I love. As for what's good about him, well...everything. Tee hee...!"

Lundel's hit points finally reached zero. He sank to all fours again, his entire body trembling.

Kaori worriedly rubbed the prince's back, but he slapped her hand away and struggled to his feet. Once he was up, he dashed straight for the door.

Before departing, he turned back and screamed, "I hate you allllllllllllll!"

After that, he sprinted down the hallway and out of sight.

Tears glistened in his eyes as he fled. His wails echoed loudly through the halls.

Lundel's dumbfounded bodyguards returned to their senses and hurried after him.

"That's youth for you."

"D-don't sound so unconcerned... It's your fault he's crying."

"Nah. I mean, I guess I started it... But Kaori finished him off."

"Grr... I can't deny that."

Hajime and Shizuku bantered as they watched Lundel's first crush wither away. Kaori attempted to go after Lundel, but Liliana stopped her. Kaori had done enough damage. Liliana had known Kaori would eventually break her brother's heart, so she was prepared for this. She'd sleep next to him tonight and comfort him as usual. Lundel would be Heiligh's king very soon. It was probably best that he experienced heartbreak once or twice before he had to deal with the rigors of kingship.

Liliana closed the door and walked to Hajime, Kaori following behind. She hadn't come here to find Lundel, but to speak with Hajime.

Liliana sat next to Shizuku, while Kaori attempted to climb onto the other side of Hajime's lap. A short wrestling match between Kaori and Yue ensued.

In the end, the girls sat on the edges of Hajime's knees, arms locked. In her old body, Kaori wouldn't have stood a chance. Yue might have specialized in magic, but her ability to control mana directly and strengthen her body had put her leagues above Kaori. In her new form, Kaori was the one with the advantage.

"Kaori... You've become so strong..." Shizuku muttered.

"Uh, Shizuku. Could you stop staring and break them up already?" Liliana replied, watching worriedly.

The shock of Kaori's death, however temporary, had turned Shizuku into a far less capable woman. Hajime wanted to avoid letting the only person in their class with common sense devolve into a blubbering mess, so he flicked Kaori's forehead and forced her onto the seat next to him.

"Aww... Why is it always Yue?"

"Tee hee! I'm the only one allowed on Hajime's lap."

"Can we get back on topic, please...?" Liliana asked hesitantly. Everyone ignored her.

"Hajime-kun..."

"Don't give me that look, Kaori. Isn't sitting next to me good enough?"

"Fine. You can have his hand." Yue said.

"Huh? Really?" Kaori turned to Hajime. "Then can you stroke my cheek like you always do for Yue? Or is that too much?"

"If that's all, then I don't mind, I guess."

"Hee hee hee! Thanks, Hajime-kun."

"Okay, I'll wait until you're all done. Then you'll finally listen to me, right? *Sniffle...*" Liliana sobbed, having completely missed her opportunity to butt into the conversation.

Hajime and the others only returned their attention to the princess thanks to Shizuku's intervention. Now that she'd had her fill of Kaori, Shizuku was back to her normal, serious self.

The fact that Hajime would indulge Kaori a little proved that their bond had grown deeper. However, Shizuku knew it wasn't the time to dwell on that.

"Ahem... I wanted to discuss the rumors you asked me to spread regarding the fate of the Holy Church, Nagumo-san. Surprisingly enough, people believe them. Aiko-san's fame as the Fertility Goddess appears to be greater than I expected."

"I see. Well, people believe what they want to, after all. Especially when the story's exaggerated and sentimental. I didn't think there'd be any problems. The real question is how well the story will hold up when people start digging deeper... Well, no point worrying."

"Indeed. Although I still find it difficult to believe that our entire faith was built upon a lie... It's fine for one or two individuals to know, but if the truth gets out, we'll have riots in the streets. Your suggestion was truly a lifesaver, Nagumo-san. Thank you."

Liliana's face had a troubled expression as she thanked Hajime. Shizuku tilted her head, wondering what they were talking about.

Hajime had asked Liliana to spread rumors about the temple's destruction. They wouldn't be able to hide the event forever, and the faster the palace provided an explanation, the better.

However, Liliana couldn't tell people the truth. Ehit, the god everyone praised, was an uncaring monster who treated humans like playthings. That would send the citizens into a panic, especially if they discovered that the priests and bishops were actually deranged maniacs.

Therefore, Hajime drafted an alternate explanation. Namely, that an evil god had brainwashed the high-ranking bishops. Liliana used that as a basis for her story, claiming that the bishops were the ones who betrayed the capital to demons.

Which was why, according to Liliana, Aiko had reluctantly taken up arms against the corrupted church.

Pope Ishtar had fought valiantly with her and died in the conflict.

Supposedly, Aiko's sword had turned into a pillar of light in the middle of the fight, which killed the demon army.

That was the story Liliana told. It wasn't technically a lie either. At the very least, the most important facts were true.

Furthermore, Aiko said this new, evil god was masquerading as Ehit. That, if the people wanted to stay true to the real Ehit's teachings, they needed to start thinking for themselves. Otherwise, the evil Ehit would lead them astray. They needed to decide what was right and wrong, and not just rely on the Holy Church's teachings. That was the only way to honor Ishtar's memory. On top of giving such speeches, Aiko also attended Ishtar's memorial service.

Hajime's plan had been to create a fictional "good Ehit" and tell people that Aiko worked for him. That way, Hajime could pretend all the problems stemmed from the fake "evil" god, and plant the first seeds of doubt in people's minds.

If both the "good" and "evil" Ehits used that name, people wouldn't just blindly put their faith in god. They would ask themselves whether anyone invoking Ehit's name was preaching good or evil.

The story also helped avert the panic that would have occurred if Liliana told everyone their god was a deranged lunatic. Most importantly, it meant that if Hajime ever had to pit himself against Ehit, he might be able to count on the people's help.

"I see. You like to plan pretty far ahead, Nagumo-kun." Shizuku looked at Hajime, impressed. "I guess that's why you only told Ai-chan the truth at first..."

Hajime simply shrugged in response. "I hope you didn't think I was a brainless musclehead. Although, usually, my plans are just things I come up with on the spot, and try in the hopes they might work. It's not too much of a loss if they don't, and I can always fall back on shooting my way through..."

"Tee hee! I didn't mean it like that. I was praising your foresight. If anything, it's reassuring."

Kaori and Yue glared at Shizuku, angry that she understood Hajime in some way that they didn't.

Shizuku flinched away from their glares and stammered. "Wh-what? What's wrong?"

Yue and Kaori whispered to each other.

"Yue, what do you think?"

"Hmm... She's still okay. They're just friends for now."

"I suppose. For now, anyway..."

"Mm-hmm... We must be careful."

Shizuku couldn't hear them, but she had the sinking feeling that she knew what they were discussing. And, once again, Liliana was ignored.

Hajime stared warily, worried about the girls' whispered dealings. When those two started colluding, nothing good came of it.

◦◦ ◦◦ ◦◦ ◦◦ ◦◦ ◦◦ ◦◦ ◦◦ ◦◦ ◦◦ ◦◦ ◦◦ ◦◦

That evening, a single figure stood before the massive monument honoring Heiligh's dead. The sun's final rays colored the palace grounds a dazzling shade of crimson, and the monument cast a long shadow into the mountain from which it was carved.

Numerous flowers and offerings dotted the monument. Many brave soldiers had perished recently.

The dead hadn't all been tallied, so the names of the most recent casualties weren't carved into the stone yet. Once all the names were in, Captain Meld's would be first.

Among the offerings, Aiko spotted a pair of weapons that she recognized. A longsword and a spear. The artifacts of choice for two of her students—Daisuke Hiyama and Reichi Kondou.

"I'm so sorry..." Aiko muttered.

Aiko wasn't even sure what she was apologizing for anymore. Was she sorry she couldn't bring the students back to Japan? Sorry that her class had caused the deaths of innocent people? Or sorry that she herself had killed so many? Dispirited, Aiko hung her head. She only stirred when she heard footsteps.

Aiko knew he made his footfalls heavy to alert her. Hajime normally walked much more quietly.

She slowly turned around. "Nagumo-kun..."

"Fancy meeting you here, Sensei."

Her eyes met his. His eye reflected the sunset's fading orange light, and he carried a single flower. It appeared that he'd come to make an offering. Aiko was surprised that Hajime of all people would do such a thing.

Hajime saw the bewilderment on her face and smiled awkwardly.

"Even I feel a little sad when people I know die, Sensei."

"Huh? Oh, uh, I didn't mean to imply that..."

Flustered, Aiko flailed wildly. She hadn't expected to hear such pain in Hajime's voice. He shrugged, indicating that it wasn't a big deal, and walked to the monument.

Aiko shot Hajime sidelong glances, but the memorial occupied his attention completely. He seemed to have no intention of talking, either.

Aiko found the silence unbearable, and spoke more to dispel the gloomy atmosphere than anything.

"Umm, is that flower...for Hiyama-kun and Kondou-kun?"

Hajime raised an eyebrow. *You seriously thought that?* "Hell, no. It's for Meld."

"Why Meld-san...?"

"Well, it's not like we knew each other that well, but I respected the guy. He was the knight commander. He could have had anything, but he still worked so hard for us. Even though he messed up, he kept trying to improve himself... He deserves at least one flower."

"Nagumo-kun... Yes, I suppose he does..."

Aiko watched Hajime with a gentle look in her eyes. She was glad there was still humanity in him. He might kill his enemies without any mercy, but he also mourned those he cared about enough to bring an offering to their grave.

In truth, Hajime just wanted to escape being dragged into the bath by Yue and the others. He'd walked through the palace halls, spotted a flower in a vase, and thought bringing Meld an offering would be a good way to kill time. Of course, he didn't mention that. Besides, he'd meant what he said. He might have visited on a whim, but he truly believed Meld deserved to be remembered.

Hajime put Meld to the back of his mind and focused his attention on Aiko.

"You're not blaming me..."

"Huh?" Aiko tilted her head in confusion.

"About Hiyama. This isn't like what happened with Shimizu. Sure, maybe monsters caused his death, but I'm the one who killed him. I killed Kondou, too... One of your precious students. Even if he was already dead, I blew his body apart. I figured you'd be mad at me."

"......" Aiko's smile vanished, replaced by a brooding frown.

Hajime waited, giving Aiko as much time as she needed.

The two stood there silently for what seemed like hours.

At last, Aiko spoke hesitantly.

"To be honest, I'm not sure it's that simple. Hiyama-kun murdered Shirasaki-san. That's not something that can be easily forgiven. Of course, I do think he should have lived to repent for his crimes, but I understand your choice. The same goes for Kondou-kun. You must have been furious, Nagumo-kun. You cared deeply for Shirasaki-san, and she was murdered before your eyes... It would be unfair to get angry at you just because this wasn't the outcome I hoped for. Besides, I no longer have the right to judge you." Aiko crossed her arms and absently rubbed her elbows, as if trying to warm herself.

"Because of what you did to the Holy Church?"

"......" She nodded silently.

Hajime's words and Tio's restoration magic had helped Aiko keep her sanity right after the event. As time passed, however, the guilt ate away at her.

There were dark circles under Aiko's eyes, hidden with makeup. She wasn't sleeping well. *She probably has nightmares about that explosion.*

Silence returned to the small field. Hajime didn't know what to say.

"Nagumo-kun..." Aiko said, unable to withstand the oppressive silence. "Doesn't it ever bother you?"

"The fact that I've killed people? No, not really. I think the time I spent in the abyss broke those parts of me."

"......"

Aiko looked sadly up at her student. It pained her that Hajime had suffered so much. That he'd thrown away parts of his humanity to survive.

"No one...blames me."

"Hmm?"

"No one blames me for killing them." Aiko's true feelings spilled out. "My students still look at me the same way, and the people in the palace even thank me for it."

It was true. Hajime's display of brutality had shocked the other students out of considering the fact that Aiko killed a couple bishops and the pope. In fact, the students respected her for fighting on their behalf. The nobles and ministers, too, were grateful that she saved them from Noint's brainwashing.

"I told David-san and the others what I'd done, but they just said they needed some time to think. Even though I destroyed the foundations of their faith, they didn't blame me." Aiko bit her lip so hard she drew blood.

She wanted someone to condemn her. After all, she was a murderer. Knowledge of that sin was a heavy burden. Only madmen and monsters thought nothing of killing. The guilt would agonize most people.

It would ease Aiko's pain if someone condemned her, which was why she sought that out. However, no one did.

Hajime was confident that Tio would have obliterated the Holy Church even without Aiko's help. It might have taken longer, but she would have done it. To Hajime, it felt as though Aiko was assuming too much responsibility for something that wasn't really her fault. He scratched his cheek, searching for the right words.

"I mean, in the end, it was Tio's breath that killed everyone. You just helped her do it, right, Sensei? You don't have to take responsibility for all of their deaths..."

"That doesn't matter! At that time...I helped Tio, knowing that it might lead to their deaths. That makes me a murderer!" Aiko retorted with more vehemence than Hajime expected. Embarrassed by her outburst, she shrank back into herself.

After a moment's silence, Hajime asked, "Do you regret helping?"

"Ah... No. I was prepared for the consequences. There was no way I could ignore what the bishops were trying to do... And I didn't want you to die. Plus, if I left them alone, my students would've suffered later, so..."

Pained though Aiko's voice was, there wasn't an ounce of regret in it. She knew Ishtar had been trying to kill Hajime. She also knew the rest of her students would be next. She'd resolved to dirty her own hands, if it meant saving the class.

Even now, Aiko still believed that was the right decision. That logic didn't ease the anguish, however. Feelings weren't rational, after all.

Hajime let out an inaudible sigh. *I'm the student here, so how come I have to give out advice? I just came here to kill time...*

He thought about Yue and Shizuku's opinion that Aiko loved him. Maybe that was why the teacher was confiding to him now. She was starting to see him more as a man, and less as a student.

Hajime glanced around, trying to think of what to say.

"Sensei, are you going to keep being my teacher?"

"What?" Aiko didn't expect that. She remembered Hajime asking something similar before.

Back then she replied, "Of course!" without hesitation. Now, however...

"......"

Aiko hesitated. Was it really all right for a murderer to guide others? She gritted her teeth, feeling incredibly conflicted.

Hajime saw that she had a hard time replying, so he continued. "If you still want to be our teacher, even after this, could you listen to one selfish request?"

"A selfish...request?" Aiko stared at him in confusion. Her face was pale, and she seemed ready to collapse.

"Yeah." Hajime turned and looked Aiko in the eyes.

There was a warmth to his gaze that sucked Aiko in. She felt reassured.

Hajime saw himself reflected in Aiko's eyes, and felt the weight of responsibility settle on his shoulders. He made sure to choose his words carefully. No matter how carefully he phrased it, though, his request was the epitome of selfishness.

"Sensei... I want you to hold that guilt you feel forever. I want you to feel burdened by it. I want you to do things the right way. Fight for the right reasons, agonize over those you kill, and cry about what you've done. To me, you're the most human person here. You feel all the emotions I've lost... You're the role model I look up to. You know what it means to be truly human. That's why I want you to suffer. Because I'm learning from you. I think, if I keep watching you, I'll at least be able to act more human when we return to Japan."

"Nagumo-kun..."

Aiko's eyes opened wide in surprise. Hajime hadn't tried to comfort or condemn her. He'd asked her to continue suffering.

Yet those words chased away the dark clouds that hung around her heart. Hajime's selfish request did what no amount of comfort or condemnation could have.

Accepting the consequences and necessity of her actions would be the hardest thing Aiko could do, especially because of how traumatizing the event had been. She had already wanted to run away from what she did, or to break down under the strain, so many times. There would probably be many more. But Aiko's personality and determination wouldn't let her break or run. That would just make her feel worse.

Aiko could only stand firm because someone was there to prop her up. Someone who'd lost his humanity, but was trying his best to remember it.

This really is the most selfish request I've ever heard. It was a mercilessly kind request. Teardrops streaked Aiko's cheeks. She'd held back the tears all this time, but now the dam finally burst.

Hajime turned away awkwardly.

"Well," he said. "If you absolutely feel like you can't bear it anymore... And there's no one else you can rely on... And I mean *no one* else... I don't mind lending you a shoulder to cry on."

"You...really are..." Aiko smiled weakly and leaned on Hajime's back. He was deliberately acting as though he hadn't seen her cry.

"In that case, I'd like to borrow your shoulder for a little bit, Nagumo-kun."

"Go for it, Sensei."

Aiko leaned into Hajime, entrusting herself to him. Weeping, she reaffirmed her dedication to being the students' teacher, and to bearing the sins she'd committed. As long as a certain selfish student of hers was watching, she could keep on going.

Their shadows elongated as the sun slipped below the horizon. Aiko's sobs were the only sound in the darkening palace grounds.

Once Aiko had cried everything out, the two returned to the palace. Aiko's flushed face and embarrassed expression raised a lot of eyebrows, and Hajime broke into a cold sweat when he realized how their arrival looked to Yue and the others.

As always, Yue, Shea, Tio, and Kaori dragged him into their room.

Shea's noisy complaints bothered Hajime a little, but what truly terrified him was Yue's silent glare.

In the end, David and the others returned to serve Aiko. Their love for her won out over any loyalty they felt towards the Holy Church.

Traveling with Aiko had introduced them to many ways of thinking, and their perspective on the world was different now. Plus, they'd grown suspicious of the Holy Church when Ishtar refused to let them see Aiko.

The news that Ehit cared nothing for them, and that the Holy Church was decimated, still came as a shock. But they couldn't hate Aiko. She'd made the right decision.

Of course, it was possible that they were just looking for something to cling to. They had converted and become adherents of the Fertility Goddess Aiko. Either way, they swore to protect her with their lives.

Their love for Aiko sublimated into a kind of cult fanaticism, but perhaps they needed that to accept the Holy Church's destruction.

"I can't believe you! Why do you keep doing this?!"

"Hajime-kun... You really should be more careful about what you say to people."

"Tee hee! I expected no less from Master. I take my eyes off him for a moment, and he has already gotten another woman to fall for him..."

The three girls complained about Hajime while eating dinner in the main hall. Hajime ignored their pointed glares and enjoyed the splendid feast laid before him.

Yue said nothing, but she did shoot Hajime a dirty look. Considering the situation, she couldn't really blame him, but that didn't change the fact that Aiko now thought of him more as a love interest than a student.

It was a complicated situation, and Yue did have sympathy for Aiko. After all, Hajime's plan to manage the teacher's feelings was to pretend he didn't notice them.

"Hajime, do you think Aiko will break down?"

When Hajime told Yue what had happened, she grew a little worried. Hajime lowered his fork and thought.

"Hmm... I think she'll be fine. If worst comes to worst, I'll just use magic to make her an artifact that'll keep her sane. Knowing her, though, I don't think we have to worry. She'll get better in time."

"I see. That's good." Yue's gaze softened, and Hajime smiled.

Shea looked shocked. "Yue-san... I should have known. You're always two steps ahead."

"Is this...what makes Yue better than me?" Kaori gritted her teeth in frustration. "Gah, I won't lose! I definitely won't lose to her!"

"Impressive. I don't know whether she does it unconsciously or on purpose... But she always knows how to tug Master's heart-strings. She is truly a master of seduction. I cannot help but be amazed." Tio watched Yue in admiration.

Yue grimaced slightly. "That doesn't feel like praise."

Hajime simply stroked Yue's hair and smiled wryly.

Kouki and the rest of the class walked in, interrupting the lively meal. Aiko was with them, so everyone from Earth was gathered in the dining hall.

Hajime raised an eyebrow. He'd asked what time Kouki and the others ate so that he could avoid them. However, his plan had apparently failed.

Well, it's not that big a deal, Hajime thought and returned to his meal. Yue went back to eating as well.

The classmates milled about uncertainly. Some brimmed with curiosity, others weren't sure how to approach Hajime and his friends, while others just felt uncomfortable in the group's presence.

They kept shooting Hajime furtive looks. The students knew that he had no interest in them, and didn't see himself as their comrade. They hesitated to speak to him. Aiko shot Hajime glances as well, but for a very different reason.

"Ah, Shizuku-chan! Come eat with us!"

"Is it really all right if I sit next to you guys?"

"Of course it is."

Hajime wasn't sure he'd ever get used to Noint's grim face smiling so openly. Shizuku didn't seem to mind, though, and took a chair next to Kaori.

The other students found it hard to believe that Kaori had really been reborn in a different body. That grin was so like her, however, that they had little choice.

Even in Noint's body, Kaori's smile had the power to make an entire room relax. Compared to the time everyone thought that Hajime had died, Kaori's temporary death was less of a shock.

Kouki sat next to Shizuku, and Suzu and Aiko settled in across from them. That put Aiko directly next to Yue.

The other classmates sat on either side of Hajime's party. Suzu appeared rather nervous around Yue. When she first sat down, she stammered some odd words.

"S-sorry for interrupting your meal, ma'am..."

Yue tilted her head, wondering why Suzu referred to her as "ma'am."

The moment Kouki and the others sat, the palace servants brought out food. It was the same high-quality fare they'd served Hajime.

As everyone ate, Aiko accidentally met Hajime's eyes. She blushed beet-red and turned away.

"U-umm, Nagumo-kun..." Aiko whispered after a few more furtive glances. "If possible, could you not tell anyone...?"

Yue felt a little miffed that the two were talking across her, but she held it in. She knew it must have been embarrassing to cry in front of Hajime, and she could understand that Aiko wanted to make sure he didn't say anything.

Hajime silently thanked Yue for staying out of it and turned his gaze to Aiko.

When their eyes met, Aiko blushed to the tips of her ears. Shizuku and the others knew it was too late to do anything about Aiko's infatuation, but that didn't stop them from glaring. Fortunately, the other students couldn't see Aiko well, so most of them didn't notice. Only Kouki and the other frontliners saw, but they didn't immediately understand.

Atsushi and the other male members of Ai-chan's guard glared resentfully at Hajime.

"That bastard. Now he's totally gotten her to fall for him," they muttered under their breath.

Yuka, Nana, and Taeko tried to look uninterested, but they were obviously attempting to sneak glances.

"What are you talking about, Sensei? Did something happen?"

"Huh?" Hajime put on a perfect act.

For a second, Aiko was confused, but then she realized he was playing dumb on purpose and smiled. "No, of course not," she replied.

Although it was a little vexing that Hajime always looked out for her, Aiko was happy about it, too.

The longer they watched, the angrier the girls got at Hajime. Only Yue was still on his side. She patted his shoulder affectionately and started feeding him.

Such was the main heroine's power. She was on a completely different level.

I really do have the best girlfriend in the world! Hajime fell for Yue all over again. As he mentally thanked her, Shea tugged his sleeve.

"Hajime-san, say 'Ahhh...'"

Shea was tired of these new rivals. She was vying for his affections too. Blushing slightly, she brought her fork to Hajime's mouth, making sure her bunny ears brushed against him. Shea was just as crafty as the others.

Hajime was used to this by now, and he let her feed him without a fight. Shea's ears and tail twitched happily.

Naturally, Tio and Kaori wouldn't let this go. The pair thrust out their forks, intent on feeding him.

"H-Hajime-kun, have some of mine too! Say 'Aaah!'"

"Master, I implore you to try some of my food. Please open wide."

"Just this once, you two."

There was only so much Hajime could eat before he tired of it. He sampled some of Kaori and Tio's meals, then put a stop to things. Both women melted when they saw him eating.

"This is...starting to get really awkward..." Shizuku muttered, her expression stiff.

Suzu, Kouki, and Ryutarou grimaced awkwardly.

For a moment, Aiko considered trying to feed Hajime as well, but then snapped back to reality and berated herself for even considering it. The students ignored her one-woman comedy act.

Fortunately, the other girls started squealing, dispelling the awkward atmosphere. They'd been afraid of Hajime, but now they gossiped about his love life. On the day Hajime fell into the abyss, no one would have imagined that he would return with a harem. It stood to reason that his classmates burned with curiosity.

Even the guys stopped being so timid around him, although that was mostly due to jealous rage.

Every single girl in Hajime's harem was a beauty without peer. Shea especially drew a lot of attention. Most guys, otaku or not, found bunny girls irresistible. The way her ears twitched when she smiled at Hajime had everyone smitten.

No matter how jealous the boys were, and no matter how badly they wanted to ask Hajime for his secret, none had the courage.

They felt bad for making fun of him, back when they'd

thought he was incompetent. The innate pressure Hajime exuded now made him hard to talk to.

Only those who had spent time with Hajime before were able to converse normally. The ones that could, like Nagayama and Yuka, were eager to ask him questions.

Before they could engage, though, Hajime turned his attention to Kaori, who blushed and looked at her fork.

After a moment's deliberation, she came to a decision, and apologetically popped the fork into her mouth. She blushed even deeper.

Hajime was about to say something scathing, like, "What are you, twelve?!"

Yue beat him to the punch, pouncing when Kaori noticed her gaze and met her eyes. "Pervert...!"

"Y-you've got it all wrong! I'm not a pervert! I-I was just eating my dinner!"

"Dinner seasoned with a side of Hajime."

"Th-that's not true! Besides, Tio's way more of a pervert than I am!" Red-faced, Kaori pointed to Tio. "Look, she's licking her fork all over!"

"Slurp! Slurp! Slurp! Hm?" Tio stopped slobbering over her fork and looked questioningly at Kaori. "What seems to be the matter?"

Tio showed Kaori her fork, emphasizing that there was nothing on it. She was definitely savoring something other than the food. Hajime tried not to think about it. Over time, Tio had transformed from a perverted masochist into a plain, regular pervert.

"Tio, stop that, before I send you flying," Hajime warned her, rubbing his temple.

"Mrrr... If you insist. But you have yet to kiss me, Master. Unless I do this, I will be unable to sate my burning lust."

Her reply only irked Hajime more.

Just then, Tio's eyes lit up.

"Oh, yes! I remember now! You still have not given me the reward you promised, Master! I demand you do so!"

"Huh? Reward?"

Hajime scrunched up his face, and clicked his tongue when he remembered. The others looked at him quizzically.

Shea asked what they were all thinking. "What's this...about a reward?"

"You see, when we fought at the Divine Mountain, Master promised me a reward if I could keep Sensei-dono safe. As you can see, she is still hale. Tee hee hee...! Master. You would never go back on your word now, would you?"

"Hey, that's not fair!" Shea and Kaori yelled simultaneously, but Tio wasn't swayed. With everyone's attention on him, Hajime turned reluctantly to Tio. He put his chin in his hands.

"All right, what is it you want? Don't forget, I promised to do anything only as long as it's reasonable."

Like the time he'd rewarded Shea, Hajime wasn't going to oblige requests like "Sleep with me."

Tio nodded in an exaggerated fashion. Then, fidgeting a little with embarrassment, she spoke.

"Fear not, I shan't ask for the impossible. I just want you to punish me...like you did when we first met."

Tio put her hands to her face and squirmed in shame. *I can't believe I really said it!* As far as she was concerned, that was a reasonable request. Hajime had done it before. Forget the fact that it was a pretty hardcore fetish.

I should have expected this from a pervert like her.

As Hajime feared, almost everyone shrank back in disgust.

They looked at Hajime as though he was some heinous criminal.

"Hell no, you perverted dragon. And stop saying that in a way people will misunderstand."

Shocked at his refusal, Tio vehemently protested.

"B-but why? Surely, this is a reasonable request! All you have to do is drive that thick, hard, black pole into me like you did last time! Then, when I beg you to take it out, you must simply ignore me and keep pushing deeper! All I wish is for you to mercilessly torment me!"

"How many times do I have to tell you, stop misleading people!"

Hajime had been upgraded from "heinous criminal" to "monster" in the other students' eyes.

"But you can't deny that that's the truth, right, Nagumo-kun?" Aiko said, unhappy that the other girls got to feed him.

Yuka, Nana, and Taeko decided to dogpile onto Hajime as well.

"She isn't lying..."

"Yeah, he really did stab her with it."

"Yeah, Nagumo-kun, you have no mercy!"

The three were ostensibly whispering, but Hajime could tell they meant for everyone to hear.

The students' suspicion transformed into certainty. They glared at Hajime.

"Hajime-san, you can't really call it a misunderstanding..."

"Hajime, it's because of you that Tio's a pervert. Accept responsibility."

Even Shea and Yue had betrayed him now.

"N-Nagumo-kun... How could you do such a thing... to Tio-san...?"

"Hajime-kun, I'm so jealous... I mean, you need to answer for your actions..."

Everyone looked at Hajime as though he was the demon lord himself. Hajime stood abruptly, his chair clattering backward. He raised his right hand high, and pulled his black pile bunker from his Treasure Trove. It was already covered in sparks.

A bead of cold sweat dripped down Tio's face.

"Okay, Tio. I'll give you the reward you request. You wanted it in your butt, right? I'll gladly stick it in harder and deeper than last time. It'll be over so fast, you won't even have time to scream."

Only then did Tio realize she'd gone too far.

Hajime had only driven the weapon into her backside last time because they'd been in the middle of a fight. Seeing everyone look at him like he was some pervert had tipped him over the edge.

Perhaps the most maddening thing was that he couldn't actually say Tio was wrong.

"W-wait, Master. I know that's what you used last time, but that doesn't necessarily mean I want you to use it *every* time. If you put that inside me, I'll truly die! I apologize for being impertinent, so please put that dangerous weapon away!"

"No need to be shy, Tio. Didn't you say you wanted this? Going to your room would take too much time, so let's just do it here."

"Oh, noooooooooo! Master's serious! Yue, Shea, Kaoriiiiii, help me! Stop him!"

Sobbing, Tio turned to Yue and the others for help. She wasn't so extreme a masochist that she wanted to die. Or perhaps she was. There was no denying the fact that she was panting a little.

Tio fled to Kaori and tried to hide behind her chair. Her terror was enough to satisfy Hajime, and he returned his pile bunker to the Treasure Trove.

Now, however, the other students were convinced that he was scarier than a demon lord. Rumors of a white-haired demon with an eyepatch circulated through the capital afterwards, but fortunately for Hajime's sanity, he never found that out.

"All right, what do you really want? I don't mind giving you a reward, as long as it's nothing perverted."

Sighing, Hajime flopped back into his chair. Around him, everyone sighed in relief.

No one present wanted to see a beautiful young woman ravaged by his deadly weapon.

"V-very well. In that case, may I request the right to sleep next to you? Usually, it's Yue and Shea. I've never once had the opportunity. Is that reasonable enough?"

"Yeah, that's no problem. You should just have said that from the start."

"My surging passion cannot be quelled so easily. Please try and understand."

Hajime turned back to Shea, who shrugged.

"I guess I have to let her," she said in a resigned voice.

It appeared that Hajime would spend the night sandwiched between Yue and Tio. Once they were in bed, Hajime had no doubt he'd be sandwiched by something else entirely.

The girls went back to gossiping, while the guys muttered angrily to themselves.

After that, Aiko treated Hajime to a lecture about how sleeping with multiple women was indecent. Although Aiko sounded modest, her issue wasn't that Hajime was sleeping around. It was simple jealousy. Shea interrupted to point out that, after the things Hajime had done with Yue, something as innocent as sleeping was hardly a problem. Yue smiled seductively and openly flirted, which led the class to get even noisier. A number of male students developed very uncomfortable boners. Needless to say, it was quite a chaotic dinner.

Hajime watched the ruckus while thinking about the day.

He'd brought Kaori back from the Divine Mountain and showed everyone her new body, watched as a gold-ranked adventurer was robbed of his family jewels, and spent an afternoon running from crazed Synergists, which had required Liliana to come end the chaos personally. He'd beaten down the crown prince, and watched Lundel's first crush wither away. After all that, he'd run into Aiko while looking for a way to kill time, and ended up consoling her. Finally, at dinner, he'd struck terror into the hearts of his former classmates.

All that, in a single day. Trouble and mayhem seemed fated to follow him, wherever he went.

Tomorrow, Hajime would leave with Liliana for the empire. He had no intention of actually stepping foot in the empire's capital, but he'd learned now never to say—or think—never.

I wonder what'll be waiting for us in the east...

Hajime smiled his usual fearless smile, ready for anything the world might throw at him.

ARIFURETA:
ARIFURETA SHOKUGYOU DE SEKAISAIKYOU

FROM COMMONPLACE
TO WORLD'S STRONGEST

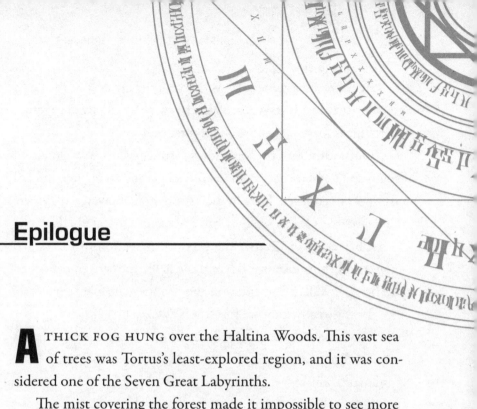

Epilogue

A THICK FOG HUNG over the Haltina Woods. This vast sea of trees was Tortus's least-explored region, and it was considered one of the Seven Great Labyrinths.

The mist covering the forest made it impossible to see more than a few meters in any direction. The forest itself couldn't be navigated through either magical or mundane means.

It was common knowledge that fending off the dangerous monsters that lurked within was nigh impossible. Beastmen, the only species unaffected by the forest's misleading mist, prowled its depths, killing any humans lucky enough to survive the monsters. For that reason, people referred to the area as the Forest of the Forgotten. Neither humans nor demons had any hope of returning once they stepped into its uninviting depths.

Precisely because of these harsh conditions, beastmen had made the Haltina Woods their home. The sea of trees acted as a natural barrier against the outside world.

At the forest's center was Verbergen, the greatest of the beastmen's cities. Inside its walls, all the beastmen races lived together. Verbergen boasted the forest's greatest military.

Outside the forest's protection, beastmen were weak. Unlike humans and demons, they couldn't use magic and were often hunted for sport or enslaved. Here in their stronghold, however, they were undefeatable. Or at least, they had been, until this fateful day.

Charred trees littered the ground. A section of forest had completely burned away. Beyond the hellscape lay a transformed Verbergen. Wails of lamentation and furious roars filled the streets.

The normally tranquil forest was ablaze.

Smoke, ash, and blood filled the streets of the beastmen's capital. Boot prints and animal tracks covered the forest floor, and many houses were burnt to a crisp.

Verbergen's assailants were no longer there. Nor were most of its citizens. They hadn't been killed, however. They'd been kidnapped.

"Hmph. They sure got beat bad. They fought to the death, and still couldn't stop these guys."

A shadow observed the decimated town from atop the ruins of the main gate.

The figure's rabbit ears flapped in the wind, and a wisp of smoke blew past them. Although people often thought of rabbitmen as adorable, harmless creatures, the one surveying the wreckage had a grizzled look.

Cam Haulia—for it was indeed him—seemed like a hardened war veteran. He was the Haulia clan's chief, and Shea's father.

One after another, more shadows alighted around him. Below, a number of rabbitmen gathered before the main gate.

They were members of the Haulia clan, and they looked like veteran fighters. Anyone who saw them would have wondered at the stereotype that rabbitmen were gentle, weak, peace-loving creatures.

These rabbitmen had killers' eyes. Even though Verbergen was destroyed, they smiled fearlessly.

"Sir, I've finished gathering intelligence from the outlying villages."

"Let's hear your report." Cam folded his arms and observed the newcomer. He was a young, imposing rabbitman, with a cross-shaped scar on his cheek.

According to his report, many non-Haulia rabbitmen living in Verbergen and the surrounding villages had been taken by this new enemy.

"Did you suffer any losses?"

"Of course not. No Haulia would be so foolish as to get caught. A few of my men are injured, but they're all still in fighting shape."

"Good. Organize a pursuit team to tail the enemy. I'll take command. Have everyone else fortify our defenses and prepare for the next attack."

"Roger!" The youth saluted crisply and vanished as suddenly as he'd appeared.

Cam ordered his men step a few paces back and took in Verbergen's destruction.

"Those damned murderers!" he spat, a dark gleam in his eyes.

After a moment's silence, Cam quietly called out orders. The other rabbitmen licked their lips in anticipation.

"The scum who invaded our homeland are still out there somewhere. They've kidnapped our brethren, and plan to work them like slaves."

A passing bearman spotted the group. He screamed and quickly fled in the other direction. Supposedly, bearmen were the strongest beastmen, but this one had just fled a group of rabbitmen. He looked like a little girl who'd seen a wild animal in the forest.

Cam ignored him and asked quietly, "Will we let this stand?"

"Never! Never! Never!"

The roars shook the trees. The people trying to organize rescue efforts shivered.

"Are we going to cry ourselves to sleep, like in the past?"

"Never! Never! Never!"

"That's right. We will never let this stand! We're not the same weak creatures who ran whenever things got dangerous, and we never will be again! In the name of our esteemed boss, we will drive these invaders from our homeland!"

Cam spoke with fiery passion. He pumped his fist in the air.

"Let's show these bastards how sharp our fangs are! We'll teach them a lesson they'll never forget! We're going to strike fear into the hearts of these worms!"

"Cut their heads off! Rip out their entrails! Gouge their hearts out! Kill them all!"

With a soft rustling noise, a wolf-like monster fled to the safety of its den. It had planned on making a meal of some of the beastmen, but after seeing the terrifying rabbitman army, it fled with its tail tucked between its legs.

The rabbitmen's bloodlust was palpable. Cam smiled in satisfaction as he glanced over the frenzied members of his clan. He sucked in a deep breath and looked his people in the eyes.

"Let's make those imperial bastards regret ever stepping foot into Haltina!"

Cam slammed his fist into his palm, as if bringing down the hammer of holy retribution.

In response, the others screamed.

"YEAAAAAAAAAAAAAAAAAAAAAAH!"

The entire forest trembled.

In the distance, alarm bells and cries of "Enemy raid!" were audible. The people remaining in Verbergen mistook the rabbitmen's bloodlust for an actual attack. All things considered, that was understandable.

Confusion and chaos spread through the ravaged city.

The rabbitmen ignored it all and continued shouting war cries. A certain monster of the abyss had trained them well.

Their anger was so great, it could even be felt hundreds of miles away.

❖ ❖ ❖ ❖ ❖ ❖ ❖ ❖ ❖ ❖ ❖ ❖ ❖ ❖

"Huh?!"

"Whoa, Shea, what's wrong?"

Back in Heiligh Palace, Shea's rabbit ears stood on end, and she jumped to her feet. Hajime yelled out in surprise, and Yue, Tio, and Kaori turned to see the source of the commotion.

"Uh, sorry, don't worry about it. I just thought my dad was doing his gangster yells again..."

"The heck's that supposed to mean?" Hajime said with a smile. "You sure you're not just overexcited, since you'll get to see your family again soon?"

Shea blushed and nodded sheepishly, rabbit ears still standing straight up. "Maybe. I hope everyone's all right. And I hope they haven't gotten themselves mixed up in anything dangerous."

"Who knows. I realize it's partly my fault... But those guys are tough. And really belligerent now."

"Gah... Now you've gotten me worried. Please be all right, guys!"

Shea's ears flopped back and forth. She hoped her prayer would reach her family. She didn't guess that at this very moment, Cam and the others were about to pick a fight with an empire. She didn't know that the war to follow would have repercussions around the world, and change the standing of beastmen forever. How could she? No one could have predicted what would come to pass.

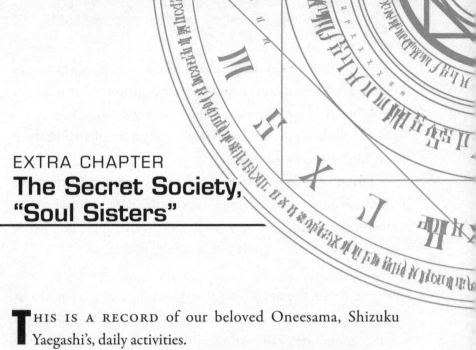

EXTRA CHAPTER
The Secret Society, "Soul Sisters"

THIS IS A RECORD of our beloved Oneesama, Shizuku Yaegashi's, daily activities.

I understand how insolent it is for someone like me, the princess's lowly royal guard, to even write about our cherished Oneesama. But I wish to leave behind an accurate record, so that historians a hundred or a thousand years in the future do not misconstrue what kind of person she was.

First, I suppose I must address the question of Oneesama's identity. She is a heroic figure, and will be spoken of for generations to come. Historians and schoolchildren alike will learn of her great deeds. For this reason, I must leave a detailed record of her true nature, as historians often distort the truth to fit their preconceptions.

Oneesama hails from another world. In her previous home, she was known as one of the greatest swordsmen alive.

No one her age could rival her, and no challenger was able to defeat her. She was, at the very least, the greatest swordsman in her country.

Her skills impressed God himself, and he summoned her here to bring this world salvation.

I must say, you picked wisely, God. A number of others were summoned with her, along with some obnoxious boy who calls himself the "fated hero." However, they are not important to the telling of this tale, so I have omitted their stories.

Let me be the first to say that Oneesama is wise, beautiful, and chivalrous beyond measure. Not only is she a master swordsman, she's academically skilled as well. Proficient with both the pen and the sword, as they say. Despite her apparent superiority, she isn't arrogant. She is a true goddess, greeting everyone with a smile, regardless of their station.

Excuse me, don't you think you're being a little too rude to the other heroes?

Very well. Allow me to write of my wondrous meeting with Oneesama, and how I came to call her that name in my heart.

Not long after she appeared in this world, Oneesama and the other heroes (God technically summoned them, so I suppose I must refer to them reverently) were training outside the city walls. The female knights had been put in charge of training the female heroes. However, there were not enough female knights to go around, so I was temporarily pulled from the royal guard to assist with the training.

I must say, you picked wisely, Captain Meld. The heroes hadn't fought in their old world, so they had trouble even with captured, weakened monsters. Occasionally, a few heroes would hesitate so long that the creatures attacked them.

Naturally, it was my job to dispose of monsters if they threatened the heroes. One time when I was killing a monster that got too close, however, someone panicked and fired a spell. I avoided it in time, but just barely. As a result, I twisted my ankle.

I was embarrassed that I'd let myself get injured, and did not wish to worry the heroes, so I pretended nothing was wrong. By the time training was over, my ankle smarted fiercely.

I slipped away and headed toward the infirmary. However, I was unable to walk properly, and the going was rough. Just as I wished a horrific curse on the hero who caused my injury—that they would sweat profusely from their armpits—I felt my body grow light.

Are you wondering what happened? Brimming with curiosity? Very well, let me tell you.

Oneesama appeared, and carried me princess-style to the infirmary!

"You hurt your leg back there, didn't you? I'm sorry I didn't notice sooner."

Those gentle words enveloped my trembling body, leaving me in a daze.

Before I knew it, she had carried me all the way.

"I understand that it might be difficult, but you don't have to be so formal with us. After all, we're the inexperienced ones. So please guide us, Sensei," Oneesama said with a dazzling smile.

Although I was just a lowly knight, she'd thought about my rank, and spoke the most comforting words.

I felt my heart beat faster, and suddenly grew embarrassed. I told Oneesama I could walk again, and asked her to let me down. Not only had I troubled our divine Oneesama, I still wore my armor! I must have been so heavy! If Oneesama actually said as much to me, I would have hanged myself then and there! And yet, all Oneesama gave me were comforting words.

"I can't do that. It's my fault you ended up like this, so at least let me carry you. Besides, even in your armor, you're as light as a feather."

Oneesama gave me a playful smile and lifted me to prove how light I was. I wrapped my arms around her. She chuckled, and hugged me back.

I was smitten.

"Oneesama..."

When I called her that, Oneesama smiled gently. Her smile seemed a little forced, but I suspect that was just my imagination.

"Umm, I'm younger than you. You know that, right?"

Her voice seemed slightly strained, but I ignored that. After all, I wanted so badly to be her younger sister. If not by lineage, then at least in spirit. I could be her soul sister! My entire world went pink.

I respect and adore my wonderful Oneesama, but if I had to mention one thing that bothered me, it's that she made everyone else want to be her soul sister too.

In fact, there was a silent but bloody conflict to decide who would be Oneesama's true soul sister. In the end, we decided to form a secret society, Soul Sisters, and keep watch over Oneesama from the shadows.

Our organization's objective was to somehow snatch the role of Oneesama's personal maid away from Nia.

There is no doubt in my mind that that vulgar girl thinks herself Oneesama's closest confidant.

How presumptuous of her. Although I must admit, I *am* jealous.

Oneesama has a single best friend, Kaori Shirasaki. We Soul Sisters have fallen in love with Kaori-sama. She treats everyone kindly, no matter who they are.

For some reason, Kaori-sama is infatuated with a fellow hero (if he can even be called that, haha!) Hajime Nagumo. She tries to woo him every chance she gets. Naturally, this means Oneesama inevitably comes into contact with him often as well.

How much of Oneesama's precious time will Hajime Nagumo take before he's satisfied? Oneesama, too, seems more interested in him than any other man. I cannot understand it. All he does is make things out of rocks... The self-styled hero, Kouki Amanogawa, is more notable. He is quite close to Oneesama, and everyone agrees that they would make a good couple. For his impertinence, I cursed him with dark magic to always sneeze at the most inopportune moments.

Captain Kuzeli discovered that I did so and punished me with a beating. How did she find out?

This is heartbreaking. Oneesama has gone to train in the Great Orcus Labyrinth.

She is no longer here. The Soul Sisters have been reduced to walking corpses.

Great news! Oneesama has returned from the labyrinth.

Well, it's not all great news, sadly. Hajime-sama perished in the labyrinth. Kaori-sama suffered such a shock that she is still unconscious.

Oneesama refuses to leave Kaori-sama's side. Although she is maintaining her composure, it hurts to look at her.

She is worried about Kaori-sama, of course, but Hajime-sama's death seems to weigh heavy on her mind as well.

Oneesama has recovered a little since Kaori-sama regained consciousness. However... I misjudged her.

I believed she was an unshakable rock, someone who couldn't be hurt. A true angel sent to us by God. However, that isn't the case.

In truth, Oneesama is like any other girl. She gets hurt, cries, and mourns like anyone else.

I know, because I've watched her all this time. Although she puts up a strong front for Kaori-sama, she is hurting just as much.

Oneesama wasn't in love with Hajime-sama, though. Her pain stems from much simpler emotions: regret that she could not save him, and fear that she might be next. These feelings, and other worries, have clearly been tormenting our poor Oneesama.

And yet, only we Soul Sisters have realized.

We cannot leave her like this. We shall formulate a plan to cheer her up.

First, we shall present Oneesama with gifts.

I pray that our burning love reaches Oneesama!

Oneesama smiled when we gave her our presents. I would like to believe that we eased her sorrow.

"Wh-why are you all calling me Oneesama? I don't even recognize some of you! When did your group get this big?!"

I recall her grimacing a little when she said that, but I do not think she was actually displeased.

Oneesama has completely recovered. She proved it by defeating the Behemoth that halted their progress before, and reaching a level of the labyrinth no one else has.

Oneesama truly is amazing.

A messenger from the empire arrived, so Oneesama returned from the labyrinth.

It would be remiss not to mention what transpired.

The emperor himself challenged our self-styled hero to a match of strength. I don't care if this hero is her childhood friend; he has no right to be so close to Oneesama. It pisses me off that everyone thinks they should be a couple, and that he acts like they should be too. I know this is petty, but I was glad to see the emperor beat the hero to a pulp. What I didn't foresee was that damned emperor proposing to our Oneesama! How dare he?!

Naturally, as the Soul Sisters' representative, I immediately cursed the emperor with dark magic that made his toes unbearably itchy.

Oneesama thought he had athlete's foot and cringed away from him! Somehow, Captain Kuzeli found out and beat me senseless again.

"Are you trying to start a war or something, you moron?!" she yelled.

Of course, my response was obvious.

"For Oneesama, I'd pick a fight with the whole world!"

I gave a very impressive salute.

I can't seem to remember what happened afterwards; my memories are fuzzy. I suspect Captain Kuzeli beat me unconscious.

I vaguely recall her muttering something odd.

I thought I heard, "She's beyond help now!" as I faded into unconsciousness. I'm probably recalling incorrectly.

More importantly, Oneesama totally turned the emperor down!

Serves you right, you smelly emperor! I must say, Oneesama looked so impressive when she faced him.

Any normal girl would have been overjoyed to marry royalty, especially since the emperor's actually rather handsome.

In fact, I'm a little worried about Oneesama's taste in men if she didn't find him attractive.

Don't tell me she really does have the hots for the hero...? If that turns out to be the case, I will have to unleash my inner wrath.

Worried, I brought up the topic the next time I saw Oneesama.

"Oneesama. What kind of guy is your type?"

"Can you stop calling me Oneesama? Also, could you maybe not sit so close to me? I can feel your breath on my face. Please get away."

"Don't tell me you're into guys like that hero? Tee hee!"

"Please don't make fun of my friends. Shouldn't you be guarding Lily right now? If Kuzeli-san finds you here, she'll throw a fit, you know that? So, get—"

"Who cares about the princess?! What matters are your preferences, Oneesama."

"How could you say that?! You're part of the royal guard. You're really creeping me out! Someone, help! Kaori! Nia! Meld-saaan! Save me!"

"Fear not, no one will interrupt us. The Soul Sisters have cleared the area. Now tell me. Don't be embarrassed."

"I'm plenty scared right now!"

"I won't leave until you answer my question. I'll follow you to the labyrinth, and even to bed if I must."

"How come you're emphasizing 'bed' more than anything?! Fine, fine, I'll tell you, so just quit it! Hey, stop touching me!"

It's quite rare to see Oneesama in tears. I know I won't forget that expression.

Oneesama backed up to the wall, trembling for some reason. Probably from embarrassment at having to divulge her tastes. Oh, Oneesama, you're so cute.

I love how she stopped speaking politely at the end there, too. She clearly thinks of me as a close sister, rather than a distant acquaintance.

For some reason, Oneesama gave my question serious thought. She trembled the whole time.

"H-hmm... I guess I'd like someone who could protect me."

So that's Oneesama's taste.

I must say, I'm quite surprised. Although, in retrospect, I should have expected it.

She blushed in embarrassment, and for a moment looked just like any other girl, not like a great hero or a master swordsman.

Unfortunately, Oneesama is one of the strongest people alive. A few people think she might be even stronger than our resident hero (heh).

I doubt even the emperor or Captain Meld could defeat Oneesama. No man is strong enough to protect her.

"I see. So, you have no interest in men at all! That's wonderful."

"What on earth makes you think that?! Also, wait, you have a really serious nosebleed! I think you need to get that checked out!"

After that, Oneesama carried me princess-style to the

infirmary. The experience was so euphoric that I passed out... Although that might have been from blood loss. The nurse told me I'd almost died, but I think it was worth putting my life on the line for the information I gathered.

I can say with confidence that Oneesama has no interest in men. She prefers women.

Devastating news. Oneesama will return to the Great Orcus Labyrinth.

The Soul Sisters' lamentations could be heard throughout the capital on the day of her departure.

Great news. Oneesama will return again.

Kaori-sama wasn't with Oneesama when she returned.
Oneesama obviously misses her. The fact that her ponytail is drooping is proof.
I must comfort her without delay!
For some reason, Oneesama tried to flee from me. However, I finally caught up to her. I may slack on occasion, but I'm still part of the royal guard.
"I wish you'd show some of that enthusiasm when you're guarding Lily."
Despite her loneliness, Oneesama is still worrying about the princess. How kind of her.

Upon further conversation, I discovered a shocking fact.

Hajime-sama is actually alive. On top of that, he's become unbelievably strong. I can't imagine that that boot-licking boy is actually powerful.

He defeated a bunch of monsters and a demon that not even Oneesama could face. On top of that, he saved her from certain death... Good going, Hajime-sama. Anyone who protects our beloved Oneesama deserves my praise.

"Shouldn't you care about how strong those monsters were, or how a demon got here, or something?"

What are you saying, Oneesama? Nothing in the world is more important than your safety.

Oneesama was almost impressed by my persistence. I took that opportunity to ask her for more details.

Upon doing so, I discovered some interesting things.

"I was really surprised. Can you believe it? He drilled straight through the labyrinth's ceiling to get to us. I think he called his weapon a 'pile bunker.' I'm not quite sure what it was, but it looked like a massive stake, and it crushed one of the strongest monsters in one hit! It actually looked rather pretty with all the red sparks shooting from its sides... Oh, yeah, what do you think was the first thing Nagumo-kun said when he came to save us? 'I see you two are as inseparable as always.' Couldn't he have said something more appropriate? He didn't look worried at all about the monsters surrounding him. It turned out that was because they weren't any trouble for him. It was ridiculous. He pulled out railguns and all these other crazy weapons you only see in sci-fi stories. He made them himself, and—"

Oneesama talked nonstop about Hajime-sama. Even though I have a photographic memory when it comes to Oneesama, I can't remember the entire conversation.

I do remember that her eyes sparkled. She must have been very excited.

I'd never seen Oneesama like that before. It was as if she'd met the hero of her dreams and—

Allow me to digress. The whole time Oneesama talked, there was a strange black sword on her lap. I'd never seen that weapon before.

I interrupted her story and asked about it.

Can you believe her response?

"Oh, this? I...got it from Nagumo-kun, actually. He said I'd need a new weapon, since my old one broke. I really owe him a lot. Did you know, my style of swordsmanship actually works better with curved blades like this? They call these 'katanas' back in my world. I'm really grateful that he made this for me. Oh, and... can you believe it...? Nagumo-kun said it would cut really well, but that was an understatement. It's enchanted or something. It can slice through anything. On top of that, it's balanced perfectly, and it's just the right weight. It feels like this katana was made just for me! It's unbelievable! The craftsmanship is amazing! Do you get what I mean?! Oh, Nagumo-kun also said—"

That settled it. I'm going to kill Hajime-sama. I can't let that bastard live. I swear that I will end his life no matter what it takes. I mean, can you blame me? Oneesama talked about Hajime-sama nonstop, hugging the sword he gave her the whole time. I was worried she'd start blushing and cupping her cheeks.

Her delight was obvious.

For my own sanity, I convinced myself that her happiness stemmed from the sword, not the fact that Hajime-sama gave it to her. That absolutely, positively, surely, must have been the case. Still, Hajime-sama deserves to be cursed.

It's time to gather, my Soul Sisters. Our foe this time is stronger than any we've faced.

After that, the palace grew strange, and I was suddenly called back home. My father is an earl, and our estate lies northwest of the capital. My grandfather had evidently passed away.

To be honest, I didn't want to leave Oneesama. However, my older brother, who was also an officer in the army, drugged me and carted me back against my will. I can't believe I was so careless. I'll never forgive him.

I've finally returned to the capital.

I'm shocked by what happened in my absence. The beautiful grassy plain is a charred wasteland. The city's walls are crumbling and full of holes. Even the training grounds look like they saw a fight.

Oh, and the king's dead.

Captain Meld and a lot of my comrades are dead as well.

What in Ehit's name happened?

When we received the report, my brother groaned and fainted. At any rate, it turns out Oneesama's safe. That's all that matters.

It's time to use my Oneesama-locating magic and jump into her arms.

"Oneesama! Aaah, Oneesama! Thank goodness you're safe!"

"Where've you been this whole... Oh, yeah, you went back home before the attack, didn't you? Or something like that? I'm glad you didn't get mixed up in the fighting."

Oneesama's words filled me with such joy that I feared my heart might burst. It sounded almost as if she'd forgotten me, but I wasn't worried. We Soul Sisters don't sweat small details.

Oneesama told me what happened.

Demons had invaded the capital. Eri-sama betrayed everyone. Many people died. Hajime-sama came back. He fell from the sky, like before. Kaori-sama is in critical condition. Quite a bit took place while I was gone.

Regardless, I now know my enemy's face. It turns out that he's the white-haired kid.

He looks so different from his old self that I hadn't even realized.

Time to die, my mortal foe. Let's start by using dark magic to curse him with explosive diarrhea.

Heh heh... I've been planning this for a long time now. I've already made sure to hide all the toilet paper in the bathrooms. I also know this curse works, because I tested it on one of those disgusting boys who are always leering at Oneesama. He thought it was food poisoning, but it was actually my curse. I made sure to steal the toilet paper in the bathrooms around the dining hall too. It turned into a pretty big incident, but now's not the time to dwell on that.

Now, suffer in shame and embarrassment before my beloved Oneesama!

Actually, forget it. I don't think I'll go through with it.

Hajime-sama saved Oneesama's life.

You did good, Hajime-sama. I'll let you go, just this once. I'm definitely not giving up because I'm scared of that golden-haired beauty who's always with him. True, she always seems to look at me the moment I'm about to cast a spell, and her crimson eyes are a terror to behold. But she hasn't cowed me!

Actually, what is it with Hajime-sama's group? Kaori-sama's pretty weird now too, and the rest of his party is crazy strong. I can feel an intimidating aura coming off them.

Oh, and all his comrades are knockouts. Well, Oneesama's still better looking.

Anyway, it looks like those hot girls are in love with him.

I can't believe they're flirting when the capital's in such dire straits. I wish they'd act more like Oneesama. Every time I see Oneesama, she's always so composed. I don't think she'd ever be caught dead—

......

......

......

Wait a second. Is Oneesama...

Before I knew it, she started hanging around Hajime-sama.

Her gaze is always fixed on him.

Why does she look so happy when he teases her? Why does she looks so lonely when other girls fawn over him? No... I must be jumping to conclusions.

Surely, her attention is really focused on Kaori-sama, who always happens to be next to Hajime-sama. Oneesama isn't following Hajime-sama around after all. She only looks lonely because he took her best friend.

That has to be it. I'll prove it.

"Oneesama. Could it be that you have a crush on Hajime-sama?" I asked straight-up when I got the chance.

"What are you talking about? Of course I don't."

She looked at me blankly. She wasn't flustered, she didn't blush at all, and she spoke without hesitation.

I knew you were better than that, Oneesama! You wouldn't fall for a guy that easily! I should've been relieved, so why did I feel like drowning my sorrows in alcohol? In the end, I drank myself to sleep that night.

Terrible news. Oneesama's going to be traveling with Hajime-sama.

Apparently, so will the princess. Even though I'm part of her guard, though, they're leaving me behind. Why? Why, cruel world? What have I ever done? This reeks of a conspiracy.

"You've neglected your duty far too often, so I'm removing you from the royal guards. Train yourself from the ground up, you stupid moron."

Kuzeli, the kingdom's new knight commander, was telling me something, but I didn't pay any attention.

I can't believe Oneesama's going to leave with that man.

This is the worst day of my life! All I can do now is pray.

Oneesama... Please don't let that man protect you any more than he already has.

Remember that the Soul Sisters will always believe in you!

**FROM COMMONPLACE
TO WORLD'S STRONGEST**

How to Use Spatial Magic

"**O**KAY, EVERYONE, it's time for my special magic lesson." Yue raised her pointer with one hand, adjusting her glasses with the other. Shea, Tio, Kaori, and Hajime sat cross-legged in front of her. They were in a room in Ankaji's palace. As thanks for purifying the oasis, Duke Zengen had given them free reign, so they could stay there whenever they wished.

"Yue, while I'm glad you are willing to teach us, you realize Kaori and I can't use spatial magic, correct?"

"I'm sure there's still some benefit to learning... By the way, Yue, what's that large crystal for?"

Yue had dragged Tio and Kaori to the lesson. They were still a little confused, and they didn't know the strange round crystal's purpose.

"Mmm, good question. This crystal is an artifact Hajime developed. It records what it sees."

Everyone turned to Hajime, who proudly explained how he'd used restoration magic to create the recording device. Seeing how Melusine had used it to produce illusions from the past had given him the idea, and he enchanted the crystal with a similar spell.

"I used this wonderful artifact to record tips on various spatial magic spells. It's very useful. I love you, Hajime."

"Please stop throwing out 'I love you, Hajime' in the middle of conversations, Yue-san. It doesn't even follow logically."

"I love you too, Yue. Glad to have been of service."

"All right, all right, we know you two flirt every chance you get. Can we just get on with the lesson?"

Hajime and Yue entwined their hands and looked passionately into each other's eyes. Shea pouted, her bunny ears flopping back and forth. Unable to watch, Kaori charged in and physically separated the couple. Since the Sunken Ruins of Melusine, Kaori had grown bolder.

"Mmm. Okay, time to show everyone how to use spatial magic. This video will explain its different uses, and the most efficient ways to wield it. Since we all fight together, I think it's important that everyone understands how this magic works."

"I understand now." Tio nodded. "This will indeed make for a good reference point, then."

The crystal began to glow.

"Wait, is that the palace?"

Shea's bunny ears perked up. Hajime and the others nodded. The video showed Yue standing in one of the palace's hallways.

She peeked at something around the corner. When she spotted Kaori, Yue gathered mana around her, making her hair float up.

"Wait, that was you?!" Kaori shouted.

A second later, the Kaori in the video smacked her forehead into an invisible wall and staggered backward in pain.

"Here is a standard example of spatial magic creating a barrier. A spatial barrier's main advantage is that you can make it invisible, as you can see."

"Don't sound so proud! It was really *you* who did that?! How could you?!"

In the video, Kaori got up and started feeling for the invisible wall, confused. She looked almost like she was miming. Around the corner, Yue snickered. The real Kaori boiled with anger. She looked ready to throw herself at Yue.

"Hmph. That's your punishment for feeding Hajime the fruit I specially prepared for him and pretending like it was from you."

"I have no idea what you're talking about. Besides, even if that *was* true, it's a certain vampire's fault for feeding me misinformation about what fruit Hajime really does like. I'm sure it was justified."

"Curse you. Fine, if that's how you want to play, I won't hold back."

Kaori whistled innocently, or attempted to whistle, while Yue glared daggers. Shea and Tio exchanged a worried glance.

"So that fruit was actually from Yue," Hajime mumbled.

The video continued, switching to a scene of Yue walking down the corridor. She was apparently trying to move stealthily, and she stopped in front of a certain door. Golden mana swirled around her, and her hair fluttered in the artificial breeze.

"Wait, isn't this...?"

Kaori recognized that door, but before she could finish, the Yue in the video completed her spell. A forty-centimeter wide portal of light appeared, and Yue stuck her head through without hesitation. A second later—

"Kyaaaaaaaaaaaaaaaaaaaaaaaaaa?!"

Kaori, sitting next to Hajime, screamed like a banshee.

In the video, Yue peeked in on Kaori, who was crouching down after having removed her underwear. Kaori moved faster than light, and delivered a powerful roundhouse kick to the crystal, which shattered. Her graceful, accurate movements captivated even Hajime. Unfortunately, she demolished the crystal beyond repair.

"Shaaaaaaaaaaaaaaaa!"

"Hmm?! You wanna fight?!"

Kaori leaped at Yue, moving so fast that she left afterimages in her wake. She used body strengthening on an even more extreme scale than Shea.

"Wait, was that the bathroom Kaori..." Shea flattened her ears in terror. "Hajime-san, there are some things you shouldn't say. You'll just hurt Kaori-san's dignity. And, Yue-san, you do some really mean things."

"I know Yue and Kaori have been growing ever more competitive, but even I think this is too far." Tio slowly backed away.

Hajime smiled bitterly as he watched Yue and Kaori catfight.

"I imagine Yue just wanted to get back at her. A few days ago, Kaori tried on Yue's underwear in front of me, smiled, and said 'I knew it! The chest is too tight! Are you sure you didn't accidentally get a kid's bra?!'"

Shea and Tio gasped. *Just how much do those two hate each other?* Yue was skilled enough with magic that she should have been able to blow Kaori away with ease, but she'd deliberately engaged in a fistfight. It was strange to see them so heated up. Yue was normally cool and composed, while Kaori overflowed with compassion for everyone she spoke to. Now, however, they snarled and growled at each other.

"You know, I think those two actually get along really well," Hajime said with a smile. Shea and Tio exchanged glances. It certainly was rare to see either Yue or Kaori express these emotions.

"You might have a point."

"Indeed."

Shea and Tio smiled, too.

"Yueee! Today's the day I end you for good, you perverted vampire!"

"Kaoriii... It's time you learned your place, you sneaky lecher!"

They certainly did seem like good friends. Probably. Hajime hoped.

**FROM COMMONPLACE
TO WORLD'S STRONGEST**

Arifureta Academy: Sports Tournament

A FEW DAYS BEFORE the sports tournament, a certain rumor started to spread. Supposedly, if someone managed to win every event, the chairwoman would grant them any wish.

Apparently, a certain magic teacher wanted to be transferred to the health department, and appointed one student's exclusive nurse.

A certain student wanted to get a certain teacher fired.

A certain other student wanted a special class just for her and her crush.

A certain chairwoman wished for a certain boy to become her master.

A certain student council president wanted to quit.

Quite a few people seemed to want wishes granted. Most students felt misgivings about the upcoming tournament, but the march of time was relentless. Soon enough, the dreaded day arrived.

"Sensei! We've got three more here! All fractured ribs!"

"Give me a second! I'll get to them as soon as I can!"

"Sensei? Kudeta-sensei, the referee, has been knocked unconscious. His wounds look serious! He took an iron ball to the testicles, and he's foaming at the mouth! He needs urgent care!"

"Take him to the hospital, then! Carriages are waiting outside!"

The poor nurse—whose position a certain vampire wanted—tried to sort through the chaos. The infirmary was full, forcing a number of students to receive treatment in the hallway. Although members of the health committee cast healing magic as fast as possible, they couldn't keep up with the incoming patients. The infirmary looked more like a field hospital. The poor school nurse—a young woman who'd just recently married, and was being pressured by a fellow teacher to go on maternity leave—finally got fed up.

"Sheesh, what the heck is going on?" she yelled, her hair splaying wildly about.

The poor nurse, unfairly hated by her coworker, was unaware of the madness outside. The sports tournament was turning out very lively... Just not quite the way people had hoped.

Over on the dodgeball field...

"Take thiiiiiiiiiiiis!" Ryutarou threw a ball as hard as he could.

"Ngh!"

Shizuku, the student council president, used a volleyball receive to lessen the ball's force. She barely managed to catch it.

"Tch. I knew you'd be the biggest problem, Shizuku..."

"You almost had her, Ryutarou-kun," Kaori said cheerfully.

Ryutarou and Kaori were the only people left on their side of the court. Meanwhile, Shizuku's team still had four members, including Shizuku. The fact that she could receive even Ryutarou's best throw put him in a tight spot. Kaori was sadly useless at both catching and throwing. Although he didn't want to admit it, it appeared that the student council team would win the dodgeball match.

"Sorry, but I really want to live a stress-free school life. I don't know if the rumors are true or not, but I'll crush anyone who gets in the way of me quitting the student council!"

The other students gave Shizuku sympathetic looks. Working on the council really *was* grueling. Shizuku passed the ball to an outfielder. Ryutarou wasn't sure if she was trying to catch him off-guard with an unexpected tactic, or just trying to finish off Kaori.

"Goddammit! You keep buzzing around like an annoying fly!"

Shizuku's teammates kept passing to each other at dizzying speeds, confusing Ryutarou. His movements grew sloppy, and the moment he let his guard down...

"Shit!"

"You're mine!"

Shizuku's teammate threw the ball straight at Kaori. The constant passes had lured Ryutarou away, and he couldn't get back to her in time. The ball wasn't thrown with as much force as Ryutarou's fastball, but it was more than Kaori could handle.

"Stoooooooooooooooop!" Ryutarou's scream echoed through the court. A second later...

"Ryutarou-kun Barrier!"

"Whaaa...?!"

Time ground to a halt. Ryutarou, who should have been far away, suddenly flew in front of Kaori and took the ball in the face. Kaori had bound him with her chains and used him as a shield. Devoid of force, the ball fell to the ground. Kaori caught it easily and threw it into the air.

"Take this! Ryutarou-kun Hammer!"

"Gwah?!"

Kaori swung Ryutarou into the ball, literally using him as a hammer. His eyes rolled back as his forehead connected solidly with the ball. Kaori's superball hit Atsushi Tamai, one of Shizuku's teammates, right in the stomach.

"Gaaah!" he screamed, and flew a good ten meters backward.

He came to a stop outside the court and lay still.

"You monster!"

"I'm just getting started!"

Kaori Shirasaki would do whatever it took to get what she wanted. I'll get that vixen fired, no matter what it takes! If I have to sacrifice a few friends along the way, so be it!

In truth, Ryutarou was screaming at Kaori to stop, not Shizuku. It was a wonder he'd made it to the finals in one piece.

Meanwhile, over at the soccer field...

"Shit! Someone, anyone, stop her!"

Kouki screamed desperately as Shea dribbled past his team, bunny ears fluttering in the wind. Saitou, one of Kouki's teammates, did his best to try and snatch the ball away. However, Shea's keen hearing alerted her to his movements, and to the fact that two others were circling behind her. Even if she dodged the first opponent, the second might still take the ball, so Shea sent the ground flying at them.

"Outta my waaaaaaaaaaaay!"

"Gyaaaaaah!"

Shea stomped hard, pulverizing the ground and sending pebbles and clods of earth flying at Saitou. He screamed in pain and staggered back while the ball soared over his head. The earth wave also hit Nakano and Kondou, who were coming in behind. They both screamed as rocks pelted their face.

"My eyes! I can't see!"

"R-referee! That was an illegal move!"

Despite Kouki's protests, the referee just looked away. This was a magical school, so using magic was allowed to a limited extent. A goalie could erect barriers to block the ball, and strikers could manipulate the wind to shift the ball's trajectory, so strengthening yourself and kicking up a chunk of earth was technically within the rules. That also meant that Shea accidentally kicking the Azantium-filled ball into the previous referee's testicles—*despite* his continued warnings not to be too rough—was technically a legal move.

Shea ran all the way to the goal and shot the ball so hard, she kicked up gravel in her wake. The ball sailed straight in, and netted her team their tenth point. Suzu, the goalkeeper, huddled in a corner of the goal, protecting herself with a barrier. When Shea took her shot, Suzu didn't even try to block it. She just attempted to make her already tiny body seem even smaller.

"Yahooooooooooooooooo!"

Shea raised both hands into the air and bellowed a victory cry. She was the kind of girl who would trample anyone in her path for victory.

Meanwhile, on the tennis court...

"Bwah?!"

The chairwoman flew across the court. She traced an arc through the air and crashed into the ground a few meters away, a tennis ball firmly embedded in her cheek. She stumbled to her feet, legs twitching. Even for the sturdiest person at school, it was quite a blow.

"Y-Yue-sensei, while I understand magic is allowed, I do not think using gravity magic on the ball is fair..."

"The ball was in."

Yue faced Tio in the tennis tournament's final match. For the past few minutes, the ball had bounced in ways that ignored gravity. It inexplicably hit Tio in her vitals every time. Although Yue looked stunning in her tennis uniform, no one had the guts to peep at her. Nor did anyone dare to complain about a teacher and the chairman playing in a tournament meant for students. No one wanted to be hospitalized. Anyone who made a fuss, whether on the court or as a spectator, was sent to the infirmary by Yue's gravity shot.

"Very well. If you refuse to adhere to the spirit of the rules, then I see no reason to either! Breath Shot!"

"Ultimate Technique—Gate Return."

"Wait, that really *is* against the ru—bwaaah?!"

The blazing tennis ball vanished through the portal in front of Yue's hand and slammed straight into Tio's back. Tio skidded across the court and came to a stop right before the net. This time, she didn't get back up.

"The ball's still in."

Yue glared coldly at the referee. As far as she was concerned, it was fair play so long as the ball was in. The referee was too terrified to argue, and so judged in her favor. Yue would stoop to anything if it meant she got to be school nurse.

Meanwhile, in the table tennis room...

The click-clack of a ping pong ball hitting the table echoed over and over.

"You're pretty good, Endou."

"You think so? Heh heh... Truth is, I actually practice quite a bit."

"I see."

Click-clack, click-clack.

"Table tennis sure is fun."

"Yeah."

Hajime and Endou conversed normally.

Click-clack, click-clack.

They continued playing a peaceful, normal game of table tennis.

In the end, the sports tournament had to be canceled, because there were too many injuries.

BONUS STORY 3
The Red Flower of Fate

"**O**H. YOU STILL have this, Yue-san?"

Hajime and the others were packing their belongings. They'd be leaving Ankaji soon. Yue stopped and turned to Shea, who held a pair of bunny ears in her hands. Tio and Kaori looked over, and almost dropped their luggage in shock.

"What?! Sh-Shea, are your rabbit ears detachable?"

"D-do they regrow if you take them off?"

"Of course not, guys. Quit turning my ears into something weird. These are *fake* rabbit ears. Yue-san made them a while back."

Shea flopped her ears back and forth to emphasize the difference. She handed the bunny ear headband to Kaori. Kaori turned it over in her hands and nodded in understanding.

"Mmm... I made those when I got jealous of Hajime staring at Shea's rabbit ears all the time. Not like I need them anymore... I've discovered that cat ears are superior."

"I-I refuse to accept that, Yue-san! Hajime-san only liked cat ears more because you were wearing them. I'm sure if it came down to a pair of rabbit ears versus a pair of cat ears, rabbit ears would be superior!"

Yue took out her cat ears and put them on, as if to say, "You wanna go?!"

Yue-nyan was ready for battle.

Shea's ears shot straight up, as if to say, "You wanna go?!"

Regular Shea was ready for battle.

Tio watched the two fight over animal ear superiority and mused to herself.

"I see... So, you are a connoisseur of animal ears, Master... Dragonmen have tails, but no special ears. Hmm. I suppose, if I wish to appeal to you, I must throw away pride, and don the ears of a cat... Or, rather, a dog. For that way, you could insult me like the bitch I am... No, wait, perhaps I should create a pair of pig ears if I truly wish to be belittled!"

Tio turned toward Kaori, seeking a second opinion. Kaori didn't hear, as she was busy examining Yue's fake rabbit ears. Although Kaori seemed fascinated, she made no move to put them on. Instead, a wicked grin formed on her face. That expression scared Tio a little.

Worried that Kaori might do something that would ruin Tio's gentle and kind impression of her, Tio called out, "Kaori, you must return to reality. Your expression is beginning to terrify me."

"Huh?!"

Kaori blushed as she realized how she must have looked. Shea and Yue stopped grappling and glared suspiciously at her.

"Confess, you closet pervert. What were you doing to my Hajime in your fantasies?"

"I'm not a closet pervert! A-and I wasn't fantasizing!"

"Oh? What do you think, Shea-san? Tio-san?"

"She's guilty!"

"All I shall say is that trying to deny it will only make things worse for you in the end."

"Ugh..." Kaori's shoulders slumped.

Yue continued glaring, silently urging her to confess, while Kaori tried to look anywhere else.

"I was thinking that the rabbit ears might look good on Hajime-kun..."

The other girls sat up straight, as if a jolt of electricity had run through them.

"A rabbit-eared Hajime?"

"He'd match me..."

"Oh ho..."

Yue closed her eyes and imagined what a rabbit-eared Hajime would look like.

"Welcome home, Lady Yue. Here, give me your hand."

A butler Hajime with rabbit ears helped Yue out of her carriage.

Shea closed her eyes and imagined what a rabbit-eared Hajime would look like.

"We'll be together forever, dear."

A rabbit-eared Hajime looked lovingly at her, his new wife, surrounded by the splendor of a grand wedding feast.

Tio closed her eyes and imagined what a rabbit-eared Hajime would look like.

"You perverted waste of space! Hurry up and give me my boxers back!"

A rabbit-eared Hajime acted the same as usual.

Kaori closed her eyes and imagined what a rabbit-eared Hajime would look like.

"I'm sorry I always cause you so much trouble, Kaori... I don't know what I'd do without you."

A rabbit-eared spy, Hajime, looked lovingly up at Kaori, who was nursing him back to health. He'd been betrayed by his partner, Yue. Kaori had found him slumped in the rainy streets and brought him home.

For some reason, Kaori's delusion was far more detailed than the others' daydreams. Meanwhile, Tio didn't need Hajime to have rabbit ears at all. At any rate, a few minutes later, bright-red showers of happiness spurted from their noses.

"Hey, you four, have you finished packing your things...? Whoa, what the heck?! What happened?! Why do you all have nosebleeds?!"

Hajime hurried over, a mixture of confusion and worry on his face. However, despite the bloody spectacle, all four girls were smiling happily.

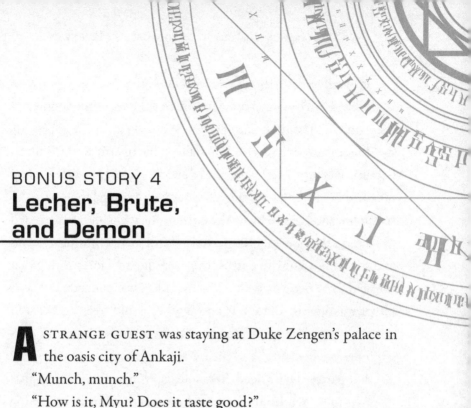

BONUS STORY 4
Lecher, Brute, and Demon

A STRANGE GUEST was staying at Duke Zengen's palace in the oasis city of Ankaji.

"Munch, munch."

"How is it, Myu? Does it taste good?"

Myu blissfully stuffed herself with Ankaji's best fruits. Airi, the duke's daughter, watched her eat with a smile. Airi was only fourteen, and still captivated by young children's antics. Beastmen were generally shunned by humans, and considered inferior, but the Holy Church gave dagons a special exemption.

Still, it would normally have been unthinkable to host a dagon at the royal palace. Especially since the duke's daughter was entertaining her. Under other circumstances, Airi's attendants would have stopped her, and reprimanded Myu for her insolence. Yet the attendants smiled as they watched Myu stuff her cheeks like a squirrel. They made no move to keep Airi from fussing over her. Myu finished her mouthful and turned to Airi.

"It's really tasty! Thank you, Airi-oneechan!"

"Heh! Don't worry about it. You're the precious daughter of the man who saved our city."

The reason Myu received such favorable treatment was indeed because her (surrogate) father had done the city a great service. Not only had he rid Ankaji of the monster that poisoned their oasis, he risked life and limb to bring the citizens the stillstone they needed to fend off the poison. He'd stayed behind in an erupting volcano, and still found a way to entrust the medicine to Tio, ensuring that it reached the people safely. As far as Ankaji was concerned, Myu's father was a hero. There was no way they could treat his beloved daughter with disrespect. Besides, Myu was just too cute.

"Hee hee hee! You're so nice, Airi-oneechan."

Airi patted Myu's head, her smile growing wider. "Hnnngh!"

"Airi-sama, while I understand how you feel, it is unbecoming for someone of your stature to look so...childish," said an attendant. "Please, at least wipe that drool from your face."

"Huh?! Oh, no... Myu's so cute it's scary."

Airi sucked her drool back in and wiped her face with a hand-kerchief. She went from looking like a pervert to a graceful lady in the span of a few seconds. Myu wasn't just scary because of how cute she looked. She also acted cute, had a cute personality, and basically, exuded cuteness from every pore. Airi was the youngest child in her family, and she'd always wanted a little sibling, so whenever Myu called her "Airi-oneechan," she lost it. Even the palace staff were enthralled.

"Mmm... Daddy...!"

Myu's face clouded as she thought of her adopted father, who was missing, and presumed to be in grave danger. Airi mentally berated herself, convinced Myu's mood was somehow her fault. She hurriedly tried to cheer the little girl up.

"M-Myu? Umm... I'm sure Hajime-sama's...well..."

The Grand Gruen Volcano hadn't erupted in centuries, and *this* eruption had been so powerful that even Ankaji's residents saw it. When the volcano erupted, Hajime was in its mouth. Logically, he should have been vaporized. In fact, most people assumed that their hero had perished valiantly. However, Hajime's comrades believed without a doubt that he was still alive, and Duke Zengen declared that he would not officially recognize Hajime's death. Thus, although the citizenry thought him dead, they held their tongues. Airi didn't know what to say to comfort Myu. Seeing her lost for words, Myu comforted Airi instead.

"It's okay. Everyone says Daddy's the strongest in the world, so I'll see him again. Daddy promised he'd come back... So don't be sad, Airi-oneechan."

"My...Myu!"

Myu patted Airi's head with her tiny hand, moving Airi to tears. Even though Myu was probably the most hurt by Hajime's disappearance, she still tried to comfort others.

What an unbelievably strong little girl. Airi hugged Myu tight, while her maids muttered, "What a brave girl," or "She's an angel," or "Myu-tan...haaah...haaah..."

"Myu, would you like to tell us about your father, Hajime-sama?"

"You want to know about Daddy?"

"Yes. He saved you from an underground auction at Fuhren, right? I heard you'd been kidnapped and were going to be sold off. I'd love to hear the heroic tale of how he saved you."

Surely this girl, who has absolute faith in her father, would love to talk more about him. Airi's guess was right on the mark. Myu's eyes lit up. Airi and her maids smiled, glad to see her happy again.

What kind of wonderful tale will Myu tell us?

"When Daddy saved me, he made all of Fuhren burn!"

"What?!"

"He made the buildings go *boooooom*!"

"What?!"

"Then he made lightning fall from the sky!"

"What?!"

"Everyone said Daddy dyed Fuhren red!"

"......"

None of them had expected a tale of death and destruction.

"Umm...ahem! Myu, I think you may have over-summarized your story. Could you please go into more detail?"

"Okay. It's story time!"

Myu cleared her throat and sat straighter. Her seriousness made Airi and the others straighten as well. They felt they'd be overwhelmed if they didn't prepare.

"When I tried to run away, I had to go through this dirty place called a 'sooer.'"

"Oh, my... You really are amazing, Myu."

Airi and the others gulped as they tried to imagine it. Just how bad must things have been, if swimming through the sewers was Myu's only choice?

"Then, when I woke up, Daddy had taken my clothes off."

"He did what?!"

"It was really warm and felt good."

"I-It felt good?!"

"Shea-oneechan was really nice to me."

"A-a threesome?!"

Although Myu wasn't lying, she'd left out the crucial detail that Hajime was giving her a bath. It was understandable that she'd skip ahead, given how young she was. Sadly, Myu's abridged explanation left Airi and the others imagining something very different.

"Then Daddy left me."

"He abandoned you?!"

Once again, Myu forgot to mention that Hajime left her in the care of an organization that helped kidnapped children return home.

"But then Daddy came back!"

Airi and the others sighed in relief.

"He said, 'How come you're soaked whenever I see you?' and gave me a blanket, because I had no clothes."

Isn't it your fault she's always wet?! Airi and the others thought.

Although Myu giggled as she told her tale, Airi and her attendants couldn't help but think that she'd been picked up by a brute of a man. And the tales of his terrible exploits still weren't over.

"Then, Daddy hugged me real tight... And blew up ten bad guys' heads!"

"Don't tell me he killed her real guardians..."

"I could believe it. Dagons are protected by law. I'm sure they didn't want her with a man who goes around making them wet."

The misunderstandings kept growing.

"Oh, he didn't blow one of them up. He crushed them instead."

"That's enough!"

A maid was covering her ears. She couldn't bear to hear anymore. Confused, Myu jumped to the end of the story.

"Then, Daddy took Myu into the sky and made an...'eggsample ...'? of everyone."

"So, that's what you meant by 'he dyed Fuhren red.'"

Airi trembled in terror. It was too much for a fourteen-year-old girl to take. Their beloved hero had another side: one that took advantage of a little girl, mercilessly killed her guardians, and slaughtered an entire city just to set an example. However, Airi was a nobleman's daughter. She quickly recovered her wits and looked resolutely at her maids. They overcame their fear and returned her determined gaze. The lot of them swore that, if that man still lived, they would never let him near Myu.

The next day, Myu left to look for her daddy. Airi and the others saw her off with tears in their eyes.

Ten days after that, Hajime, who had miraculously survived, returned to Ankaji. He'd seemingly done quite a bit more for the city, but that didn't matter. Airi was going to give him a piece of her mind.

"You lecher! Brute! Demon!"

"Wh-what the heck did I do?!"

Hajime wrinkled his nose as he endured a barrage of insults from Airi and her maids.

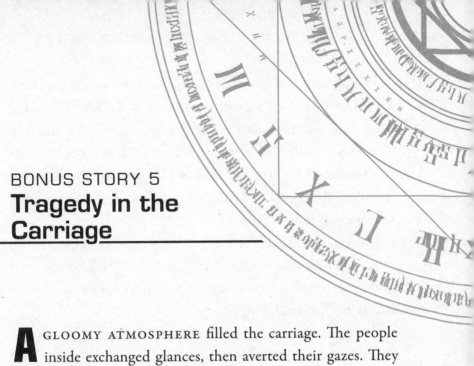

Tragedy in the Carriage

A GLOOMY ATMOSPHERE filled the carriage. The people inside exchanged glances, then averted their gazes. They all wanted someone to do something, but no one wanted to volunteer.

"Haaah..."

"......"

A sigh heavier than a neutron star escaped Kouki's lips. The others in the carriage, Ryutarou, Shizuku, Eri, and Suzu, twitched.

Ryutarou shot an unexpectedly timid glance at his best friend, who had caused the gloomy atmosphere. *He's totally dead...*

Suzu somehow read Ryutarou's thoughts, and retorted with a telepathic message of her own.

He's not dead! Though he might as well be, the way he looks.

Indeed, Kouki was still alive, but he resembled a corpse. His head drooped onto the windowsill. Although he looked out at the vibrant countryside, his eyes took none of the landscape in.

He had none of his usual vitality. He might as well have been a zombie. There were a multitude of reasons for Kouki's languid demeanor, but the main one was discovering that Kaori was in love, and had left his party to travel with Hajime. Kouki wasn't sure if he loved Kaori or not. However, he had thought she would be by his side forever, no matter what. Kaori's confession and subsequent elopement shocked him.

Worse, Kouki had let his emotions get the better of him, and challenged Hajime to a duel. Not only had Hajime not even bothered to humor him, Kouki ended up falling into a pit without so much as scratching his opponent.

"I just want to crawl into a hole and die..."

"You already did the crawling into a hole part. Do you have any idea how hard it was to dig you out?"

Ryutarou meant it as a lighthearted joke, but his wisecrack was the final blow that crushed Kouki's soul.

"Waaaaaah! Ryutarou-kun, you moron! Kouki-kun! Are you all right! Pull it together! Everything'll be okay! Right, Eririn?!"

"Wait, you're asking me?! U-umm, yes, of course. Everything will be just fine, Kouki-kun!"

Their attempts to reassure him only made things worse.

How is anything going to be okay?! Kouki thought painfully. He didn't notice Suzu smacking Ryutarou over the head, or Eri trying her best to comfort him, or Shizuku looking tiredly at the ceiling. That was how bad his depression was.

Suddenly, with the determination of someone resolved to go to battle and never come back, Suzu stood.

"I-I'll tell him a one-liner that'll definitely make him laugh!"

The others looked at her in awe. *What a hero!* Suzu shrugged off their stares. She would prove that she could cheer people up, even in this gloomy atmosphere.

"Hmm. Where did they go? I can't find them! I could have sworn I took them with me on this trip, but they're not here!"

Suzu patted her clothes and looked around the carriage. As usual, Kouki couldn't ignore someone in need. He looked at Suzu, momentarily returning to the real world.

"Suzu, what did you—?"

"I just can't seem to find my boobs!" Suzu said with a flourish, patting her sadly flat chest.

For a one-shot gag, it was pretty painful. Silence filled the carriage. Time stopped. The only sound was the soft clop of horse's hooves.

"I'm sorry for being born."

Suzu slumped into her seat. She leaned her head against the carriage and stared at the ceiling with dead eyes. She'd completely self-destructed.

"H-hey, Suzu, are you all right?"

"Next, please enjoy Ryutarou-kun's impersonation attempts."

"What?!"

Ryutarou's reward for his concern was to be placed on the chopping block. If Suzu was going to die, she'd take everyone down with her. Eri backed away in horror. Ryutarou sat in his seat, cold sweat pouring down his back. When Kouki once again looked out the window with dead eyes, however, Ryutarou made up his mind and stood.

"O-okay, fine. I'll do my best impression of Colonel William Stuart!"

Ryutarou sucked in a deep breath and flexed, showing off the full glory of his considerable muscles. Stuart was from a film called Die Hard. Getting even more into his act, Ryutarou flexed harder. However, it was not received as well as he would have liked.

"This is too macho for me."

"S-sorry, I can't bear to look."

"It hurts to breathe."

Suzu, Eri, and Shizuku glared at Ryutarou. His impersonation apparently brought the girls nothing but pain.

"I'm sorry for being born."

Ryutarou collapsed into his seat. He looked out the window with the same dead expression as Kouki.

"Eririn... You'll have to carry out our will."

"Suzu?! I thought we were friends!"

Eri shot Suzu, who still gazed blankly at the ceiling, a murderous glare. Suzu was asking the impossible! Suzu and Ryutarou's sacrifices hadn't been in vain, however. Kouki turned around and focused on Eri. With one more push, they might really bring the hero back.

"Very well... I shall sing!"

Eri raised her hands to her mouth, as if holding an imaginary mike, and sang in a beautiful voice. Her pitch was perfect, and she had a great sense of rhythm. It was the kind of voice that enthralled people. Or it would have been, had she not picked one of the most depressing love songs known to man.

"Th-thank you for being such a silent and attentive audience."

They'd been silent, all right. In fact, they were deathly pale. Despair and loneliness sapped their mental fortitude. Kouki looked as if he'd aged ten years. Eri's proud smile faded as she saw the effect of her singing. She quietly plopped back into her seat and hid her expression behind her glasses. Things didn't look good.

"Shizushizu, you're the only one left," Suzu mumbled in despair.

Shizuku was desperately trying to hide her presence. She jumped. Timidly, she raised her head to see everyone but Kouki staring at her.

"You don't think you'll be the only one to get out of this, do you?" their gazes seemed to say.

Tears welling, Shizuku got to her feet. She covered her eyes with her ponytail, and said in a high falsetto, "Eh, Nagumo-kun did what? I don't believe it! He always seemed like a quiet, low-profile guy."

"......"

Shizuku seemed to be acting out a fake interview with the other students.

"Nagumooo..." Kouki groaned. He wanted to forget all about Hajime.

Why the hell did you have to bring HIM up?! Suzu and the others glared at Shizuku. Trembling, Shizuku slumped to her knees and wrapped her arms around herself. Her ponytail still covered her eyes. Now she was the one who wished she could crawl into a hole and die. In the end, nothing but corpses remained in the carriage. The only sound was the horse's steady clopping.

A few hours later, the group stopped for a rest. Nagayama and the others got out of their respective carriages to stretch. When they noticed that no one had emerged from Kouki's carriage, they grew curious.

"What happened to them?" Meld wondered aloud, approaching.

Although he knocked on the door and called everyone's names, no one came out. A little worried, Meld opened the door and peeked inside.

"Wh-what happened to you guys?! Why do you all look dead?! Guards! Guards! Kouki and the others need medical attention! Who's the best healer here?!"

Meld panicked and ran to find a healer.

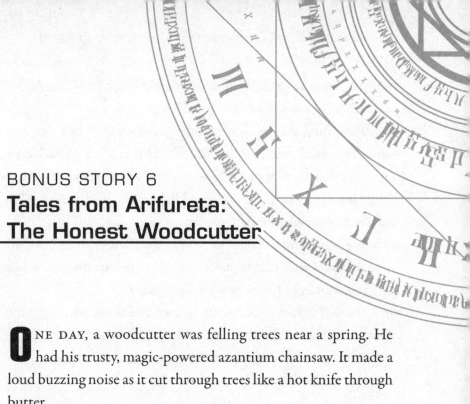

BONUS STORY 6
Tales from Arifureta: The Honest Woodcutter

O NE DAY, a woodcutter was felling trees near a spring. He had his trusty, magic-powered azantium chainsaw. It made a loud buzzing noise as it cut through trees like a hot knife through butter.

With his trusty chainsaw, the young man could chop down anything he pleased, whether boulders or steel walls. The chainsaw was just as useful on a battlefield. Anyone who wielded it could easily mow down hordes of soldiers. Swords, shields, and even plate armor couldn't withstand the weapon.

As for why a mere woodcutter possessed such a powerful tool, well, that's not important. Why he was *still* just a woodcutter, despite having this ability, was also unimportant.

With a resounding crash, a tree fell to the ground.

"Phew! Looks like work went well today, too."

The day's job was done. It had only taken the young man five minutes, but still, he wiped a bead of imaginary sweat off his brow.

Just then, he sensed something trying to kill him!

"Tch! Die, you worthless mutt!"

The young man set loose a string of violent curses that you wouldn't expect from a village woodcutter. He then pulled loose an L-shaped piece of metal from his pocket and took aim. A second later, he loosed a streak of red light through the trees. A lot of things were sure being set loose.

The last thing to come loose was the head of the "mutt" he had shot at, a wolf-like monster hiding in a nearby thicket. When the streak of light hit its head, it blew clean off.

There wasn't just one wolf, however. The woodcutter fired a series of flashes that brutally obliterated the entire pack. The scene was gruesome enough to be censored, and the peaceful forest was dyed red with monsters' blood.

"Tch! As always, all you've got is numbers. Hmm? Shit, the goods!"

Until now, the young devil painting the forest red had been perfectly composed. However, he lost his cool when he noticed a wolf sneaking towards his precious goods.

By "goods," the woodcutter meant the splendid tree he'd just chopped down. The wolf heartlessly activated its special magic and shot a fireball at the tree. Even if the woodcutter slaughtered the monster, the fireball would burn the tree beyond recognition. The woodcutter flung his L-shaped weapon aside, raised his chainsaw in both hands, and charged toward the fireball.

"Like hell I'll let you!"

With a spirited cry, the woodcutter split the fireball in two. He then swung the chainsaw back up, slicing right through the wolf's stomach. Another red flower blossomed amidst the green trees.

"Phew, I made it...! Oh, yeah..."

Once again wiping imaginary sweat off his brow, the woodcutter looked for the weapon he'd thrown. When his gaze passed over the spring, he noticed ripples in the previously still water.

"Crap! I can't believe I threw it in there!"

The woodcutter walked to the spring's edge. Since he couldn't find his weapon anywhere else, it had likely fallen in. He slumped his shoulders and sighed.

"Man, what do I do? Without that thing, it'll take more time to annihilate monsters and thieves. God, what a pain."

The spring was wide and deep. Diving to the bottom to search for the weapon would take considerable time and effort.

"Maybe I should just throw burning taur down there and vaporize the spring," the woodcutter muttered ominously.

Taur burned at an impressive 3000 degrees Celsius, so that was certainly possible.

The spring suddenly began to sparkle, as if reacting to the woodcutter's terrifying words. Surprised, the man turned on his chainsaw and got ready to fight. From within the spring's depths, a person emerged.

"Wow..."

The usually curt and cruel woodcutter gasped in wonder. That was the power of the beautiful goddess who emerged from the spring. Nothing could match her splendor. Her golden-blond hair sparkled in the sunlight. Her long eyelashes and deep crimson eyes captivated all who gazed upon her. Her porcelain-white skin was tinged with the faintest blush. She appeared to be no more than twelve or thirteen, but her passionate gaze and seductive smile made her seem much older. She was quite the captivating goddess. Her slender limbs peeked out from a pure white gown. When she spotted the woodcutter, the goddess crouched in front of him. She thrust both hands into the spring and pulled something out in each. The woodcutter had expected her to use magic, not something as mundane as her own hands.

"Is this your crafty rabbit? And is this your perverted priestess?"

The woodcutter didn't know how to respond. The goddess pulled two people out of the spring. Bunny ears grew from one's head, while the other wore priestess robes. They were both soaked through and seemed rather miffed. From the sound of it, the goddess had plunged them into the spring against their will. It seemed that this goddess kidnapped people.

"Ugh. Hey, you... Mister with the chainsaw. Won't you please pick this poor rabbit? If you do, I'll devote these bunny ears to you for life!"

The woodcutter wasn't sure what it would mean to have bunny ears "devoted" to him, but he was certainly tempted. The bunny girl had an impressive bust, and she made sure to emphasize it.

I see now, she definitely is crafty.

"U-umm, you over there! The guy who turned this peaceful forest into a battlefield, I mean! Do you think you could help me? If you pick me, I'll do anything you ask!"

The woodcutter wasn't sure what she expected him to ask of her, but he could tell by her blushing and fidgeting that it wasn't wholesome. The priestess buried her face in her hands, but peeked coyly through her fingers.

I see now, she's definitely a pervert.

"I didn't drop anything living into the spring, you know."

"Huh?!"

The crafty bunny girl and perverted priestess looked at him in shock.

"Mmm... I suppose that's understandable. We don't need these, then."

"Hey, don't you think that's a little rude?!"

"Y-you're so mean, Ha—"

The goddess dumped both women back in the spring. They didn't reemerge.

"Then, is this your—"

"Oh, is it my turn already? Very well, Master. Please insult—"

The goddess dropped what she had picked up before the woodcutter even had a good chance to look at it. "Next."

From the woodcutter's quick glimpse, he assumed it was some strange creature.

The goddess stuck her hand into the spring once more and fished around. After a while, she found what she was looking for.

"Mmm... Is this your thirty-five centimeter long, taur-made, azantium-coated, Lightning Field-powered, six shot revolver, capable of railgun-enhanced shots, and named after the German word for thunder, 'Donner'?"

What a frighteningly detailed description. It was hard to believe the goddess had just seen Donner for the first time. It was almost as if this goddess had been watching the woodcutter all along.

The woodcutter's expression stiffened. He realized, perhaps too late, that this goddess was dangerous. Chills ran down his spine, and he opened his mouth to say that Donner was his. However, the goddess interrupted him.

"Or..."

She took her empty hand and placed it elegantly on her own chest.

"Is this your goddess?"

"Like I said, I didn't drop anything living into that spring." The woodcutter retorted. The goddess narrowed her eyes. It was the look of a hunter eyeing her prey.

"This is your goddess, isn't it?"

Now she was pushing herself at the woodcutter. However, he wasn't one to be swayed.

"No, I dropped Donner in. The gun you're hiding behind your back. Please give it back to me. Hey, wait, don't throw it away! What? I have to pick you if I want it back? Now you're blackmailing me!"

The goddess attempted to throw Donner back into the spring, tears in her eyes, while the woodcutter did everything in his power to stop her. The noise of their life and death struggle resounded through the woods. In the end, their tale ended just as it was meant to. For his honesty, the woodcutter received everything the goddess offered him. That, of course, meant that he received both his revolver, and a smiling goddess.

AFTERWORD

Hey everyone, chuuni lover Ryo Shirakome here!

Thank you so much for picking up *Arifureta* Volume 6.

Were you confused by the girl on the cover? Until now, the cover character has always been one of the heroines. This time, a new girl who hadn't shown up in any illustrations suddenly got the front page.

Be honest, how many of you were like, "Who's that girl?!"

And how many of you went "Wait, that's Eri!" when you saw the name on the inside flap? Me and everyone in the editing department planned this little surprise, so if it worked, we're really happy.

Anyway, Kaori sure did a lot in this volume. And now she's in a real apostle, Noint's, body.

Now that I think about it, that's overkill. Kaori already had cheat-level healing magic that got powered up in the last labyrinth, and now she's got physical stats as good as Hajime's. Oh, and she can use Noint's disintegration magic, and possesses all the skills to wield the apostle's greatswords proficiently. I'm starting to think Kaori is scarier than Hajime.

At any rate, congratulations on joining the ranks of monsters, Kaori! Speaking of monsters, Shea was really happy when Mikhail called her that.

Were you charmed by her smile when you saw the illustration? Can you believe she killed Mikhail while smiling that sweetly? I guess she really is a monster! Thanks for giving us such a great image, Takayaki-sensei! It's wonderful to see Shea go from worthless rabbit to overpowered bunny girl.

There sure was a lot packed into this volume. The invasion of the capital, Eri's betrayal, all those deaths, the Holy Church's destruction, the unveiling of the Soul Sisters, Hajime's duel with Noint, his classmates' changing feelings... I think I've said it a bunch of times already, but this volume really does mark the big turning point for Arifureta.

It feels like time has passed in the blink of an eye, but it also feels like it took forever to get here.

At any rate, I think that with all the revisions, additions, and extra stories, the light novel has become a lot more complete than the web novel. I promise I'll keep downing gallons of coffee and working hard to bring Arifureta to you all, so I hope you stick with me.

Before we go, I'd like to give thanks to everyone who made this volume possible.

First and foremost, a big thank you to Takayaki-sensei for his wonderful illustrations. Next, huge thanks to my editor, who really helped me flesh out Kaori as a character. I also want to thank my proofreader for picking out typos with the accuracy of a sniper. Plus, thanks to RoGa-sensei for all his wonderful work on the Arifureta manga, and to all the people in the publishing division that made this book a reality.

Lastly, I'd like to thank my readers. Both the ones who supported the web version, and the ones picking this book up in stores.

Thank you so, so much for your support.

I pray we meet again in the next volume.

—Ryo Shirakome